Faith Unbroken

Book 4 of the *Moving Mountains* series

ISBN: 978-1-9991282-7-2

One

If Hannah stood in precisely the right spot, she could see the entire city laid out before her like an ocean of light. She'd spent most of the night hovering near the window, where her reflection made her feel less alone. The odd part was, she hadn't been alone at all: up until about twenty minutes ago, the room had been quivering with lively discussions about politics, women's rights, and Indigenous history. Logan's friends were a chatty bunch—too chatty for Hannah's taste. Most of them were older too, with well-paying jobs in fields like law and education. Why Logan had invited her Hannah didn't know. Every puzzle box had one piece that didn't quite fit, and this time, she was it.

Hannah picked up the empty martini glass and cocktail napkin from the coffee table. Of course, Logan's party guests had not been able to stay and help clean up due to the presence of other commitments—or maybe they were only pretending to be busy in order to feel less lonely, like Hannah was doing now. She swiped a forgotten beer bottle off the console table and delivered it, along with the martini glass and napkin, to the kitchen.

"Thanks for helping me clean up," Logan said in the middle of packaging leftover mini quiches.

"No problem. It's the least I can do."

As Logan snapped the lid on the Tupperware, she said, "Be honest: what did you think?"

"Of the party? It was nice. And it seemed like everyone had a great time."

Logan added another plate to the dishwasher. It was strange to feel envious about an appliance, but every time Hannah noticed the sleek, grey machine and its cage of pristine white racks, a knot formed in the pit of her stomach. Logan had worked tirelessly for years to afford a place of her own, but that didn't stop Hannah from wishing it was hers.

"I can never be sure," Logan explained, her brows pulling together as she rounded up more dirty dishes. "Do you ever find yourself in the middle of a crowded room with no idea how you got there? It's like everyone else knows what to say and do, but you're just observing." She shook her head. "I mean, of course I *know* how I got here, but then I look at my friends and I think they're all doing better than me. Winning the Game of Life."

Hannah smiled, grateful that Logan had been able to articulate her own feelings so eloquently. "I wonder what Jo would have thought of the party."

"I think she would've said there wasn't enough alcohol. Speaking of which—"

Logan reached for the bottle of champagne. Hannah had only had champagne two other times in her life: once to celebrate her engagement to Ray, and again on the night of her graduation from university. On both occasions, she'd been filled with hope for the future. But earlier tonight, when Logan had gathered everyone in the living room to toast this exciting new chapter in her life, Hannah had been hit with an icy wave of dread. Somehow, she'd stumbled on the starting block and fallen behind. Most of her friends had vanished into thin air, and her student loan debt wasn't going away anytime soon. Nonetheless, Hannah was determined to get away for a while. She had to, if only to prove that she, too, was going somewhere.

"What did Jo say that one time?" Logan asked, producing two glasses from the cupboard. "We were sitting on her living room floor eating sushi and she said…"

"'To new beginnings and old friends.'"

"Right. Well, I think it applies here." Logan emptied the remaining bubbly into Hannah's glass first, then her own. She set down the bottle, picked up the glass, and raised the golden liquid above her head. "To new beginnings and old friends."

"Cheers," Hannah said, pulling in a long drink.

Logan lowered her glass. "I never really got a chance to talk to you tonight. I mean, I wanted to, but…"

Hannah waved her hand. "It's okay. You were making some really good arguments about why Hillary Clinton should be the next president, and I didn't want to interrupt."

"The world needs more women in power." Logan took a sip. "How are the wedding plans going?"

"Slowly. I'm hoping that changes when I get to Colorado."

"I can't believe you're getting married in seven months. Seems like just yesterday Joanna texted me with the news."

Hannah merely smiled. In seven months, she would be a wife. Ray would be her husband. She'd never set foot in Logan's condo or Ruth's Flower Shop again. But at least she'd finally have a permanent home, which was what she'd wanted all along.

As she drained her glass and looked over at the clock on the microwave, Hannah said, "I should get going. I still have a ton of stuff to pack."

"Did you want me to drive you home?"

"That's okay. I was going to call for an Uber."

"Cool. Well, thanks for all your help tonight. If you ever need anything, I'm only ever a text message away."

Hannah placed her glass in the dishwasher and walked down the hall to the front door. As she bent to zip up her boots, blood rushed into her cheeks and her head felt like it was filled with cotton balls. It wasn't often that she drank, but tonight, the alcohol had saved her from having to discuss her career choice or defend her political views. Straightening, she pulled on her coat and lifted her purse onto her shoulder.

"Good luck in Colorado. Say hi to everyone for me," Logan added awkwardly.

"I will." Hannah opened the door and stepped into the hallway, passing artificial plants and No Smoking signs on her way to the elevator.

As Hannah stood on the curb, waiting for her ride, she noticed the high-pitched ringing in her ears brought on by the ineluctable buzz of chattering, satisfied partygoers. It was in moments like these that Hannah missed Ray the most—when there were no car horns, police sirens, disgruntled customers, or blaring TVs to distract her thoughts. Despite her best efforts, she hadn't been able to convince him to move to Canada. His home was in the mountains, and there was more than enough room for both of them to grow on the ranch. Soon, a pair of yellow headlights emerged from the haze. Hannah confirmed the details on her phone, then opened the rear passenger door and ducked into the car's warmth.

"Thanks for not being a dude," her driver, Libby, said. "They're the most obnoxious passengers, especially around Christmastime when everyone is lonely." Libby flipped on her turn signal. "Going to a party?"

"Just leaving one, actually," Hannah replied.

"Good call on using Uber. Alcohol and cars don't mix, you know."

Hannah masked her sorrow with a trained smile. "All too well."

When Hannah arrived home, she opened the door on a dazzling display of lights. The Christmas tree in the living room bloomed with golden bulbs, illuminating the gifts spread at its base. She quietly closed the door and removed her scarf in a couple of turns. Andrew and Jeanette had been kind enough to let her stay with them until she got back on her feet, but so far, Hannah had merely dusted herself off and watched her peers pass her on the next lap.

As she crossed the foyer to the stairs, she heard a voice in the living room say, "You're home earlier than I thought you'd be."

Hannah looked at her mother, tucked into the corner of the sectional couch with her arms crossed and her hair undone. As always, a stack of files sat on the coffee table, accompanied by a cup of tea she hadn't touched in hours.

Hannah replied, "I was tired. And I need to finish packing."

"Do you have a few minutes to talk?"

Hannah nodded and sat down beside Jeanette. She could've stayed for one more Christmas, seen her grandparents one last time before the wedding, and been happy enough to smile for the ensuing pictures. But she wanted to see Ray, and Laney wanted to see her, and even though her parents hadn't come straight out and said it, Hannah knew she'd overstayed her welcome here, outgrown her childhood home the way she'd outgrown retainers, Barbie dolls, and ice cream dates with her dad.

"How was the party?" Jeanette asked.

"It was okay. The condo's beautiful."

"I remember when you wanted a condo," her mother went on, her wistful tone taking Hannah by surprise. "And, instead, you settled for a cattle ranch in the middle of nowhere."

And we're back, Hannah thought, fixing her gaze on a recap of the six o'clock news. "I didn't *settle* for anything. I chose Ray."

"But at what cost? Your dreams? Your career?"

"Mom, can we not do this tonight? Please?"

Jeanette puckered her lips before conceding with a sigh. She'd enjoyed having her daughter at home again, even if the circumstances behooving her return had been subpar. They'd talked a lot in these last several months, and for a time, it seemed like Hannah was finally coming to her senses about things. But it was a losing battle… and the boy always won.

Jeanette angled toward the Christmas tree, her right hand reaching to pat Hannah's knee. "I almost forgot—I wanted to give you your present before you leave." She crouched next to the pile of gifts and picked up a small container wrapped in green and silver paper.

Hannah held out her hand to accept it. "Shouldn't we wait for dad?"

"He already knows what it is." This time, rather than curling up on the couch, Jeanette perched stiffly on its edge, watching her daughter unwrap this latest peace offering. As Hannah lifted the lid on the box to reveal a glass bird nestled in paper straw, her mother asked, "Do you recognize it?"

"Of course. It's the ornament from grandma and grandpa's tree." She picked the decoration up by its string and watched it spin in the cornucopia of light, throwing out pulses of white and gold.

"You always loved that little bird," Jeanette said. "As you know, this ornament has been in the family for generations. And now, your father and I are giving it to you."

"Thank you. I promise, I'll take good care of it."

"You know, it's not too late to change your mind," Jeanette hedged.

"About spending Christmas in the States?"

"About getting married."

Hannah returned the ornament to its box and set it on the table. Unlike Laney, who'd appointed herself wedding planner the instant Ray proposed, Jeanette had avoided becoming too involved. Now, four years later, Hannah found herself with no venue, no dress, and no inkling of what the future might hold for her and Ray, aside from the knowledge that couples who wed young made up a troubling percentage of the divorce statistics. This, at least, had proven Jeanette was not entirely indifferent to their plans.

"I'm not going to change my mind," Hannah said quietly.

"I'm just saying, weddings are expensive and you have student loans to repay. Why not wait a few years? Statistically, the more a couple spends on their wedding—"

"The more likely they are to file for divorce," Hannah finished. "I know."

"Hannah, you know I'm not trying to rain on your parade. I'm your mother, which means I only want the best for you. And sometimes the best thing is to be honest."

"I know," Hannah said again, "but those statistics apply to normal couples, and Ray and I are far from being a normal couple. We've been living in two separate countries for six years and we're still in love. That's not normal—that's extraordinary." She added, "He's the only one for me, mom. Young or not, we're going to make it work."

Jeanette's attention slid back to her unfinished paperwork. Even after six years, she knew less about her future son-in-law than she did about the characters in the TV show she would inevitably watch to help her fall asleep. She'd made her living guiding couples through the arduous journey of reclaiming their independence, yet here was Hannah, about to throw it all away for the statistically improbable chance at eternal happiness.

Sensing a shift in her mother's mood, Hannah announced, "I should go. I have lots of packing to do."

"I'm glad we had a chance to talk," Jeanette replied. "And, please, think about what I said. For your sake."

The second floor was quiet, with Andrew sleeping soundly in the master bedroom and Hannah herself feeling too exhausted to analyze her mother's often contradictory displays of affection. In two days, she'd be in Colorado, celebrating Christmas with Ray's family and planning their long overdue wedding—a joyous end to a year that had been fraught with pain, uncertainty, and the unassailable promise of change.

Hannah had been lucky: two weeks before graduating from the University of British Columbia, she'd been offered a job at CPS, working with society's most vulnerable members. In many ways, it had been a dream opportunity—and dreams sometimes had a way of evolving into nightmares. For every child she'd helped rescue from an abusive home, ten more went overlooked, slipping through the cracks and disappearing forever. Some she'd tried to remember, others she'd tried to forget. At night, alone in her overpriced apartment, she'd journaled her way through the guilt and the powerlessness to no avail. By the end of August, faced with the prospect of investigating yet another case of child neglect, she'd taken lunch in her car and driven straight to the hospital, knowing it was the safest place to be when she inevitably cracked under the pressure.

In the weeks that followed, she'd met with countless doctors and therapists. Their assessments all seemed to point to some form of burnout, and several had recommended taking a leave of absence to allow her mind and body to heal. The tug-of-war between her guilt over leaving and the hypocrisy of inflicting her trauma on others raged for weeks until, on a cool, crisp autumn day, Hannah had looked at the leaves browning outside her window and realized it was time to let go. That afternoon, she'd packed up her desk, returned her apartment key, and driven home to Kamloops.

Hannah opened her bedroom door and switched on the lamp. Her eyes gravitated to the suitcase, upright but slightly slouched in the corner. Hannah lovingly patted the bulky case and turned her attention over to the newer, shinier carry-on. Rather than wait until she and Ray were married to transfer her belongings to Colorado, she'd decided to bring a little more of home with her on each trip: photo albums one summer, cherished childhood treasures the following Thanksgiving, until the bulk of her life occupied the American side of the border.

Hannah gazed around the nearly vacant room, letting its emptiness consume her: the white bookcase with its thin layer of dust, the wooden desk where she'd planned everything from trips to the mall to university open houses, the queen-sized bed, and the standing mirror propped against the wall. Perhaps her parents would turn the extra space into a storage room, or push the bed into the corner and finally invest in that treadmill her mother had always wanted.

Kneeling beside the carry-on, Hannah removed the handful of items and laid them out on the floor. As she carefully rearranged her possessions within the suitcase's frame, a light knock came at the door, prompting her to turn around.

Andrew smiled. "You're home early-ish."

"I know. Did I wake you?"

"I couldn't sleep. After all, the phrase is 'sleep like a baby,' not 'sleep like a father.'" Andrew approached the bed and seated himself on the edge. "Is all that going to Colorado with you?"

"Yeah. And probably straight into the attic when I get there." Hannah reached for another item and gently squeezed its pillowy, bubble-wrapped edges. "A lot of my stuff is in boxes in the basement. You and mom can get rid of it if you need more space."

"We have plenty of space. Besides, this will always be your home, even after you're married."

Hannah set the jewellery box in the suitcase. She'd need somewhere to store her engagement ring and future anniversary gifts, she'd reasoned after a days-long inner debate over whether some silly trinket was worth additional baggage fees.

"I can't believe I'm leaving again," Hannah said, almost to herself. "It feels like I'm always on a plane, flying somewhere else."

"I can't believe it either. It feels like we just brought you home from the hospital." Andrew indicated the walls with a nod. "Did you know this used to be your nursery?"

"I thought my nursery used to be the spare room. That's why the walls are still yellow."

"Well, your mom would argue they're peach, but no—the guest room was your playroom, once you got old enough to be left alone. When you were a baby, you slept in here. Your crib was where the dresser is, and over there" – he pointed to the corner of the room where her most valuable possessions once decorated the bookcase – "we had a rocking chair. I read a lot of bedtime stories in that chair."

"Do we still have it in the basement?"

"Somewhere. I don't suppose you plan on packing that, too?"

Hannah shook her head. "I'm moving to the country. There will be plenty of rocking chairs, I'm sure."

Andrew ran a hand through his hair and tried to ignore his reflection in the mirror. "True. Anyway, you probably want to get some sleep."

"Yeah. I should." But as Hannah studied her father's face, she felt far from tired—only concerned about the future and all the endings that hadn't yet passed. She wondered if this was how Ray felt every time he looked at Laney.

"One more thing," Andrew said upon reaching the doorway. "When you get married, people are going to give you all kinds of gifts. So, don't feel like you have to take everything, unless Ray's house has a lot of extra bedrooms."

"They never have enough space. Not in the house, anyway."

"See? Now might be a good time to let a few things go." He grasped the doorknob and smiled again. "Night, cookie."

"Night, dad." As the door closed, Hannah removed the jewellery box from the suitcase and carefully peeled off the bubble wrap to expose the white, wooden container. Tiny purple flowers with green stems had been painted on the lid, complementing the gold latch and matching hinges. Inside, the velvet-lined compartments jingled with personal accoutrements, from chunky charm bracelets to delicate silver pendants.

Hannah dipped her finger into the mishmash and unearthed Cameron's promise ring. Its narrow gold band was embedded with an artificial diamond, cut and shaped to resemble a heart. *Unbreakable and everlasting,* he'd said the day he gave it to her. *Just like my love for you.*

Hannah shook her head as the memories faded. "So much for keeping your promise," she muttered. She raised her left hand to admire the peridot engagement ring from Ray. Even after all these years, it had never lost its lustre. It had survived Emma's passing, the inevitable purge that proceeded her death, and more than a few years in Jim and Laney's basement. And now, after four years of university, it was still wrapped around Hannah's finger, unaltered by the everchanging landscape of her life. As true love should be.

She placed Cameron's ring back in the box and shut the lid. Then she stood up, carried it over to the bookcase, and set it on the shelf where it belonged, forever.

Two

It was late afternoon when the black pickup truck pulled into the driveway towing a red horse trailer. Normally, when Ray agreed to work with a horse, he arranged to have it delivered in the morning to give the animal time to settle in—yet here was Marcus, roughly two hours before sunset, carefully maneuvering their creaky two-horse transporter down the icy laneway leading to the barn. No warning, no notice, not even a text message explaining where he'd gone or why. Ray drove another nail into the fence board he was repairing, then set down the hammer and went to meet his brother.

"That trailer better be empty," Ray said as Marcus stepped out of the truck.

"It will be once I unload it."

They walked around to the trailer's rear. Through the narrow gaps along the trailer's sides, Ray spotted a pair of russet-brown ears and heard the hollow clanging of hooves as the animal inside shifted, causing the flimsy bumper-pull to quake.

Marcus said, "Before you get mad, you should know he was being neglected. A couple of hikers were cutting through an abandoned property when they heard whinnying coming from the barn. When they looked inside, they saw this guy standing in about six inches of manure, with no food or water in sight."

Ray grimaced. "How is that not going to upset me?"

"It should upset you. It certainly upset Laney…" As Ray prepared to protest, Marcus raised his hands. "You know she can't help herself."

"And neither can you."

"So, can you do anything with him?"

Ray peered into the dingy, metal shell. The gelding's rump was facing the door, allowing him to see the scaly grey patches where the hair had either rubbed off or fallen out, as well as the bony protrusions of his hips.

11

The neck seemed insufficient to support the weight of the animal's head. Even his brows were sunken, leaving two deep wells above his eyes that appeared totally black in the waning light.

"How long was he in the barn?" Ray asked.

"Hard to say. His teeth and feet are overgrown, so maybe a couple of months. But he wasn't lying down, so Laney thinks there's a solid chance he'll make a full recovery." Marcus added, "She doesn't think he'll ever be rideable. According to her, this horse has a severe case of PTSD."

"I've never heard of a horse having PTSD," Ray muttered. He knew horses experienced trauma like humans did and had long memories when it came to pain and suffering, but to slap such a generic label on the problem only made his job more difficult. He would need to get back to basics here, unravel each mystery as it came, and who knew how long that would take? "If he isn't rideable, why should I bother working with him? Why would Laney agree to take on a horse that no one wants?"

Marcus shook his head. "I don't know."

"Well, I don't have time to figure it out. This is a working ranch, Marc. I need horses that make my life easier, not harder." Ray turned away from the trailer, his thoughts jumbled and his patience short. As Marcus fell into step with him, Ray said, "I have a million things to do before Hannah comes tomorrow, and training some half-starved horse with PTSD isn't exactly on my list of priorities."

They stepped into the barn. Winter in the mountains meant snow as far as the eye could see. Blazing white peaks bit into a clear blue sky and tree branches drooped under the weight of built-up ice. Ray and Marcus had moved what they could away from the doors, gates, and water pump, but the snow kept coming, carried on the wind each time it blew. As Ray's eyes adjusted to the darkness, he pictured the abandoned barn to which the horse had been confined, with the snow piling up against the entrances and choking off access from the road. People could be criminally selfish when it came to non-human lifeforms. At least while the horse was in his care, it would be adequately fed and watered. Maybe a second chance was all the gelding really needed.

"So, I guess this is a bad time to mention that Laney wants to see you," Marcus hedged.

Ray squinted. "See me?"

"When I went to pick up the gelding, she said she was expecting an old friend around three. I asked her why she wanted you to be there, but she wouldn't give me a straight answer."

"I don't have time to meet another one of Laney's friends. Hannah's coming tomorrow, the house is a disaster, and we have no food."

"I'll go get some groceries. And Hannah doesn't care about the mess. She's seen how we live."

Ray grappled for another excuse to avoid a trip to Fitzgerald Farms, but his mind came up blank. It would have to be a short visit, but if he left now, he'd still have plenty of time to clean his room, do the laundry, and figure out where to put the gelding so his presence wouldn't disrupt the other horses' routine.

"Laney knows how busy you are," Marcus said, "and she wouldn't ask you to take time out of your day if it weren't important."

With a nod toward the trailer, Ray replied, "I think Laney and I have a very different idea of what's important."

"Just go see her. Tell her you can't stay long, now that you have a new horse to work with."

"Fine. Put him in the sand ring for now. I'll figure out what to do with him when I get home." Ray pulled his keys out of his pocket and trekked across the hard-packed snow to his truck, leaving Marcus to unload the trailer.

As Ray headed down the driveway, he glimpsed the rearview mirror to find the gelding with its nose pressed up against the gate, breathing in the mountain air. Ray rolled down his window and did the same, but his mind didn't clear, and his worries, like the snowdrifts around the house, only grew larger.

*

13

Twenty minutes later, Ray steered into the Fitzgeralds' driveway and drove toward the house expecting the worst. Laney had been in poor health recently, and being unable to work in the barn meant she'd had to find other ways to occupy her time. Knitting demanded a level of dexterity that her arthritis no longer allowed, and she was finding it increasingly cumbersome to keep up with the handful of TV shows Marcus had recommended on account of the memory issues triggered by her stroke. When it became clear that he was the only one taking care of them, Jim had been forced to sell the last of their horses: Laney's prized brood mare, Katarina, and her steadfast pinto gelding named Chip, who'd lived at Fitzgerald Farms his entire life. Now, as Ray parked in his usual spot under the trees, he tried to push aside the blooming seed of sorrow at the thought of what the future might bring—and who it might take away.

It wasn't until he stepped outside that he noticed the second truck: a brawny silver Ram 1500 with the words *Windreach Farms* stretched along the bed and accompanied by a silhouette of a horse and rider sliding through a cloud of dust. The front door of the house was unlocked, so Ray stamped the snow from his boots and went inside, where he was greeted by the smell of coffee and the jubilant crescendo of laughter.

"Oh, you had to be there," Laney exclaimed, wrapping her hands around her mug as Ray entered the dining room looking perplexed. "I don't think I've ever seen Jim look so surprised."

"The way you tell stories, I feel like I am," a man in a starch white shirt and crisp blue jeans replied.

Ray cracked a grin. "Am I late to the party?"

The visitor turned around as Laney raised her eyes to Ray's. Her face brightened encouragingly, and the pallor of the last few weeks drained from her skin.

"Ah, no, you're just in time," she announced. "Raymond, I'd like you to meet a dear friend of mine. This is Wilbur McCullough. Wilbur, this is my godson, Raymond, the one I was telling you about."

Wilbur stood and offered his hand. Tall and narrow as an aspen, he had a suntanned face webbed with creases, uniformly ashen hair, and

14

watery blue eyes that fixed on Ray with inexplicable intensity. A firm grip completed the picture of a man who'd once occupied a position of considerable power and wasn't keen on letting it go quite yet. "Nice to meet you, son."

"Likewise." As Ray reclaimed his hand, he looked at Laney and asked, "Is everything okay?"

"Never better. There's coffee in the kitchen if you want to join us." Laney plunged back into her lively narrative as Ray helped himself to the steaming elixir and stirred in milk and sugar. Marcus would be thrilled to know their godmother was not only awake, but apparently thirty years younger. Sprawled in Jim's seat at the head of the table, Wilbur was talking about a woman named Anita and looking at Laney like Ray wasn't there at all.

Ray took a seat across from Laney and placed his coffee on the table, capturing Wilbur's interest.

"So, Ray," the older man started, "may I call you that?"

"Of course."

"Laney tells me you have something of a gift for fixing unrideable horses. Where did that come from?"

Ray faltered, his gaze sliding back to the mug's contents. "I'm not sure. I wouldn't call it a gift, exactly. It's just a part of what I do, having grown up on a ranch."

Laney chimed in, her voice noticeably more subdued than it had been a few minutes ago. "His father had a remarkable talent for working with horses. Never met one he couldn't train—not that I always agreed with his methods, but the results were hard to argue with."

"Well, there's your answer, son: you were born with the magic touch." Wilbur picked up his coffee and pulled in a deep sip.

Ray nodded, trying to wrap his head around everything he'd just heard. His memories of his father were blurry at best, although he could recall a handful of moments where he'd witnessed—even admired—his father's skills. For instance, when Ray was six, one of their horses had become ensnared in a rusty coil of barbed wire, carelessly abandoned in a field where the fence had been torn down years before. The yearling had kicked and whinnied fruitlessly, growing exhausted in its attempts to tear free of the metal teeth. When his father had approached it, the young animal had merely lay still, terrified and resigned to its fate.

Ray's father had laid a hand on the horse's sweat-dampened neck and stroked soothingly. He'd often been described as gentle and reassuring, although Ray couldn't say those qualities ever extended to him, his brothers, or his mother, who'd needed it most.

"What's the most important thing you need to know about horses?" his father, Bernard, had asked, his voice pitched low to avoid frightening the filly.

Ray had answered, "They're prey animals."

"And what's the main emotion prey animals feel?"

"Fear."

"That's right." Bernard's hand had moved down the horse's neck, toward its shoulder, flank, and hindquarters. Dozens of small, bloody cuts marred its tender flesh. As he'd lifted the wire from around the horse's hooves and untangled its limbs one by one, Bernard had said, "If you want a horse to trust you, all you have to do is take away its fear."

Take away its fear, Ray thought now, pushing his father out of his mind as easily as Bernard had pushed him and his siblings away. Of course, nothing was ever that simple, but the basics were as good a place as any to start, especially when it came to a horse with PTSD.

"Tell him about Chief," Laney prompted, bringing Ray back into the conversation. "After all, that's why I invited him here."

"Right. Chief." Wilbur cleared his throat. "He's my best horse: a two-time National Reining Horse Association Futurity winner and Team USA prospect. He's worth a fortune—a true champion in blood and spirit. Chief is everything I could want in a reining horse: flawless lead changes, lightning-fast spins, and long, clean slides. I've never had a more promising colt, and I probably never will."

"He does sound pretty special," Ray agreed.

"Of course he does. He's my best horse," Wilbur reiterated, lightly thumping his fist against the table to emphasize his point.

"So, what's wrong with him?"

Wilbur sighed. "I don't know. Chief's been working with my best trainer, Kathleen Devaras, for the past two years. She's never had an issue with him until recently. She says he feels... pokey."

"Pokey?" Ray looked to Laney for clarification.

"I think what Wilbur means is he isn't himself lately," she ventured, clutching her coffee cup with both hands. Ray leaned forward, his brows furrowed with focus. "We were hoping you might have some idea of what could be bothering him."

Ray was acutely aware of Wilbur's stare, heavy with expectation, on his face. High-level performance horses were still horses, and, like humans, even the best among them were prone to bad days. Usually, when people sought Laney's expertise, it was because they'd exhausted all other options. Ray hadn't expected her to hand the metaphorical reins to him. All he could do now was hold on tightly and hope he didn't disappoint her.

"What did your vet say?" Ray asked, beginning with the most obvious question he could think of.

Wilbur answered, "He said Chief's the picture of health—no swellings or sores anywhere to be found."

"Any changes to his diet or training regimen?"

"Not a chance. He's on a strict schedule—and I have only the best people watching him around the clock, making sure he gets plenty of food, fresh air, and exercise."

No surprises there, Ray thought. He ran through his mental checklist one more time before taking a leap of faith. "What about Kathleen?"

"What about her?"

With a quick glance at Laney, Ray hedged, "Maybe she's doing something he doesn't like, like using different tack or not grooming him as well as she should. It doesn't take much to upset a horse, especially one that's under constant pressure to perform."

Wilbur's eyes widened, scandalized by such an egregious suggestion. After a tense moment, he tore his eyes from Ray's, picked up his coffee, and said, "I'll have a talk with her, but I doubt she's doing anything differently. She and Chief are inseparable. That's why I trust her to know when something's wrong."

"Well, without actually seeing Chief for myself, I can't tell you what's bothering him," Ray said. "What I can tell you is that the longer a problem goes on, the worse it gets. I see it in my own horses all the time: what starts out as a bad day turns into a week of stall rest."

"Perhaps Raymond should pay a visit to Windreach," Laney suggested, looking at Wilbur as she spoke. "You know as well as anyone that you can't judge a horse based on what anyone else says. Raymond has worked with many of my horses in the past, and he's always delivered."

"Is that so?" Wilbur assessed Ray with an inscrutable expression. "All right. Come over tomorrow afternoon and we'll see what you've got."

"Tomorrow? I'm afraid that won't work."

"Why not?"

"My fiancée is coming to stay with us for a little while. Her flight lands at two o'clock and I promised I'd be there to pick her up from the airport."

Wilbur waved his hand. "That's fine. You can bring her. But I still want you to look at Chief as soon as possible." He pushed back his chair and rose from the table. "Laney… it's been a pleasure seeing you again. I'm sorry it took me so long to get around to it."

"Pleasure's all mine." Her smile lingered on his back as he headed for the door, lifted his white Stetson from the coat tree, and pressed it onto his head. As Ray watched Wilbur pull on his coat and walk back to his truck, his thoughts once again turned to his father, wondering what he would've said about Chief if questioned. Across the table, Laney was studying the pattern on her mug, her mouth still bent upwards at the corners.

Ray smirked. "A dear friend, eh?"

"Very dear," his godmother replied. "Wilbur and I met when we were young. We lost touch for many years, but that's the mark of a true friendship—the ability to pick up where you left off as if nothing's changed." She raised her gaze to his. "Wilbur is highly respected in this industry. He used to be a member of the Professional Bull Riders Association before leaving the world of pro rodeo to train and show reining horses. Wilbur is very well connected too, and has had dinner with Mickey Hammond on several occasions."

"Mickey Hammond?" A knot formed in Ray's stomach at the mention of the self-proclaimed Horse God. Four years ago, Ray had had the misfortune of working with one of Mickey's horses, a quarter horse mare named Blaze, who'd nearly killed Mickey's young son in a riding accident. Blaze had been one of Ray's more challenging project horses, but eleven months and one broken ankle later, he'd felt comfortable enough to let Hannah take her out on the trails. From the unwanted to the unrideable, Ray's belt was bursting with experience. But up until now, he'd only ever worked with the worst, never the best.

Sensing his apprehension, Laney said, "If I didn't think you were capable of working wonders with Wilbur's horse, I wouldn't have suggested he talk to you. But I told him you're one of the best."

"That seems to be a very popular word tonight," Ray muttered.

"You have a gift. I know you don't want to hear it, but your father was the same way. He denied having any sort of special talent, but in my experience, the people who are lucky enough to have a gift never consider themselves gifted. That's why I recommended you."

Ray sighed and avoided her gaze. The deep velvet of dusk had already descended on the sky, making the snow-covered backyard appear more grey than white. He had to go home, get back to his life as a fourth-generation cattle rancher. But for some reason, he couldn't make his feet move.

Laney cocked her head and asked, "What are you so afraid of, hon?"

"I'm not afraid. I'm just not sure why you think I can fix Chief. I breed Black Angus. That's who I am. I'm not a horse god like Mickey or a successful businessman like Wilbur."

"Breeding cattle is what you *do*. Who you *are* runs much deeper. Who you are is defined by the choices you make, not where you come from."

"Well, I come from a working ranch—and right now, I have to get back to it."

"All right."

"Do you need anything before I go?"

"No. Jim will be in soon. He's going to attempt to make chicken pot pie casserole."

"By himself?" Ray placed his empty mug in the dishwasher, trying to picture Jim moving around the kitchen as efficiently as Laney did. Or had.

Doubt rang clear in her voice. "That's the plan. Of course, I'll be directing him every step of the way."

"Of course," Ray chuckled. At least Laney had found a new pastime. He bent to kiss her cheek and said, "Thanks for the coffee."

"Good luck tomorrow. And give my best to Hannah."

"Will do." Ray smiled, slipped into his coat and boots, and stepped outside.

When he got to the ranch, Marcus was walking back to the house, his silhouette barely visible against the dark shape of the barn behind him. Ray parked his truck and met him halfway. To his surprise, the sand ring was empty, prompting both confusion and panic.

"Where's the gelding?" Ray asked.

Marcus looked up from the noisy tread of his boots and replied, "In the barn. We're supposed to get a cold snap tonight, and he's not in good physical condition as it is—certainly not well enough to stay outside in a light blanket."

"I'd think a barn's the last place he wants to be, given the circumstances." Ray felt his anger building. "Not that I really want anything to do with him, but you don't take a horse that supposedly has PTSD and stick it in an unfamiliar barn overnight. He needs to work up to that slowly. *I* need to work with him until I know he won't hurt himself trying to escape."

His brother fixated on him with a quizzical stare. After a moment, Marcus narrowed his eyes and asked, "What does Laney want from you this time?"

"It doesn't matter."

"Yes, it does. The gelding is fine. You're not. What's going on?"

Ray chose his words carefully. Marcus would insist he was overreacting to Laney's request, but to him, no favour was too great if it made her forget about her declining health. Wisely, Ray decided not to mention their father, which would trigger Marcus's anger as easily as the gelding's untimely arrival had triggered Ray's.

"Do you know a guy named Wilbur McCullough?" Ray asked.

"The name sounds familiar. Another friend of Laney's, I'm guessing?"

"Yeah—and, apparently, he's friends with Mickey Hammond. Or acquaintances, at least."

Marcus's brows shot up. "The Horse God, Mickey Hammond?" When Ray nodded, Marcus asked, "So, where do you fit in to all this?"

"Wilbur has a horse he needs help with, and Laney recommended me. I agreed to go over to Wilbur's place tomorrow and see what I can do."

"But Hannah's coming tomorrow."

"I know. Wilbur said it's okay if she comes with me." Ray added, "Laney seems to think I possess some 'gift' for training horses, only I can't see it."

"You can't," Marcus replied flatly.

"So, you agree with her?"

"As much as it pains me to admit this, you're a lot like dad. Not in the way that you'd ever walk out on this family or hurt Hannah, but he was a cowboy, you know?" Marcus's expression softened with an emotion Ray couldn't identify. "That's what you are. Old stock."

"And you're a moron."

"Maybe." Marcus kept walking up to the house until his footsteps faded from Ray's awareness.

Inside the barn, the sweet smell of fresh hay rose thick in the air. Ray walked down the long aisle, naming each horse as he passed its stall, until he reached the box at the end. Pressed into the back corner and shivering under the nylon blanket, the latest addition to their herd trained a wary eye on Ray as he leaned on the door.

Ray glimpsed the sprinkle of hay under the water bucket. "Not hungry, eh?" The gelding swiveled its ears in the direction of Ray's voice, but didn't move from the safety of its dark corner. "You must've been trapped in that barn for a long time. You've forgotten how it feels to be a horse."

Marcus's voice cut into Ray's memories: telling him about their father without bitterness or reproach, how he was "old stock," which Ray had taken to mean that the old ways of doing things were still the best ways they had, methods that had kept them in business generation after generation. But this horse standing in front of him would need a different kind of help.

"What are you so afraid of?" Ray asked. The gelding turned its head toward him, even dared to take a small step toward the hay. "Are you afraid of being abandoned again?"

The gelding sniffed at the air, where the unfamiliar scents had swirled into one. Horses navigated the world by smell, creating detailed mental maps of the places they'd been so they'd know what to avoid in the future. Ray held out his hand for inspection, felt the coarse whiskers of the gelding's muzzle against his skin, and smiled at this glimmer of progress.

"Yeah. I think I'm afraid of that, too." Ray backed away from the stall as the horse began to nibble on a few bits of alfalfa. He walked toward the door and switched out the light, leaving the barn's occupants to a warm slumber.

Three

"Is this it?" Hannah asked.

"I think so." Ray steered into the driveway. A large wooden sign erected a few yards beyond the entrance proclaimed the property 'The Home of Champions since 1984' beneath the words *Windreach Farms*. A Coverall arena rose out of a sea of dark green firs in the distance, its canvas peak gleaming in the afternoon sun.

Beyond the house, the driveway branched in three directions. One of the snowy prongs widened into a parking lot enclosed by a white-painted fence. The second led directly to a barn, oddly shaped to resemble a plus sign instead of the classic rectangular foundation. Wilbur must've been using the additional space for wash stalls and other show barn amenities, since Ray didn't see any rusty water pumps outside. The third, and longest, branch pointed to the Coverall arena. Like Laney, it appeared the McCulloughs had spared no expense in the property's construction, left no detail to chance. Ray parked the truck alongside several others and turned off the engine.

"Thanks for coming with me," he told Hannah. "I promise, this won't take long."

"That's okay. I've spent too much time indoors today. And it looks like the arena's heated." Hannah indicated the spectators in the stands, whose light sweaters and nylon vests pointed to an alternate heat source. A man like Wilbur could afford every comfort, and the cost to heat a space as large as the Coverall must've been astronomical.

The inside of the arena had been divided into two separate spaces: a sandy area enclosed by a low wooden wall where horses and riders trained and performed, and a row of metal bleachers where viewers could sit and observe. At one end of the sandy portion, a man on a bay gelding was instructing a group of students on lead changes and counter-bending. A short distance away, a palomino colt was cantering in circles. The woman riding him wore a black cowboy hat, dark blue shirt, and full-length leather chaps over her jeans. After a couple of laps, they steered toward the centre of the ring, completing a swift figure eight and flying lead change before repeating the pattern in the opposite direction. By all accounts, this was a horse bred for performance, able to remain calm and focused in even the busiest settings. The duo circled inward again, picked up a bit of momentum, then, in a perfect imitation of the decal on Wilbur's truck, slid to a stop in a spray of sand. The woman reached down to pat the palomino's neck before reining him toward the gate.

Wilbur was leaning on the wall, his forehead creased beneath the rim of his white Stetson. "Well?"

"You saw as well as I did. He's still holding back." The woman dismounted and lifted the reins over the palomino's head.

"A horse like Chief doesn't hold back without a good reason. I don't care what it costs me—I *will* find out what that reason is."

Ray slipped his hands into his pants pockets as he approached the wall. At the sight of him, Wilbur's face split into a grin.

"Ah, you made it," the older gentleman exclaimed, offering his hand for Ray to shake. "I was starting to think the idea of working with my best horse might've scared you off."

"No way. Besides, I think I'm more afraid of disappointing Laney."

Wilbur nodded. "You're a smart kid." As Hannah joined the group, he added, "And a lucky man, from the looks of it. Pleasure to meet you, darling. I'm Wilbur McCullough." His hand went out to her, along with a charming smirk.

"Hannah," she returned with a smile.

"By the way, I hear congratulations are in order. When's the big day?"

"July 25th. We were going to get married this year, but Hannah finished university a few months ago and we couldn't really afford it," Ray explained.

"Well, that won't be a problem when you're working for me." Wilbur swept an arm out across the arena to where his best horse and rider awaited introduction. "Ray, I'd like you meet Chief and Kathleen. Kathleen's my head trainer and knows everything there is to know about Chief."

"So, what's wrong with him?" Ray asked.

"That's what we're trying to figure out." Kathleen stroked Chief's neck, obviously troubled by the lack of answers. "Wilbur's had everyone you can think of look at Chief and give their expert opinion: farriers, veterinarians, even an equine acupuncturist."

"And now you," Wilbur told Ray, propping his elbow on the wall. "Laney was supposed to be my last hope. But seeing as she's unwell, and you come so highly recommended, I'm eager to hear your theories."

Ray directed his focus at Chief. The palomino was a shining example of what time, money, and proper care could do to a horse. If Laney were here, what would she ask? Which piece of the puzzle had gone overlooked?

"Mind if I take a closer look at him?" Ray asked.

"Be my guest."

Ray entered the sand ring and conducted a head-to-toe inspection of Wilbur's pokey prize-winner. Chief's eyes were clear and bright, as they should be. A quick peek in his mouth revealed no abscessed teeth or bit sores. As Ray palpated the horse's neck and throat, ruling out grass mumps and strangles, a memory of his father flashed to mind. At just seven years old, Ray had watched his father's hands the way other children watched TV, mesmerized by the ceaseless motions. Sometimes, the motions were gentle and soothing. Other times, those same hands looked like nothing Ray had ever seen, smeared in blood and dirt, the callouses as thick as a horse's chestnuts. Now that he was older, Ray understood that things often appeared quite different on the surface compared to what lay below. If he wanted to help Chief, he had to look past the coat conditioner and the flashy tack, get his hands dirty, and uncover the truth.

"Well?" Wilbur said. "You must have some idea by now what's bothering him."

Ray ran his hands down both of Chief's back legs, found them cool to the touch, and straightened.

"There's no physiological explanation as far as I can tell," he said, patting Chief's rump. "Are you the only one who rides him?" Ray asked Kathleen.

"Yes. Although sometimes Don fills in for me." She indicated the man in the background, who'd moved on from lead changes and was now explaining proper finger position on the reins.

"Has he noticed anything different?"

"Not as far as I know. Then again, he rides so many horses, he wouldn't necessarily notice if one of them is out of sorts." Kathleen spoke directly to Chief now, as Ray imagined Laney would do if she were here. "I'm sorry, buddy. I promise, we're working as fast as we can."

"My dad always used to say if horses could talk, we'd realize how little we know about them," Ray said.

"Your dad sounds like a wise man."

Ray declined to comment as he and Kathleen exited the arena, with Chief plodding between them. Wilbur led the group across the dusky yard to the barn. Bright, airy stalls lined the aisle on both sides, and each door had a wide scoop in the middle so that the horses could look out and observe their surroundings. Two rows of arctic-white fluorescent bulbs hung from the ceiling and illuminated the small, metal nameplates mounted to the doors. Everything had its place here, from the winter blankets folded over their metal rods, to the bottles of Showsheen lining the caddies on the floor.

Hannah stood off to the side, feeling out of place as she watched Kathleen unsaddle Chief. Then again, this year been unusually cruel in terms of making Hannah believe she didn't belong. Vancouver had been too expensive, the job at CPS beyond traumatizing. Back in Kamloops, she'd stood in Logan's living room and tried to ignore the reality that she was merely a guest, not a friend or a roommate, as she'd been so many times before. She'd come to Windreach as a way to support Ray, but it was apparent he could've handled the visit on his own.

Kathleen slung the honey-brown saddle over the stand and proceeded to remove Chief's boots. "You're dressed fancy for the barn," she said above the ripping of the Velcro straps.

Hannah came back to herself, glanced at the skirt peeking out from under her coat, and replied, "This is what I wore on the plane. Well, not the boots. Ray brought them from home."

"Do you travel a lot?"

"I have to, if I want to see my fiancé in person."

Kathleen removed the skid boots on Chief's rear legs and set them on the seat of the saddle. Spirals of steam curled along the horse's back. The saddle pad had tramped down his pale golden coat, leaving a damp, grey impression between his withers and his hips. Another outline, this one encircling his girth, marked the location of his cinch.

"I used to be married, once," Kathleen stated. Reaching for the cooler draped over the front of one of the stalls, she spread it over Chief's back and fastened the necessary clips to hold it in place. "Thank God that's over."

"What do you mean?"

Kathleen ducked under the crosstie and took a seat on a nearby footstool. One by one, she undid the buckles on her chaps, her voice taking on an air of nostalgia as she spoke.

"Cue the happy memories. I was young and in love—we both were, but I was young in that way that made me feel like I had something to prove. So, Hank and I got married. As soon as that ring was on my finger, I knew I'd made a huge mistake. Of course, I couldn't admit that to my friends and family because, as I said, I was trying to prove I was ready for a lifelong commitment."

"Were you and your husband together for a long time before you got married?" Hannah asked.

"Oh, about four years. Hank kept saying, 'If we haven't broken up by now, we never will.'" Kathleen smiled wryly, coaxing a tiny wrinkle from the corner of her mouth. "To be fair, four years feels like a lifetime when you're twenty-five. That quarter-life crisis came at me like a runaway train."

The weight of Kathleen's confession settled on Hannah's shoulders like a humid August afternoon. She'd be turning twenty-five next year, four short months before she and Ray said "I do." Even in the most colloquial sense, *tying the knot* had the audacity to sound like a threat. Rather than a scrapbook of highlights from their life, Hannah now pictured their marriage as a length of rope, with both of them pulling against the other's weight, the other's hopes and dreams for the future. Kathleen was right: four years *had* felt like a lifetime to Hannah when she was in university, writing to Ray in the evenings and wondering what he was doing during the day. But they'd made it work, hadn't they? She was here, wasn't she?

Ray and Wilbur reappeared. At some point in Hannah and Kathleen's conversation, Wilbur had offered to give Ray a tour of Windreach's facilities. Now that the men were back, and Chief nearly cool to the touch, Hannah felt herself growing restless. It had been a long day of traveling, and her body ached for a warm meal, a hot shower, and Ray's delicate touch. He extended a hand toward her arm and squeezed lightly, as if to apologize for how long things were taking.

"Anyway, you can think on it," Wilbur said as Kathleen led Chief into a stall. "As I said, I pay generously, and I know all the right people. Chief's my best horse, and I wouldn't trust his wellbeing to just anybody."

Ray said, "I'm glad we had the chance to meet. I should have an answer for you by tomorrow morning."

"Pleasure's all mine." Wilbur shook Hannah's hand again. "And good luck on the wedding plans. Not that luck has anything to do with making a marriage last."

Kathleen laughed. "I wish someone had told *me* that. I fell into the trap of thinking love conquers all."

"I've been married thirty-eight years," Wilbur went on. "There were plenty of times I wanted to quit. Some days, we couldn't stand each other. All marriages are like that. You have to remember it's a team effort, like Kathleen and Chief here. You work together—that's the secret. Making it look easy is hard work."

"Thanks for the tip," Ray said. The couple said their goodbyes, then headed back to the truck, letting the crunching of snow under their boots fill the silence.

"What did Wilbur say?" Hannah asked.

"He wants to offer me a job working with Chief."

"For how long?"

"As long as it takes. I asked if I could have some time to think about it, and talk to you."

Ray reached for the passenger door so Hannah could climb into the truck. Meanwhile, Don and his students were still refining their technique inside the fully-illuminated Coverall. As Ray drove past the barn, parking area, and house to reach the road, Hannah said, "You don't need my permission to work with Chief. I know I came here so we could plan our wedding, but I don't want those plans to interfere with your life."

"I know. But maybe I need a second opinion."

"On whether you should work with Chief?"

"Yeah. I mean… Wilbur's offering me a lot of money. And it's his best horse."

Hannah narrowed her eyes. "How much money are we talking about, exactly?"

When Ray revealed the precise amount, Hannah asked him to repeat himself, certain she'd misheard. "That's a lot of money," she agreed.

"I know." Ray pried his focus from the road and smiled tentatively. "That's mainly why I want to take the job. Wilbur says he has a lot of connections, and I'm thinking they might help us attract more business to the ranch…"

His voice trailed off, prompting Hannah to ask, "So, what's stopping you from giving him an answer tonight?"

"I don't know. Maybe I need some more time to think about it." He added, "It *is* a lot of money."

Hannah smirked. Here was a chance to put her newly-minted psychology degree to use—a place where it might actually do some good. "Have you ever heard of Imposter Syndrome?"

"No, but it sounds serious. Should I be worried?"

"No. Imposter Syndrome is the feeling that you're a fraud, or that you won't be able to achieve something because you're underqualified. From what I've seen, you're neither of these things."

Ray turned a smile on her. "What would I do without you?"

"You'd be doing what you've always done: raising cattle, training horses, and putting up with Marc," Hannah replied.

"And what would you do without me?" Ray asked, steering down the tree-lined road leading to the ranch.

Hannah thought about her answer for a minute, watching the truck's headlights bob over the snowy rifts. "I don't know. I've never wanted to think about it."

When they arrived at the house, the lights in the kitchen were on, as well as those in the upstairs study. A line of smoke from the fireplace curled through the winter sky. Hannah breathed in its comforting sweetness as she stepped outside and felt for the first time that day like she'd finally come home.

Ray unloaded her luggage from the truck and carried it into the house. As Hannah walked through the door and placed her purse on the bench, footsteps pounded down the stairs and Marcus appeared wearing a faded red t-shirt and blue jeans.

"Look who it is," he exclaimed, taking Hannah into a hug. "Welcome back."

"Thanks," she replied.

Marcus addressed his brother, "How'd it go with Wilbur?"

Ray set down the suitcases and removed his coat. "It went well. He showed me around and introduced me to his best horse and trainer. I said I'd call him in the morning so we could discuss next steps."

"Next steps," Marcus repeated as they moved into the kitchen, where the table had already been set with three plates and three sets of cutlery. "What does that mean?"

Ray approached the stove and lifted the lid on the largest pan, where three chicken breasts simmered in a bath of spices that Laney had grown, picked, and dried herself. Marcus was leaning on the back of one of the chairs, still awaiting an answer as Hannah helped herself to a glass of water.

"It means he wants to offer me a job," Ray replied. He went to the fridge. "Do you want a beer?"

"Sure." As Marcus accepted the bottle, he took a sip and steered the conversation back on track. "How much is he offering to pay you?"

"Enough. How's the PTSD horse?"

"The PTSD horse?" Hannah said, quirking a brow.

Marcus idly swirled his beer and explained, "Laney got a call about a horse that was locked in a barn. A couple of hikers found him. Now, he's in our barn, and Laney's expecting Ray to perform a miracle."

"Which I can't do because I'm not the Pope," Ray said testily, "and if I decide to work with Chief, I'll have even less time. Oh, and let's not forget I'm trying to plan a wedding here."

"So, you guys just went onto someone else's property and took their horse?" Hannah asked. Ray had done a lot of questionable (and, at times, dangerous) things in the name of helping a horse, but trespassing seemed like a step too far.

Marcus replied, "You make it sound like we did something wrong. This horse hadn't been fed in weeks and the house was abandoned. What else were we supposed to do?"

"I don't know. Call the humane society?"

"Laney said she did that already. Hopefully they can figure out who owns the horse, and we can get this mess sorted out in a couple of weeks." *Then the gelding will be someone else's problem*, Ray thought with a twinge of compunction. He pulled out one of the chairs. "Let's eat."

After dinner, as Marcus cleared the table and washed the dishes, Ray helped Hannah carry her suitcases upstairs. The bedroom was tidy, but cool, the window open a crack to facilitate the flow of fresh, wintery air. Hannah set down the carry-on just as Ray walked through the door and closed it behind him.

"I see you cleaned up," she said, surveying the room, which was normally cramped and cluttered.

"Enjoy it while it lasts. I won't have many opportunities to clean over the next few weeks." Ray leaned her suitcase against the wall and shut the window. As the supply of fresh air was extinguished, Hannah was overcome by the scent of pine and damp denim she'd come to associate with life on a working ranch. Ray smirked and stepped toward her. "Speaking of opportunities…"

His hands cupped her face, drawing it toward his own as the cool caress of his lips numbed the light pink crease of her mouth. It was the first kiss they'd shared since she'd landed, and Hannah allowed the hungering motions of his tongue to feed into her desire for comfort. She pressed into him, biting the fleshy protrusion of his bottom lip until Ray pulled back with a soft chuckle.

"Missed me that much, eh?" he said, wiping his hand across his mouth.

A blush warmed her cheeks. "A little." Hannah wrapped her arms around Ray's waist. "So, are you going to take the job?"

"Probably." He cocked his head, "By the way, why were you so upset about Laney rescuing the gelding? I thought you, of all people, would understand."

"I don't know. I just… worry sometimes."

"You worry too much." Ray pressed a kiss to her forehead and turned away, going to his dresser for a change of clothes.

Hannah couldn't deny this, so, as Ray left to take a shower, she lifted the larger suitcase onto the bed and began transferring her clothes into the dresser. Each time she visited, Hannah treated the unpacking of her suitcases like a sacred ritual, but tonight, the process felt harried, and she wondered how much her conversation with Kathleen had contributed to her unsettled state.

"You can put those in the closet, if you want," Ray offered as he entered the room a few minutes later. It wasn't like Hannah to be so careless, especially when it came to her clothes. "I can probably find some more hangers if you need them."

"No, this is fine." She quickly shut the drawer, snagging a grey wool cardigan in the process. After stuffing the material down, she returned to the bed and hunted for something else.

Ray approached her and placed both hands on her shoulders. He could still feel the blood throbbing in the spot where her teeth had pinched his mouth. Had she thought he was rejecting her when he pulled away in surprise?

"Hey," he said. "What's going on?"

"Nothing."

"Like hell it's nothing. Five minutes ago, you were ready to rip off my clothes. Now you can't even look at me." Ray fought the urge to scowl and lost. "I wasn't rejecting you, you know. I've been deprived of human touch for far too long to say no to anything."

"I know," she replied, sighing. Her facial features relaxed slightly as she unburied another item from her suitcase. "I'm sorry. It's not you, okay? I want you."

Ray spread his arms. "Great. I'm glad we cleared that up."

"No, Ray, you don't get it. I've always wanted you. I've always *needed* you." She paused, swallowing the uncomfortable feeling in her throat, and took a seat on the bed.

Hannah continued, "When you were with Wilbur, Kathleen told me about her husband and how they had gotten divorced. Even my own

34

mother talks about how young couples always end up growing to hate each other. I never wanted to believe her, but if she's telling me all this, then it must be true—"

"It's not. Nothing could be farther from the truth," Ray insisted, taking a seat beside her.

"But what if it is? We're so young. I met you when I was eighteen. I wasn't even done high school, at that point. And now we're getting married…" Ray reached for her hand. "Maybe I'm scared. I don't want us to end up hating each other."

"We're not going to hate each other." Ray raised his other hand and gestured toward the window. "Those other couples out there, they're not us. They haven't survived what we've survived. And I know you're scared, but you've always been strong, and I'm always going to be here for the times when you're not." Using his thumb to turn the peridot toward the light, he whispered, "I love you. That's never going to change."

Hannah nodded, a hint of a smile lining her face. Brushing the tears from her cheeks, she appraised the jumble of belongings spilling out of her suitcase and sighed at the seemingly insurmountable task that lay ahead. "I think I overpacked."

"That's okay. We have lots of room."

"We're going to make this work, right?" she asked.

Ray smiled easily, like he'd never had a single worry in his whole life. "We always do, don't we?"

Four

"All rise."

Everyone in the courtroom stood up. As the Honorable Judge McKay proceeded to the bench, Adrianna hoped justice would prevail, and that the faith she'd put in her lawyer, Odessa Hanson, had not been misplaced. The obliging shuffle of chairs and feet quieted at last, and a thick silence fell over the room. Judge McKay took a seat and spread his files across the bench before finally addressing his audience.

"Please be seated," he said. Chairs were filled, and any breaths that had been withheld emptied into the surrounding clamor. Adrianna tucked her chair under the table where she and Odessa had been instructed to sit and aimed to look composed, rather than tense, as she faced the front of the room. Her midnight-blue skirt and matching jacket, buttoned over a white blouse and accented with a string of pearls, had been specially purchased for the occasion. Four years after Doug had cornered her in a dark parking lot and ravaged her dignity, Adrianna knew that in order to sway the jury, she'd have to convince them that she'd been the victim of a crime rather than the result of an improperly thought out choice. She couldn't just speak her truth—she had to kill the doubt, too.

Judge McKay began, "Thank you all for being here today. For those directly involved in the case, I appreciate your cooperation with regards to some last-minute scheduling changes. Now, without further ado, I'll call formally the case of Bishop v. Alderman. Are both sides ready?"

"Yes, your Honour," Odessa replied, rising to address the judge. At a neighbouring table outfitted with two wooden chairs, Doug's attorney, Marshall Newman, stood as well, quickly buttoning his jacket in the process.

"Yes, we are, your Honour," he said in a voice that filled the room.

"All right. You may be seated." Odessa and Marshall returned to their seats as Judge McKay continued, "We'll start by hearing opening statements from the Crown followed by the defense. Once both parties have had a chance to present the details of the case, we will proceed with witness testimonies and the examination and cross-examination of the witnesses. Prosecution, you may deliver your opening statement now."

Odessa stood up.

"Good afternoon, your Honour," Odessa said. "My name is Odessa Hanson, and I will be representing my client, Adrianna Bishop." She paused briefly, casting a glance at the men and women assembled in the jury box. "Four years ago, my client was walking back to her car after work when she was approached and assaulted by the defendant. As a result of the attack, my client suffered physical, emotional, and psychological hardship that persists to this day. In a single second, my client's life was forever changed. During the course of this trial, the court will hear testimony from the victim and character witnesses. It is my hope that, at the conclusion of the jury's deliberations, truth will prevail, and my client will be able to reenter society safe in the knowledge that her attacker has been brought to justice. Thank you." With a nod at Judge McKay, Odessa sat down once again.

"Thank you, Ms. Hanson. Defense, please present your opening statement."

Marshall got to his feet. "Thank you, your Honour." He cleared his throat, then pointedly addressed the jury. "Four years ago, my client, Douglas Alderman, found himself down on his luck. The end of his engagement resulted in emotional and psychological hardship that negatively impacted his professional, personal, and social life. Not long after that, my client was accused of committing a violent crime against the complainant—a claim I will attempt to prove is not only false, but infinitely damaging to the defendant's reputation."

Adrianna quelled the urge to scoff. If Doug's reputation was the only damage he'd suffered, then he was clearly the winner in this situation. She corrected the hem of her skirt and arranged her facial features into a veneer of indifference. Perhaps if she didn't acknowledge Doug's self-destruction, the jury would be equally compelled to retain their sympathy.

37

"Thank you," Judge McKay said. After a bit more shuffling, he raised his gaze to Adrianna's. The ticking of her heart filled her ears. She clung to life by a single, shallow breath as she waited to be summoned to the witness stand, where she would testify against the man she'd once sworn she couldn't live without.

"And now," Judge McKay stated, "we'll hear the victim's testimony."

Steeling herself, Adrianna scraped back her chair, straightened the fit of her jacket, and made her way to the stand, where she'd be able to see every face watching from the gallery. Seated near the back of the room, Victor issued a subtle nod of encouragement. Heather sat beside him, next to Adrianna's mother, who'd worn matching pearls as a gesture of solidarity. Adrianna worried her skirt again, then threaded her fingers together in her lap until her hands stopped shaking.

"Thank you for being here, Ms. Bishop. Now, in your own words, could you tell the court what happened the night of the crime?" Odessa asked.

"Yes." Adrianna flicked her eyes toward the accused, but Doug merely waited, masking his true feelings behind a look of boredom. His attorney observed her shrewdly, ready to pick apart her testimony in the cross-examination.

Odessa raised her brows. "Ms. Bishop? Do you need a moment to collect yourself?"

"No." Adrianna sat up in her chair, channeling her words out over the courtroom. "Four years ago, I was walking back to my car after a twelve-hour nursing shift at Aspen General Hospital when the defendant approached me in the staff parking lot. I could tell he'd been drinking—"

She faltered and stared down at her skirt, rumpled by her anxious fumbling. Twelve pairs of eyes, seven women and five men, trained on her with a look of thinly-veiled skepticism.

"What happened next?" Odessa prompted. "You encountered the defendant in the parking lot and you observed that he was inebriated. Did you and the defendant have any verbal interaction?"

"Yes."

"And what was said during the interaction?"

"I asked him what he was doing here, at the hospital."

"What did he say?"

"He said that he came to see me. He wanted to know if I'd received the flowers."

"Flowers?"

"He brought me flowers at Christmas. I threw them out." Adrianna looked at Doug as she spoke, as if she were addressing him personally.

"At the time that the defendant brought you flowers, what was the status of your relationship?" Odessa went on.

Adrianna replied, "The defendant and I were not dating at that time. I was living alone. In fact, I was seeing someone else."

Her attorney nodded, her expression solemn. *Good.* "Ms. Bishop, you claim that the defendant was intoxicated when he approached you in the parking lot. Would you say Mr. Alderman has a drinking problem?"

Marshall cut in, "Objection, your Honour—leading question."

Judge McKay addressed Odessa. "Counsel, please rephrase the question for the witness."

"Of course, your Honour. Ms. Bishop, can you tell us how you were feeling in that moment?"

"I was terrified. Doug appeared distraught, and I'd known him long enough to anticipate that the situation would escalate."

"And did it?"

"Yes. He started swearing and calling me names. When I tried to deescalate the situation, that's when he attacked me."

Silence hung over the courtroom. Before long, Odessa, satisfied with this account, said, "Thank you," and returned to her seat.

"Defense will now cross-examine," Judge McKay announced.

As Marshall rose to take Odessa's place, Adrianna once again found her hands tangling with the fabric of her clothes, just as Doug's hands had done the night of the attack.

"Ms. Bishop, you said the defendant brought you flowers at Christmas. Any idea why he might've done this?"

"He said it was his way of apologizing for everything that had happened between us."

"So, the defendant did try to apologize to you directly."

"You have to understand that Doug's apologies—"

"Please answer the question, Ms. Bishop."

Adrianna relented. "Yes, he did."

"And after the defendant attempted to apologize, did you consider trying to fix the relationship?"

"No."

"Why not?"

"Because I'd made it clear to Mr. Alderman that we were no longer a couple. I'd moved out and ceased contact with him."

"Let's talk about what happened in the parking lot," Marshall went on, tucking both hands in his pockets. "What time did you get off work?"

"Around 9PM."

"Was it dark?"

"Of course. It was 9PM."

"If it was dark, how did you know the defendant was under the influence of alcohol?"

"I'm a nurse, Mr. Newman. I'm quite familiar with the symptoms of intoxication. Plus, when he got close enough to me, I could smell it on his breath."

"All right, so let's review the facts: Mr. Alderman had attempted to not only apologize to you for his behaviour, but he also brought you flowers at your place of work. Would you say his alcohol use was a direct result of you shunning his attempts at reconciliation?"

"Your Honour, that's pure speculation," Odessa interjected, "my client is a nurse, not a mind reader."

"I'll allow it," Judge McKay said.

"Yes," Adrianna said at length, "I think that's a fair and reasonable conclusion."

"No further questions, your Honour." Marshall returned to his seat on the opposite side of the room. Doug was looking more smug by the minute, but there were still several witnesses to interview and more truths to uncover. Plenty of opportunities to call his bluff, Adrianna hoped.

"Now that both sides have had a chance to examine the witness, I will ask the Crown to once again approach the stand and clarify any details of the testimony for the jury," Judge McKay explained. He leaned back in his chair, his broad shoulders sagging beneath the black robe.

Odessa smiled peaceably. "Ms. Bishop, I want to make sure your testimony is accurate and complete for the record." As Adrianna indicated her assent with a nod, her attorney said, "After you and the defendant ended your relationship, he made several attempts at reconciliation despite your desire to have no contact with him. He repeatedly approached you at your place of work, and on at least one of these occasions, the defendant was under the influence of alcohol. Do I have everything correct so far?"

"Yes."

"All right. Now, moving on to the attack, the defendant made inappropriate remarks that caused you emotional and psychological harm. In my opening statement, I also made reference to physical hardship. At this time, I would like to submit, as evidence, the results of Ms. Bishop's Sexual Assault Forensic Exam. I have also obtained a copy of the complainant's medical records from the night of the crime."

Odessa made her way back to the table. Before the hearing began, she'd painstakingly organized her paperwork into piles, flagging, highlighting, and colour-coding where appropriate. There was one pile for the evidence, another for copies of relevant documents submitted by the defense, and a third for the notes she'd compiled on the case. Her fingers rifled through the stack of evidence and liberated a copy of the rape kit results. She handed them to Adrianna.

"Ms. Bishop, could you please read what's highlighted for the court?"

Adrianna accepted the document. "Following a thorough examination of the victim and collection of samples, our laboratory has identified the DNA contained herein as belonging to Douglas Wade Alderman." She clamped her teeth over her bottom lip. To see it written so plainly, so irrefutably, and so publicly, it seemed impossible to lose the jury's faith. She relinquished the document and glimpsed Doug's face. No reaction, as expected.

"Thank you," Odessa said. Compassion compelled her to add, "I know this must be difficult for you."

Adrianna declined to comment. No point in stating the obvious, even if it was the truth. As she prepared to return to her seat, Marshall stood abruptly. He slotted the finicky button on his jacket through its hole and asked, "Your Honour, may I approach the witness?"

Judge McKay faltered. Adrianna, who was halfway out of her seat, sank back into its wooden embrace. She'd served her time on the stand, told the jury the whole truth about why they'd been assembled. What had she missed? What had Doug told his attorney when the eyes of the room were on her?

"Counsel, this isn't how we do things in my courtroom," Judge McKay intoned.

"I'm aware that this is an odd request, but I'd like the jury to have all the facts," Marshall replied. "If I may, your Honour, I have one more question for the witness."

He then turned to Adrianna, smiled as if they'd known each other for years, and took a pointed step in her direction.

"Ms. Bishop, given your personal history with the defendant, as well as the results of the forensic exam, which only prove that my client was present on the night you claim to have been attacked... how can the court be sure that you did not consent?" Marshall's snakelike eyes narrowed on her. "How do we know you didn't ask for this?" He undid his button and returned to his seat. "No further questions, your Honour."

Five

An artist's brush couldn't have painted a more picturesque scene, from the sunlight that slanted through the trees, to the two-lane highway that curved through the mountains as gently as a stream. Yet, even as Adrianna was admiring the cloudless blue sky and distant white peaks, Marshall Newman's words played on repeat in her mind, drowning out the latest hit country song thrumming through the radio.

Victor reached for the dial and switched off the music. "You're still thinking about him, aren't you?"

Adrianna faced the driver's seat and forced a smile. "No, not really. I thought the whole point of getting out of town was to forget about the trial."

Victor raised a brow disbelievingly. His lip quirked as his focus returned to the road, flanked on both sides by pale aspens and several meters of snow. "Exactly."

"You're not thinking about the trial? At all?" Adrianna didn't believe he could forget it if he tried. He'd been at the hospital the night of the attack and seen firsthand the damage Odessa had alluded to in her opening remarks. When news of Doug's arrest had broken, Victor had sat with Adrianna on the kitchen floor as she sobbed into the phone, telling her mother that it would all be over soon.

Victor steered down the snowy, less-traveled road leading to the ranch. A blinding panorama of windswept fields, ice-encrusted fence boards, and hardy evergreens shouldering a thick layer of white drove a stake of dread through his gut. He may have grown up here, but this place wasn't home to him anymore.

"Of course I am," he replied softly. "I'm always thinking about it."

Adrianna leaned forward and rummaged through the cloth bag at her feet. As Victor approached the house, she folded back the cover on *Today's Bride* and said, "This is kind of pretty. I'm not sure if it's Hannah's style though."

Victor glanced at the image of a blushing bride sheathed in an ivory mermaid gown. Lace flowers bloomed on the bodice and skirt, while the train spilled in a sheer waterfall down her back. "You'd look amazing in that," he said.

"Too late—we're already married."

As she continued to leaf through the pages, he asked, "Do you regret that we eloped?"

"No. It saved us a ton of money and stress."

The old farmhouse came into view as they rounded a copse of trees. Ray's truck was parked in front of the porch. Down near the barn, a few of the horses were digging through the snow in search of elusive grass. Victor guided the truck down the pathway leading to the paddocks, parked by the barn, and took a deep breath.

"Remind me why we're here," he mumbled.

Adrianna tilted her head, a thin smile softening her face. "We're here because you haven't seen your brother in weeks. Plus, I want to give Hannah these magazines."

"Yeah, but Ray's probably busy. No sense disturbing him."

"You're not backing out of this," she told him with finality, "and if you won't do it for Ray, then do it for me."

Victor heaved a sigh and reached for the door. A dimple appeared on his right cheek as he said, "Fine—but you owe me later."

As the couple entered the barn, they found Blaze cross-tied in the aisle and Hannah, dressed in jeans, knee-high riding boots, and a green vest, aggressively scouring the mud from the horse's coat with a curry comb. Ray was in the background, moving from stall to stall to break up the ice that had formed in the water buckets. The frozen shards clinked into the plastic containers like glass.

"Long time, no see," Adrianna said as she slipped her hands into her pockets.

Hannah turned away from the caddy of grooming supplies and smiled. "It has been a while," she agreed, ducking under Blaze's crossties in order to hug Adrianna. "How are you?"

"I've been better," Adrianna admitted. "Victor and I are headed up to Vail for a little weekend retreat, but when we heard you were back in town, we decided to drop by for a visit."

"We can't stay long, though. Traffic gets pretty heavy around this time," Victor added. As Ray emerged from a stall wielding a hammer, Victor motioned to the isolation pen, where the rescue horse was sheltering in the lean-to. "New project horse?"

"Yeah. And it has PTSD, apparently." Ray set the hammer on the workbench alongside the other tools.

"He looks in bad shape."

"Laney said he was found in an abandoned barn by a couple of hikers. He hadn't been outside in months, and no one had been coming to feed him either. I've been giving him alfalfa every six hours to start with, then I'll mix in some timothy hay once I know he can handle the extra nutrients."

Victor nodded. Even under a heavy winter blanket, it was evident that the gelding was severely malnourished. When he'd arrived at the Fishers' ranch, his tail had been an unsalvageable tangle of dead hair and manure; Marcus had described it as trying to comb a brick. In a fit of mercy, he'd opted to cut off everything below the tailbone, leaving a scraggly orange tassel that would take months to regrow.

"I don't understand how anyone can be so cruel," Hannah said, referring to the gelding.

Adrianna merely shook her head; she couldn't understand it either.

"By the way," she said, holding up the bag of magazines, "these are for you—well, you and Ray, but mostly you. I'm sure you probably already have a million ideas, but a few more can't hurt."

"Thanks." Hannah peered into the bag. There had to be thirty magazines in this thing, all of them flaunting gorgeous models and audacious promises on the cover.

"You're welcome. I held on to them thinking Victor and I were going to have a traditional wedding with church bells and cake, but elopement was a better fit for us."

"I'm glad you did. Ray and I have been trying to pin down a venue for months, and I haven't even started dress shopping." Hannah smiled, trying to appear grateful for Adrianna's foresight instead of overwhelmed by the task at hand.

As Hannah turned her focus back to Blaze, Ray said, "I'm glad you guys are here—especially you." He nudged Victor's arm, causing him to stiffen. "I need help putting together the round bale feeder. I don't like leaving the hay on the ground, and Marc's at Jim and Laney's…"

"I would, but as I said, we have to get going." Victor glanced at his wife, hoping that something in her expression would convey the urgency he felt. After all, the mini vacation had been her idea—two whole days of nothing but peace, quiet, and each other.

She smiled. "We have time. Go help your brother."

The steel contraption designed to hold the hay contained two semi-circular halves that would need to be assembled using thick bolts and considerable elbow grease. It wasn't the kind of project that could be cobbled together in five minutes. Nevertheless, Victor arranged his facial features into the most congenial look he could manage, and trailed Ray out of the barn.

Once Victor and Ray were gone, Adrianna turned to Hannah and said, "Looks like you two have been busy around here."

"Yeah. Too busy to plan our wedding, apparently." Hannah clipped a lead rope to Blaze's halter and removed the crossties. "Marc's been gone a lot lately. He's worried about Laney and wants to spend as much time with her as he can. Unfortunately, that means Ray and I have to do all the work ourselves."

"Would it be easier if you hired help?"

As Hannah led the mare out into the sunshine, she explained, "I suggested it. Ray said it was a possibility, but he doesn't have time to interview people right now, especially since he picked up another job."

"Another job?"

"He's working for Wilbur McCullough, an old friend of Laney's. Wilbur has this futurity prospect named Chief who's underperforming. If Ray can figure out what's wrong with him, then Wilbur might ask him to work with some of his other horses."

"Sounds pretty promising."

The paddock gate creaked open and Blaze marched in, eager to be reunited with the herd. Once she'd removed the horse's halter, Hannah shut the gate and led the way back to the barn, leaving Ray and his brother to bicker about the most effective way to position the feeder. "Since you're here, would you like to come in for coffee?" she asked Adrianna.

"Coffee'd be great. And I'm sorry if it seemed like Victor was trying to get out of a favour. He's been anxious about the hearing and really needs some time to unwind."

"I understand." In fact, Hannah was completely sympathetic. When she'd broached the idea of spending Christmas on the ranch, she'd told Ray it was because she wanted to plan their wedding in person, which was true. But it was equally true that she'd wanted to get away from everything that had gone wrong in Canada: the job at CPS she'd been forced to leave, her shrinking social circle, and the realization that her life was progressing at a rate much faster than she'd anticipated, with no pit stops along the way to regroup and unwind.

They crunched up the snowy path to the house. As they walked through the door, Hannah removed her boots and set the bag of magazines on one of the kitchen chairs. Adrianna hung her coat and scarf on one of the pegs and gazed around at the cozy living room, replete with equestrian-themed decor. The sofa, love seat, and armchair were all made of worn, red leather, the cushions sagging from years of use. Adrianna studied her reflection in a Christmas tree ornament as Hannah prepared the coffee in the kitchen.

Hannah offered her a seat at the kitchen table and placed a stony blue mug in front of her. Adrianna wrapped her hands around the coffee's warmth as Hannah poured a cup for herself and sat down on the opposite side, where she'd be able to keep an eye on Ray. So far, he and Victor had managed to clear a spot in the snow where the feeder would sit, but building it required something neither of them had in abundance: patience.

"This is good coffee," Adrianna said after taking a sip.

Hannah smiled sheepishly. "It's that Pike Place one from Starbucks. One of the conditions of my moving in is that we splurge on the high-quality stuff."

"Then I guess it's a good thing Ray picked up another job."

Hannah's smile faded. She let her gaze sink to the cup of overpriced java and said, "I hope you don't mind me asking you this, but did getting married change your relationship with Victor?"

"Yes and no. Yes, because we have to work things out now, no matter how difficult they get, and no, because we're still best friends." She took another sip. "Are you worried things are going to change between you and Ray?"

"Terrified."

"That's normal. Marriage is a huge adjustment." Adrianna went on, "I don't think you have anything to worry about. I mean, how many couples can say they've made the long-distance thing work for six years? That's unheard of."

"That's what Ray said—that we're not like other couples. He's always been comfortable with the idea of getting married, and I've always been..." Hannah gnawed on her bottom lip, but the right words eluded her. "We're just very different. He goes with the flow and I plan everything to death."

"Sometimes a marriage needs that contrast," Adrianna countered. "Look at me and Victor: he's painfully shy, and I love going out with friends. If we were the same, we wouldn't be able to help each other grow."

49

"I guess you're right."

"Look, I know we've never really spent much time together, but you seem like a responsible person, and it sounds like you've given marriage a lot of thought."

"I have. Too much, I think."

"Do you love Ray?"

Hannah's eyes once again flickered to the pane of glass. "More than anything."

"Then you'll be fine." Adrianna reached into the bag and pulled out one of the magazines. As the faint scent of paper and ink flirted up her nose, she said, "So, still no venue yet, eh?"

"We have a few ideas. Laney wants us to have a traditional Catholic ceremony, but I'm an atheist and Ray hasn't been to church in years. We're meeting with the pastor tomorrow morning just to make her happy."

"What do you guys want to do?"

"Something non-denominational, like a barn wedding. Or maybe something fully outdoors: an afternoon ceremony on the hill where Ray proposed, with the mountains in the background."

"Both of those options sound beautiful. By the way, if you're still in need of a dress, I'll send you the info for the boutique I went to. The girls there are fantastic and believe that the dress should fit *you*, not the other way around." Adrianna thumbed through the glossy pages and turned the magazine toward Hannah. "I bet this would look great on you," she said of the mermaid gown she'd been ogling in the truck.

Hannah leaned forward and frowned. "It's gorgeous, but I don't think I could wear something so slender."

"What kind of dress did you have in mind?"

"I'm not sure—maybe something with a little more coverage? I need a dress that says 'I had a baby and never got my figure back.'"

As Hannah rose to place her empty mug in the sink, she saw more clearly the fences and paddocks that made up much of the front yard. A few steps beyond the gate, the hay feeder was officially upright and ready to serve its purpose. As some of the more inquisitive horses approached the circular trough, Ray and Victor climbed into Victor's truck for the short ride back to the house.

Moments later, after kicking the last bit of snow off his boots, Ray opened the front door and announced, "Feeder's up. That's one item off my never-ending to-do list."

"It looks great," Hannah replied. As Ray poured himself a cup of coffee, she said, "Now that that's done, maybe we can plan that wedding we keep talking about?"

"We will. I promise. As soon as I call the vet about the gelding and check in on Laney, we'll sit down and go through those magazines." Ray settled into his seat and placed his mug on the table. He took a sip and told his brother, "We're meeting with Lionel Kincaid before the sermon tomorrow morning."

"Father Kincaid? Why?"

Ray shrugged. "Laney wants us to have a Catholic ceremony."

"But you don't go to church anymore."

"It's just four walls and a roof. We need a place to get married, and we've known Father Kincaid for years. I don't see what the problem is."

"You and Hannah should do what's best for you guys, not what's best for Jim and Laney. Why do you think Addy and I eloped?"

"I thought you eloped because you hate crowds and tradition," Ray replied, his lip turning up on one side. "Anyway, we're keeping our options open. Hannah wants to have the wedding here, but there's no hope of getting Marc on board. So, the search continues."

Adrianna closed the magazine and stood up. "Well, thank you for the coffee, but we really do need to get going."

Victor had already stepped outside and was halfway to his truck by the time she finished zipping her coat and knotting her scarf. As Hannah reached for the door to close it, Adrianna faced her and said, "Best of luck with the wedding planning. I know how stressful it can be trying to get every detail right, even if you're just going to the courthouse. And don't hesitate to reach out if you ever need a break from the boys."

"Thanks."

Adrianna trotted down the porch steps and climbed into the passenger seat. By the time the couple disappeared from view, Ray was standing behind Hannah in the entryway, where a gust of wintery air fluttered the pages on the wall calendar. She quickly shut the door, then returned to the kitchen to sift through the magazines.

"Maybe we should take a vacation," she said idly as Ray leaned in the doorway, staring at his phone. "Go somewhere for a few days, just us. I wouldn't mind seeing more of Colorado."

Without looking up from the screen, Ray replied, "And who's going to look after this place, if Marc's always at Jim and Laney's?"

"Well, maybe Marc can post a Help Wanted ad on Craigslist or something."

Ray laughed. "Craigslist. That's funny." He lifted his gaze to hers. "This is a working ranch. We don't really take vacations around here: the animals need to be fed, stalls need to be cleaned, something always needs to be fixed." Ray gestured to the feeder for emphasis. "Don't get me wrong—I'd love to whisk you away to a nice hotel, but I just can't right now. Besides, we need money to pay for our wedding."

"I understand."

He slipped his phone into his pocket and stepped toward her, pressing his lips to her forehead. On his skin, Hannah could smell the rust from the paddock gate and the sweet, cloying scent of hay that was omnipresent in his clothes. When she'd accepted Ray's proposal, she'd known the long, hard days were part of the deal—and that their marriage would be anything but ordinary. She smiled as Ray angled toward the door, off to feed, clean, or fix something outside.

"You should show those magazines to Laney," he suggested as he pulled on his boots. "I'm sure she has tons of ideas."

"I'm sure."

Ray grinned despite the hesitation in her voice, then turned the knob and left the warmth of the house behind.

Six

"Are you ready to go?" Ray asked from down the hall.

Hannah tugged her ponytail into position and stood back from the mirror to appraise the slim black cardigan hugging her shoulders and waist. Though her wardrobe had never included anything that would be considered appropriate for church, her midnight black pencil skirt was conservative enough to give the appearance of a regular attendee. She'd skimped on makeup, but permitted herself to wear a simple gold chain around her neck to draw attention away from the dark circles under her eyes. It wasn't much, but for today, it would have to do.

"I think so," she called back, tucking a wayward strand of hair behind her ear.

Ray walked into the bathroom. The collar of his shirt was popped and a tie was draped over his shoulders.

Hannah turned to him and spread her arms. "What do you think?"

"I think you look like you're going to a funeral."

"Well, what did you expect? I pretty much avoided religious establishments after Cameron died."

Ray moved in front of the mirror. As he fashioned a knot in the tie in a series of turns and tucks, he said, "I kind of expected you to be excited."

"I *am* excited. I just… there's a negative association for me, whenever I think of a church. It's something I have to work through. Plus, I haven't exactly been behaving like a good Christian up to this point."

He looked over at her and smiled. "You think I'm a perfect Christian? I'm surprised I don't burst into flames every time I walk into a church."

After a bit more fiddling, he slid the knot up to his throat and smoothed down the collar of his shirt. Hannah had chosen to perch on the edge of the tub, and her gaze was on his back, taking in the unfamiliar sight. Most days, Ray's wardrobe leaned toward practicality and comfort, but she could get used to seeing him like this, dressed in a white, button-down shirt, grey slacks, and a tie. He cleaned up well, for a man who lived and breathed the great outdoors.

"We're still keeping our options open, right?" she asked, nibbling the corner of her thumbnail out of habit.

Ray spat out the mouthful of toothpaste. "Of course."

"Good."

As he returned his toothbrush to the holder, he said, "But it might be kind of nice to continue the tradition. The church has been around since my grandparents were kids. They got married there, and a few decades later my parents did the same. Now, it's our turn."

Hannah smiled indulgently. "I guess."

"Is it that you don't want to get married in a church, or that church in particular?" Ray leaned against the sink with his hands in his pockets, watching her closely.

"Both. I don't believe in God, and getting married in the presence of something I don't believe in seems like an awful way to start a marriage."

Ray nodded. "Do you want to know what I believe?"

"Yes."

"I believe that God is something we have to define for ourselves. So, getting married in the presence of God means getting married in a way that makes sense to you and me, not to Laney or anyone else in the congregation."

"Good luck convincing her of that. She's been texting me Bible verses ever since I got here."

"She's just a little bored right now, with it being winter and all. It doesn't mean anything."

"I hope you're right." Hannah stood up, smoothed down the front of her skirt, and crossed the room to the door. "In that case, we should get going."

"Hannah?"

She stopped in the doorway, tucking her hair back again as she faced him.

A smirk stretched over Ray's face. "You look good from the back too, in case you were wondering."

"Let's go," she said, hoping the firm tone of her voice would squelch the colour rising in her cheeks.

"Maybe we should start going to church," he continued. They headed downstairs to the front door, where the rest of Hannah's belongings sat in a neat pile of matching black accessories. "I'm not saying that because of how you look. I'm just saying it might be nice to be a part of something bigger."

As Hannah zipped up her coat, she replied, "I'm sure it would make Laney ecstatic."

"This isn't about Laney. It's about us building a life together." Ray watched as Hannah sat down on the bench and slipped on her shoes. Even with her hair pulled back, a short lock of it dangled above her right eye in a feathery brown loop. He reached forward to sweep the strands aside.

"Think about it, okay?" Ray said. His fingers rode over the curve of her ear until the hank of hair stayed put.

Hannah smiled. If there was a God, then He'd made Ray perfectly, from the tips of his fingers to the deep brown of his eyes, which always seemed to see her in ways she couldn't see herself. His hand was still at her cheek, so she pressed a light kiss into his palm and stood up slowly.

"I will," she promised.

*

The parking lot was empty when they arrived. As Ray pulled into a spot near the trees, Hannah sized up the church. Its white stucco exterior gleamed with flecks of snow and the circular window above the doors had seen better days, but given its remote location and family-like atmosphere, she couldn't help feeling a little charmed. Having Ray here, donning his Sunday best, wasn't exactly hurting the situation.

"This brings back memories," he said.

"Good ones?"

"Mostly. Shall we go inside?"

"We shall."

A musty smell wafted up from the floorboards as they stepped into the church. Two rows of pews flanked the narrow aisle leading to the pulpit, behind which stood a staid wooden cross. Along the walls, a series of stained glass windows depicted holy figures and religious symbols illuminated by the winter sun. But what really stood out to Hannah was the silence. It filled the rafters to the ceiling and lingered in the prosaic benches where countless lost souls had found solace. It drew attention to her heart beating steadily in her chest and the breath she'd interrupted in a moment of reverence.

Ray took her hand and a step forward. "Think you might change your mind?"

"Maybe." Their footsteps synchronized as they made their way down the aisle. "Could we fit everyone in here?"

"Everyone on *our* guest list, sure. Everyone on Laney's guest list… maybe not." Ray indicated one of the pews. "My family and I used to sit there when we attended Sunday service. Mom sat closest to the aisle so she could talk to the neighbours. Dad sat by the window, and the three of us sat in between them."

"I assume you stopped going to church when your mom got sick?"

"We stopped doing a lot of things. Laney would encourage her to read her Bible from time to time, but it didn't do much good. Laney eventually dragged me and my brothers back to church, but I never felt loved the same way again. Not until I met you."

They reached the front of the room and turned to look back at the vacant seats and hazy, filtered light. From this vantage point, it wasn't difficult to imagine the faces of their friends and family flushed from the July heat, the rose petals sprinkled on the floor, or the ancient doors propped open to break up the stifling humidity.

From somewhere behind them, the echo of footsteps on a wooden staircase heralded the arrival of a man in a black clergy shirt, dark khakis, and a white collar. His brown beard had been oiled to a luscious shine, while the hair on the top of his head had been combed back into a tight, brassy knot. Hannah clutched her purse with both hands, striving for a look halfway between innocent and composed. Beside her, Ray did a double-take, keeping his hands in his pockets and his eyes on the young priest who'd come to greet them.

Upon seeing Ray's confusion, the priest said, "Oh, you must've been expecting my dad. He told me you'd be coming by."

"We're supposed to be meeting with him to talk about our wedding," Ray explained with a glance at Hannah. "Is he here?"

"He's in Florida—said he needed a break from the cold. I'm taking over for him." The priest stepped forward, offering his hand to Ray first, then Hannah. "I'm Isaac, at least when the congregation's not around."

"Ray," he said, shaking Isaac's hand, "and this is my fiancée, Hannah."

"Nice to meet you," she chimed in, loosely gripping Isaac's warm, soft palm.

"Pleasure. So, Laney's told me all about you two. Long-distance for six years, huh?" As the couple confirmed this feat with small nods, Isaac smiled. "That's incredible. And people say long-distance relationships never work."

"Well, it hasn't always been easy," Ray admitted, casting another look at Hannah, "but for some reason, she said yes, so here we are."

Isaac's smile widened, revealing a set of straight, white teeth.

"I've got an office downstairs," he said, indicating the door behind him with a flick of his thumb. "If you folks will follow me, we can sit down and talk about what kind of wedding you'd like."

As Ray and Hannah fell into step behind him, Ray said, "Laney has her heart set on a traditional Catholic ceremony, but Hannah and I would like to keep our options open. We were even thinking we might do something on the ranch, but I'm not sure if you—or your dad—would be willing to travel."

"I'm cool with it. Have you picked a date yet?"

"July 25th," Hannah answered.

"I'll talk to my dad and see what we can do. I doubt he'll be in Florida then, but you never know with old folks."

They stepped through the door and descended the staircase. Underneath the church was a collection of rooms and a long, carpeted hallway that softened the tread of their feet. A quick peek behind one of the doors revealed several rows of child-sized desks positioned in front of a chalkboard. Adjacent to it, a small daycare offered stimulation in the form of board books, toy cubbies, and multi-coloured floor tiles. Isaac steered into a room on his right, and Hannah was taken aback by the disorderly state of his study. A wooden desk stood in the middle of the floor. Dozens of cardboard boxes were pushed up against the walls and piled on a lumpy green sofa, with handwritten labels such as "Flyers" and "Dishes" to differentiate one container from the next. It wasn't what Hannah had been expecting, but there was some comfort to be found in knowing that a man like Isaac, who was arguably in a position to judge other people, wouldn't mind if her life was a little messy.

"Grab a seat," Isaac said, indicating the chairs facing the desk. As Hannah and Ray sat down, Isaac approached the TV table in the corner and asked, "Coffee?"

"Coffee would be great," Ray replied for both of them.

"Cool. Give me a sec to grab some water, and we'll get started." Grasping the empty pot's handle, Isaac slipped into the hall, humming to himself as he disappeared.

Hannah leaned forward to set her purse down by her feet. "I like him," she said softly as she gazed around at the unkempt piles of paperwork. "What do you think?"

Ray pressed his lips together in contemplation. Laney should've probably mentioned that Father Kincaid was on vacation, but it wasn't her fault she'd been so forgetful lately. "He's okay. A little young, though."

Hannah shrugged. "He only needs to say a few words. And he might be open to a mixed-faith or non-denominational ceremony."

Isaac reappeared. He was still humming what sounded like some old choir song as he emptied the water into the machine, spooned some grounds into the filter, and pressed one of the buttons. Hot, fresh coffee burbled into the pot. Isaac planted himself in the chair on the opposite side of the desk, then steepled his fingers and studied the couple in silence.

"So, July 25th," he said suddenly, having come to some conclusion about the situation. "Why that date?"

"Summer weddings are popular," Hannah replied. "And Colorado is so beautiful in July."

"Plus, we wanted it to be a positive experience," Ray supplied.

Isaac quirked a brow at this peculiar word choice. Glimpsing the coffee maker to check on its progress, he asked, "Are you concerned about the rigours of marriage? Or is this more of an issue with the in-laws?"

"I think what Ray means is… we went back and forth on a date for a long time, and I said no to most of them because I tend to associate certain months with certain memories. For instance, I didn't want to get married in March or April because of some bad things that happened during those months."

"Ah," Isaac said, drawing out the lone syllable to emphasize his confusion. "What happened in March and April, if you don't mind me asking?"

"In April of 2008, my ex-boyfriend was killed in a drunk driving accident. It's been years since he died, but I don't know if I could be excited for the wedding while also reflecting on his death."

"I'm very sorry for your loss. I'm sure God and His angels are taking good care of him up there," Isaac offered. As Hannah nodded, he asked, "And what about March?"

Her pulse quickened. Despite the daycare centre, the sofa, and the coffee maker brewing its heavenly black gold, this was still a church, with a doctrine as rigid as the walls that surrounded them. Isaac may have been young, but age had never stopped anyone from assuming the worst, especially when it involved an unwed mother.

In the midst of Isaac's polite stare, Ray stated, "Too wet and cold. And we're always busy with the spring calves."

"I imagine you are. Well, we can perform a traditional Catholic wedding ceremony at any time of the year, even during major holidays. A simple Rite of Marriage ceremony can take up to forty-five minutes— longer if you want a full mass and communion afterwards."

Isaac stood up. From a box labeled "Dishes," he removed three mugs and transported them to the TV table, filling each one and adding milk and sugar as requested. This brief intermission allowed Hannah to gather her courage, and when the accommodating young priest handed her one of the mugs, she resolved to clear the air once and for all.

"Actually, it's not because of the cold. Or the calves." Hannah cradled the mug in her hands, letting its heat seep into her fingers. "in March of 2010, I gave birth to a daughter. Ray and I decided we weren't ready to be parents, so I arranged for a couple in Toronto to adopt her. Having her was the most difficult and rewarding experience of my life. I figured we had eleven other months to choose from—why take hers?"

"What's her name?" Isaac asked.

Hannah smiled mildly. "Denver."

"That's a great name." Isaac relaxed into his leather chair once more. He stroked his beard with one hand, appreciating its silky fullness as the conversation reclaimed its original purpose.

"So, how familiar are you both with Catholic weddings?" he asked.

"I grew up in the church. I know they involve a lot of singing and praying," Ray volunteered.

"I don't know anything about Catholic weddings," Hannah admitted, "but I'm willing to keep an open mind."

"Excellent. Well, to start with, we'd get all your nearest and dearest together in the church. The procession would then make its way to the altar, beginning with the groom and best man, and ending with the bride being escorted down the aisle by her father. Now, does the groom have a best man?"

"My older brother, Marcus," Ray answered.

"Terrific. And Hannah, have you selected a Maid of Honour?"

"I think so. But we haven't talked in a while, so I can't say for sure."

Ray said, "Laney's offered to read the Liturgy of the Word. I don't know if she'll be strong enough to stand for that long though, so I was thinking we could have someone stand up there with her, in case she gets tired and needs to sit down."

"Sure, whatever you want."

"Hannah's parents are flying in from Canada and I really want them to feel included, even though they're not religious. Would it be all right if they both gave her away?" Ray went on.

Again, Isaac had the decency to not look scandalized. "Of course. God is about love, and love has no rules. As long as you end up married at the end of the day, that's all that's important."

"Great." Ray leaned forward and offered his hand, along with a warm smile, to the priest. "Thanks for agreeing to meet with us, and also for the coffee. We'll let you know what we decide to do."

"Alrighty. And I hope you both know you're welcome here anytime. When my dad gets back from Florida, I'll fill him in on your wedding plans and we'll go from there."

Ray led the way back upstairs. As he and Hannah emerged behind the pulpit, she turned to look back at the cross mounted to the wall. She tried to picture herself standing under it, vowing to love Ray in good times and in bad times, in front of a room full of sweating, smiling beloveds.

"That wasn't so bad," Ray said, sounding relieved. He looked over at Hannah, her expression unreadable. "Did you still want to go see some more venues?"

"Yes. This church is beautiful though…" She wrapped a hand around his arm as they walked back down the aisle and left the warm glow of the church behind.

As she climbed into Ray's truck and buckled her seatbelt, Hannah asked, "Would you still believe in God if it weren't for Laney dragging you to church?"

"Of course." Ray started the engine, making the instrument panel rattle and the floorboards tremble. Every time she rode in his truck, Hannah expected it to break down and leave them stranded in the middle of nowhere.

"You don't regret that we didn't save ourselves for marriage?"

Ray glimpsed the passenger seat as they pulled out onto the road. "No. Like Isaac said: God is love, and what better way to honour Him than to love each other in the deepest way possible?"

"I'd never considered that. I always saw having sex before marriage as breaking some cardinal rule."

"I don't think love is supposed to have rules. Or plans." Even though the interior of the truck was still freezing, when Ray's hand glided over her thigh, his skin was warm enough to permeate the fabric of her skirt. Without taking his eyes off the road, he slid his fingers under the hem and along the black mesh of her tights, forcing the muscles in her belly to tighten.

"You're a very bad boy," Hannah scolded playfully.

"Yes, I am."

She bit her bottom lip to stifle a small noise of surprise, or maybe pleasure. She didn't have to look down to know his hand was no longer on her leg, although one would never know it by the unchanging landscape of his face—his eyes calm and focused, with a slight dimple in his right cheek as the only indication of his own enjoyment. Hannah reached for his hand, but didn't remove it.

"You should wear a skirt more often," Ray said evenly, "and not just on Sundays."

Hannah closed her eyes. She was just about to say something about his own attire when the truck drifted toward the shoulder and came to rest on the gravel, with the engine chattering loudly in her ears.

"Did we break down?" she asked, looking around in confusion.

Ray undid his seatbelt and threw it over his shoulder. "No."

Comprehension dawned on her face, and she shook her head at his intrepidness. "Wait, here? Now?"

"That's all we ever have, isn't it?" Ray wrestled out of his jacket and it landed on the driver's seat behind him. Hannah's lips parted eagerly to receive his tongue, and his weight settled over her like a blanket, fueling the fire in her loins. "Thank God for bench seats," he roughed.

Hannah gave herself over to their solitude. *Thank God for country roads,* she thought as the heater roared in the background, blurring the windows into a temporary screen.

Thank God, indeed.

Seven

For Hannah, the best part about Ray's new job at Windreach was being able to watch him do what he did best: turn young, stubborn, or unbroken horses into willing partners and promising athletes. The Coverall arena was empty today (Wilbur had rescheduled a clinic, led by Don, so that Ray and Chief could have the place to themselves), and the sun was streaming through the canvas top, highlighting the unfilled stands. Halfway up the rows of seats, Hannah sat alone, clutching a thermal mug of coffee and breathing in the familiar stink of dirt and horse sweat that permeated every equine establishment. For once, she wasn't thinking about anything other than Ray and Chief, connected by a lunge line in the sand ring below.

"You sure this is going to work?" Kathleen asked. She leaned on the wall encircling the ring, her leather chaps and cowboy hat replaced by old jeans and a coat with a broken zipper that flared open every time the wind blew.

As Chief cantered past the gate, Ray replied, "It works on all my horses. Granted, I don't breed futurity winners, but slow and steady is the best way to go when you need answers fast." He flicked the untethered end of the line to maintain Chief's momentum. The palomino thundered in a wide circle around him, his creamy white tail streaming like a banner between his hind legs. Ray added, "He doesn't seem to be stiff, so we can rule out injury as the cause of his underperformance. I'll do a few more laps with him here, then you can get on and tell me if you notice any improvement."

Kathleen nodded. "What if you got on instead?"

"On Chief?"

"Yes, on Chief. Please tell me you're not one of those guys who only performs miracles from the ground."

"I can ride," Ray assured her as Chief whizzed past her again, "most of the time, I can even stay on."

Hannah took a sip of her coffee. As Ray continued explaining his methods to Kathleen, a monstrous red pickup truck parked outside the Coverall. The headlights dimmed, and soon, a man emerged and pressed a brown, felt cowboy hat onto his head. He braced his hands on his hips, drawing attention to the belt buckle gleaming in the sun, and surveyed his surroundings as if expecting to see a welcome wagon at any moment. His arrival going unnoticed, he swaggered through the doorway and into the arena. Even his boots had barely more than a scuff on them, and Hannah questioned whether he'd gotten lost looking for the nearest Outback Steakhouse.

The mysterious man made his way toward the stands. As Hannah stiffened, he eyed the space beside her and asked, "This seat taken?"

She shook her head. The visitor sat down and immediately turned his attention to the action on the ground. Chief, now exhausted from running circles around Ray, stood quietly while he positioned a saddle on his back and drew up the cinch to hold it in place. Kathleen handed him the bridle.

"What's wrong with the horse?" the man asked.

"We're not really sure. Ray was just putting him through his paces. He does that with all his horses as a way to check for lameness and burn off extra energy."

The man chuckled. "I know what lunging is for. I've done it a few thousand times myself."

She tried to mirror his amusement. *Not just a pretty face, then*, she thought, unsure why they were talking about Ray at all. Besides, someone who was intimately familiar with the practice of lunging a horse should have known better than to show up to the barn dressed like an extra in a western movie.

"Are you here to see Wilbur?" Hannah asked, setting her mug on the bench.

"No. I'm here to see him." The stranger pointed to Ray.

"Ray?" Hannah furrowed her brows. "Do you two know each other?"

66

"Not yet. I know Wilbur, though. He called me and said there was someone I had to meet, and here I am." He went on, "I've traveled all over the country, met all kinds of people who call themselves cowboys. Only a few are the real deal. They're the ones who can look a horse in the eye and know what it's thinking. They're rare, but when you find them, you have to hold them tight."

Hannah smiled. "That's Ray, all right. His brother says he's 'old stock.'"

"I believe it." Finally, the stranger offered his hand to her. "Mickey Hammond."

"Hannah."

Mickey stood up and lifted the brim of his hat out of his eyes with his thumb. "I better go down there and introduce myself. It was a pleasure meeting you, Hannah."

"You, too."

Ray placed his left foot in the stirrup and pulled himself into the saddle. So far, so good—not that he expected anything less from a horse of Chief's caliber. Ray turned his heels inward and lightly squeezed the palomino's sides. One thing Ray had learned about working with horses was to never be in a hurry to take control. Horses were curious by nature, and any attempts to erase this instinct usually resulted in an animal that refused to learn anything. Chief soon settled on a direction, and Ray went to work on figuring out the rest.

Mickey sidled up to the wall. It felt strange being the observer, but even an experienced showman like himself needed to see how it was done from time to time. Besides, the kid obviously had some experience: he kept his hands quiet and didn't throw his weight around, hoping the horse would tire before he did. Wilbur McCullough had a long and well-established track record of churning out champions; he wouldn't trust his horses' care to just anyone. But he might trust their care to someone everyone should know.

Kathleen, apparently noticing Mickey for the first time, exclaimed, "You're a long way from home."

"Home is wherever my tour bus is parked."

"So, what brings you to Windreach?"

"Him," Mickey answered, nodding to Ray. "I'm on a talent-scouting mission today. Wilbur tells me this one has potential—and you know I can't resist potential."

"I know. You've based a whole career on it." Kathleen swept some hair out of her eyes. As a fellow professional, she'd held entire arenas captivated, but as a long-time follower of the Horse God, she was overcome with butterflies to be standing in the presence of greatness. Her coat belled around her waist again, so she folded her arms and shifted the focus back to Ray, who was loping circles in the middle of the ring. "I'll admit, I had my doubts, but Chief's looking better than he has in weeks."

It was at this point in the conversation that Hannah decided to join them. She took up a new post near the gate and watched as Ray guided Chief through a figure eight, his body leaning inward toward the dusty track before veering off into the distance once more.

Ray soon reined Chief to a stop and bent down to pat his neck. Across the arena, three figures stood by the low wall. Ray rode toward them at a walk, trying to place the face in the middle of the lineup. Chief's flanks heaved under him, and his coat twitched from the insect-like pressure of the reins against his skin. When he was only a few feet away from the gate, Ray dismounted and lifted the reins over Chief's head to lead him out of the ring.

"Well?" Kathleen prompted. "What do you think?"

Ray chose his words carefully. Commenting on Chief's performance after only one ride was like trying to understand a person after only one date. He couldn't build a relationship on that, but he could decide if it was worth fighting for, or if he was going to end up walking away bitter and bruised.

"I think you need to change up his routine," Ray said, "get him out of the arena and take him somewhere he's never been. If it works for people, it'll work on Chief."

"How can you be sure?" Mickey asked.

"I can't. But I know that if I was under this much pressure to perform, I'd want a break every once in a while, too." Ray ran a hand over Chief's face, scratching all the places where the bridle rubbed or pinched.

Mickey nodded, appreciating this small nugget of wisdom. Here was someone who understood how horses thought, he mused. What made them tic. He approached Ray as he and Chief exited the arena and started down the path toward the barn.

"You know your way around horses," Mickey remarked.

Ray shrugged. "It's all I've ever known. Some might call it my gift."

"Well, it would be a shame to let it go to waste now, wouldn't it?" The Horse God offered his hand. "Mickey Hammond."

"Ray Fisher." He pulled up short as reality hit him. In that moment, Ray didn't feel like some kid from Colorado who could usually stay on a horse. Instead, he felt sweaty and panicked, like the yearling his father had freed from the tangle of discarded wire all those years ago.

"Pleasure to meet you, Ray. I hope you don't mind me dropping in unannounced, but when Wilbur told me he'd hired a new trainer for his best horse, I had to come and see for myself."

"You know Wilbur?"

"I know a lot of people." Mickey waved his hand, as if this fact was of little importance. "And now I know you. I have to say, I'm impressed by what I just saw in there. Have you ever started a colt?"

"Sure. What rancher hasn't?"

Mickey smirked. "Would you be willing to do it in front of a live audience and a camera crew?"

Ray resumed his pace. There was a breeze today, and as it lifted, it stripped the excess heat from his cheeks, calming some of his anxiety. "I don't really like having an audience. It tends to distract the horse."

"And that, *right there*, is what people want to see: someone who puts the welfare of the animal ahead of his own self-interest. I've been in this business for twenty-five years, Ray. You meet all kinds in this industry, but at the end of the day, people pay good money for the real thing. And you strike me as someone who values authenticity."

They stepped into the warmth of the barn, where grooming caddies and saddle stands littered the aisle. Wilbur's staff were in constant motion—mucking out, throwing hay, and escorting his prize-winning steeds to and from the paddock. Within moments of their arrival, a young groom named Koda materialized from one of the stalls. Ray handed him Chief's reins, then turned back to Mickey as the palomino was led off in the direction of the wash stalls.

"I appreciate that you came all this way," Ray started, darting a glimpse at the door as Hannah and Kathleen appeared, "but whatever it is you're offering, I don't think it's what I'm looking for. I don't know what Wilbur told you, but I'm not some horse whisperer or budding showman. I'm a fourth-generation cattle rancher, and training horses is just part of the job."

Mickey repositioned his hat again, prompting Ray to wonder why he hadn't bothered to find one that fit properly in the first place. If he couldn't spot poor craftmanship, then what business did the Horse God have pontificating about authenticity?

As if divining Ray's thoughts, Mickey removed the faded brown Stetson and lovingly traced its wide brim. The stitching that held the sweatband in place around the crown's inner rim had become dull and frayed in certain spots, and completely detached in others. It was the only part of his wardrobe that wasn't sparkling with newness—the only thing, Ray thought, that made Mickey redeemable.

"I'm a fourth-generation rancher myself," Mickey said, "that probably explains why I took a liking to you immediately. And I think other people will like you too, once they get a taste of your gift. Young talent never gets old."

"You're very persuasive," Ray said shrewdly.

Mickey shrugged. "I'm a showman. It's part of the job." He lowered the hat back onto his head and met Ray's gaze. "I'm hosting a colt starting clinic in Boulder at the end of the month, and to be honest, I could use a co-host. You'll have three days with a colt of your choosing, during which time you'll gentle him, saddle him, and make him rideable. I'm almost fully booked up, so I need an answer relatively soon. Something tells me you're going to say yes."

"And what is that 'something,' exactly?" Ray asked, not wanting to look too intrigued as he propped an elbow on the door of a nearby stall.

"Simple: you're a cowboy." Mickey quickly checked his watch, then, startling when he saw what time it was, offered his hand again. "I'd love to stay and chat more, but I'm late for a meeting. Let me know when you've made a decision." From a hidden pocket inside his coat, he produced a matte black business card. Reluctantly, Ray accepted it.

"I will," he said, skimming the reflective gold lettering that spelled out *Performing miracles, one horse at a time.* By the time he'd finished reading the opposite side, the Horse God was gone.

Eight

"Please state your name for the record." The clerk's voice, always loud and clear, echoed around the courtroom. Adrianna forced a breath into her lungs and stared at the face of the woman on the stand, her hair falling to a point just below her chin and her eyes brimming with exhaustion.

"Denise Elliott," Denise said, leaning slightly toward the microphone as she spoke.

"And what is your relation to the victim?"

"We used to work together at the hospital, when I was still a nurse."

These details, once committed to paper, seemed inconsequential. Denise Elliott, former nurse and coworker, had much more important information to share with the jury—a testimony that could ultimately sway these strangers in Adrianna's favour. Denise had agreed to serve as her character witness and, according to Odessa, was expected to paint a picture of a woman who didn't have a bad bone in her body and couldn't anticipate Doug wanting to harm her. It wasn't the impression Adrianna wanted to leave on the jury—that she was a poor, helpless girl anyone could take advantage of—but if it helped the case, she could live with their pity.

Odessa rose from her seat.

"First of all, I'd like to thank you for agreeing to testify," Odessa began as she approached the stand. "I know how busy you are, being a mother of toddlers myself."

Denise smiled. "After a career in nursing, being a mother feels like a vacation."

Check, Adrianna thought. She glimpsed Doug and his lawyer at the neighbouring table to gauge their reaction to Odessa's setup. An exhausted, overworked nurse wouldn't have time to concoct some plot to get back at her former fiancé, was how Odessa had framed it. But, unlike some of Adrianna's patients, Doug had a more reliable memory: he'd remember all those times she "stayed late" in order to delay an argument, or how she'd gone to see Victor on the night of Laney's stroke while claiming to have gotten held up at work.

"How long have you and Ms. Bishop known each other?" Odessa asked.

"About eight years."

"And in the time that you've known the victim, have you ever had reason to believe her relationship with the defendant was unhealthy?"

"Yes. In fact, Adrianna often told me she felt unsafe around Doug."

"Could you please elaborate on this statement?"

"Of course." Denise's gaze found purchase, temporarily, on Adrianna's face. "There were many times when Addy told me she didn't want to go home, even after a fourteen-hour shift. She told me Doug was going to be upset about the wait."

"And was the defendant aware of the demanding nature of Ms. Bishop's work?"

"I'd assume so, but that didn't matter to Doug, as far as I could tell."

Odessa nodded. Denise's testimony was turning out better than she'd hoped, and a few members of the jury had visibly flinched at the mention of Doug's volatility. *Time to turn up the heat.*

"Mrs. Elliott, have you ever worked in a psych ward?" Odessa asked.

Marshall bounded out of his seat. "Your Honour, I object to the insinuation that my client is mentally unstable."

Judge McKay chewed on this conundrum for a moment, then turned to address Odessa. "Counsel, please rephrase your question."

"Of course, Your Honour." Her mouth hinted at a smirk, which she pointedly directed at the floor. "Mrs. Elliott, in your professional opinion, has Ms. Bishop ever displayed behaviour that you would consider to be irrational or unpredictable?"

"Never," Denise answered without hesitation. "In fact, quite the opposite—Addy has always been very calm and composed, even under extreme pressure."

"And you would be able to tell if she was lying?"

"Absolutely."

"Mrs. Elliott, I have only one more question for you," Odessa said. She paused, holding the room spellbound. "How soon after the crime did Ms. Bishop return to work?"

"Almost immediately. She said she had to come back for her patients."

"No further questions," Odessa said, taking a seat once more.

Adrianna looked over at Doug and Marshall's table. Doug was scribbling something on the legal pad. Marshall was nodding, his eyes hard and focused. As he pushed away from the table to cross-examine Denise, Adrianna wondered what Doug could have possibly written to upend an otherwise solid testimony.

"Mrs. Elliott, did you ever spend time with Ms. Bishop outside of work?" Marshall began.

"Yes."

"What about the defendant?"

"Sure. They were a couple."

"And when you saw my client and Ms. Bishop together, did you ever have reason to believe their relationship was, as Ms. Hanson put it, unhealthy?"

Denise considered her answer. Her eyes ricocheted off the prosecution's table, as if seeking permission to proceed. At Odessa's urging, she did.

"Not specifically, but it's not uncommon for victims to maintain a certain… image while out in public with their abuser."

"So, what happened on the night of Ms. Bishop's 22nd birthday?"

Adrianna crossed her arms over her stomach. The steady beat of her heart marched into her ears, drowning out the ambient noise of shuffling feet and bated breaths. *Not this story*, she pleaded. *Anything but this.*

"Mrs. Elliott, would you please answer the question?" Judge McKay prodded.

Denise swallowed. She was sitting back from the microphone, and even from her position at the front of the room, Adrianna barely heard her reply. "I don't remember."

"Mrs. Elliott, I shouldn't have to remind you that you're under oath," Marshall said. "Now, can you remember anything from that night? Did you and Ms. Bishop go out to celebrate?"

Denise blinked several times and slipped some hair behind her ear. "Yes, we went to The Kicking Mule. It's a pub downtown."

"And was the defendant with you?"

"He was."

"Did anything notable happen that night—something that you felt was out of character for Ms. Bishop?"

Again, Denise looked away, her fingers toying with a button on the cuff of her shirtsleeve. The fidgeting was all too familiar to Adrianna: a precursor to the fight-or-flight instinct most people kept buried under rational, predictable behaviour. Victor had a tendency to fiddle with things when he was under pressure too, and the similarities brought her no comfort in this setting.

"It was a long time ago," Denise whispered. "If there was anything… off about Adrianna that night, I just chalked it up to work stress."

"I see." Marshall prowled around the room, laying his traps ever so carefully. "Well, I think we can all relate to being stressed at work. And if we're dealing with challenges outside of work—say, increased conflict with a partner or spouse—we may resort to unhealthy coping mechanisms."

"I agree," Denise said tonelessly. "What was your question, exactly?"

"Did Ms. Bishop have a problem with alcohol?"

"No. That I can say with absolute certainty."

"But she did consume alcohol, on occasion."

"Yes."

"Including the evening of her 22nd birthday?"

"It was a pub. We all had a couple of drinks."

"And the bartenders—what were they like?"

Odessa stood up, her chair scraping indignantly across the floor. "Your Honour, I don't see what any of this has to do with the case."

"I agree. Counsel Newman, the jury only needs to hear the facts. Please try to keep your questions on topic."

"Apologies, Your Honour." With that matter settled, Marshall turned a frigid grin on Denise. "Mrs. Elliott, would you consider Ms. Bishop to be promiscuous?"

"No." Denise's voice, like the dark, red wood that paneled the walls, was firm and inescapable. "How dare you?"

Marshall retreated. "No further questions."

Judge McKay said, "Prosecution, you may re-examine the witness now."

Odessa was on her feet in a heartbeat. The fog of endless debate had settled over the room: a dozen wilted faces lined the jury box, and dozens more fleshed out the gallery, seeing no end in sight. But Denise had given her an opportunity too good to pass up—a chance to set the record straight once and for all.

"You said you all had a couple of drinks," Odessa said. When Denise nodded, she asked, "Could you tell us who else was at the pub that night?"

"Other than myself and Adrianna, Doug and my husband, Cody."

"How many drinks would you say the defendant consumed?"

"I'm not exactly sure, but I remember Adrianna drove them home."

"Why?"

Denise flicked her eyes at Marshall and Doug, the latter slouched in his chair. His grey suit was rumpled, presumably to give the jury the impression that he was down on his luck, as his lawyer had so audaciously claimed at the hearing's outset.

Denise looked directly at him as she spoke, "Because Mr. Alderman was intoxicated."

"Your Honour, my client's dependency on alcohol has already been discussed," Marshall cut in. "Must we continually rehash it?"

"Counsel, you've had your chance to speak," Judge McKay said. He turned to Denise, now visibly squirming in her seat. "Thank you. You are excused." With that, Denise was led out of the courtroom through a door behind the bench.

Odessa faced the jury. "As you can see, Mrs. Elliott's testimony aligns with the witness's memories of the crime. If Mr. Alderman does indeed have a drinking problem—especially one that causes him to become violent—I urge you to consider what allowing a man like that to go free would mean for my client and others."

"Thank you, Ms. Hanson." Judge McKay shuffled his papers and consulted the clock on the wall, unclenching his shoulders in relief when he saw what time it was. "Court is now adjourned. We will reconvene at a later date, at which time both parties will deliver their closing statements." He picked up his gavel, banging it sharply to signal the day's conclusion.

Adrianna's head was spinning as she rose from her seat. As Judge McKay made his exit, and the jury was escorted in an orderly fashion out of their wooden pen by an apathetic bailiff, she felt a hand on her arm and turned to find Victor standing on the opposite side of the bar. "Are you okay?" he asked.

"I think so." It was only when the room began to empty that she noticed the tension in her head and the dryness in her throat. Nothing a hot bath and a glass of wine couldn't cure. She stepped into the narrow aisle and walked with Victor toward the doors, breathing a sigh of relief as they passed into the cool expanse of marble floors on the opposite side.

As they rode the elevator to the main floor, Victor removed his phone from his pocket and read the message on the screen. It had been another excruciating day, and he hadn't given much thought to Hannah and Ray's wedding plans. Nevertheless, as the elevator opened and they joined the stream of suits and briefcases trickling toward the doors, he said, "Ray and Hannah met with Father Kincaid's son. Hannah really liked the church, but they're still going to check out a few more places."

"That's great." Adrianna tried to shake off her dread about the jury's decision. As her heels clopped across the parking lot to the truck, she said, "I can't believe Doug would mention the birthday dinner. All it does is paint him in a bad light."

"I agree."

"The jury can't possibly acquit him after that," she went on, "I mean, just *look* at him! He's practically giving them puppy dog eyes, at this point."

Victor looked at her from over the truck's roof. "He's not going to win, Addy. Regardless of what his character witnesses say, the evidence says he was there that night. Pretending to be innocent doesn't make him so."

"I know." She shook her head. "I guess I'm just so used to everyone taking his side. It was like that in high school too, with Jason. The star quarterback could do no wrong."

A smile stretched across Victor's face. "Let's go home, okay? I'll draw you a bath and make dinner."

As Adrianna was about to duck into the passenger seat, a voice called out, "Addy, wait."

She froze, keeping one hand on the door as she turned toward its source. Doug was standing on the sidewalk. His hands were in his pockets, and his eyes were dark and downcast, striving for a look of penance. Seeing him, Victor rounded the front of the truck to stand beside his wife, who merely stared at her attacker.

"What?" she finally managed to ask.

Doug's gaze flickered to Victor, then settled on the grey line of the horizon.

"I know you don't really want this, Addy," Doug said, cocking his head at her. "It's not like you."

Indignation throbbed in her temples. She knew better than to talk to him, but couldn't stop herself from saying, "You don't know me, Doug."

"All those things Denise said were true—you are kind and compassionate, and you don't want to hurt anyone."

"You hurt *me*," Adrianna reminded him. "You think I'm doing this to hurt you, Doug? Revenge has nothing to do with it. This is about me moving on with my life. *Our* life." She indicated Victor, who had his hand on her back, trying to urge her into the truck.

"And what kind of life will you have if you lose?" Doug's eyes darkened. "The press will tear you apart."

"Addy, let's go," Victor said.

It's true, a voice in Adrianna's mind whispered. The trial was already tearing her family apart, pitting cousins against cousins and grandparents against grandparents. The general public knew her even less, if they knew her at all. But if she backed down now, everyone would know who was really in control—or worse, think she'd fabricated the whole story.

At last, she heeded Victor's advice and ducked into the truck. Doug continued along the sidewalk, carrying himself with the lightness of a man who refused to take responsibility for his actions. As Victor climbed behind the wheel, he looked over at Adrianna and wished there was something he could say to put her mind at ease. Instead, he started the engine and pulled away from the courthouse. Adrianna stared at her reflection and watched the clouds gather in her eyes, welcoming the impending storm.

Nine

The Fitzgeralds' dining room table was covered in bright pink Post-it notes, each one bearing a single name in permanent marker. In hindsight, leaving Laney in charge of the guest list and seating arrangements was a huge mistake, but Hannah didn't want to appear ungrateful by asking her to pare down the size of their party. Instead, she gripped her coffee mug more tightly and watched as Ray tried to make heads and tails of the mess.

"Now, remember: the list hasn't been finalized," Laney called from across the kitchen. "The important thing is making sure that everyone who *should* get an invitation, gets an invitation. Which reminds me: have you decided on a venue yet? If you need more room, Jim and I would be happy to rent out the yard. It's so beautiful here during the summer, and the pond is perfect for taking pictures."

"Laney, you're inviting half the town to our wedding," Ray deadpanned. "Even *your* yard isn't big enough for that."

Laney frowned as she carried a plate of shortbread cookies over to the table. She was rather proud of her yard, and any affront to its size or capability triggered what could only be described as a maternal instinct, as if her exquisitely lovely plot were a small, defenseless child in need of endless care.

"It's big enough for what matters," Laney stated curtly, setting down the plate and taking a seat.

"Maybe we should start by separating friends from family," Hannah chimed in. "From there, we can figure out where everyone is going to sit."

"Good idea, hon. Raymond comes from a large family, but not all of them live in Colorado."

"I'm not even sure if half of them are still alive," he muttered. His eyes flickered to his fiancée. "Why don't we start with your family?"

Hannah picked up the black marker and hesitated. Unlike Ray, she had no siblings and very few cousins. Her paternal grandparents, who lived in Salmon Arm, British Columbia, rarely left the comfort of their armchairs, and her mom's parents had been so scandalized by Jeanette's decision to marry a man of non-Jewish faith that they'd refused to have anything to do with Hannah for the first thirteen years of her life. In the absence of strong family ties, she'd anchored herself to friends like Joanna, only for that cherished, sister-like bond to vanish, too.

"Marc's my best man," Ray said in the midst of her stalling. He tapped the seating chart and asked, "Where is he sitting?"

"Well, if you want to go with a more traditional seating arrangement—which I suspect you do—then Marcus will be on Hannah's left. You'll be on her right, and the Maid of Honour will be on yours."

"That doesn't make any sense," he protested.

"Would you rather have a sweetheart table—just the two of you?"

"I want the wedding party to stay together. There wouldn't be much of a wedding without them."

Hannah stared down at the blank Post-It. She could probably fit her whole family at one table... the smallest table available.

In a fit of embarrassment, she scribbled *Mom (Jeanette)* on one pink square and *Dad (Andrew)* on another. She stuck them to the table next to Ray's elbow and, when he raised his brow in puzzlement, said, "I don't even know for sure if they're coming."

"They're your parents. Of course they're coming to our wedding."

As the group continued categorizing their nearest and dearest, Laney said, "By the way, I keep meaning to ask how things are going with Wilbur's horse. I forget its name."

"Chief. And they're going well."

"Wilbur's very fond of you. I've known that man a long time, and his respect is like gold—difficult to come by, but infinitely valuable."

"Well, I got it, and more," Ray said, looking at his godmother as she politely wiped crumbs from her lips. "Mickey Hammond dropped by, said he wanted me to co-host a colt starting clinic with him at the end of the month."

Laney narrowed her eyes. "You said yes, I hope."

"Not exactly."

"Why not?"

"Because I'm not gifted. I'm not good in front of a camera, and I'm not the kind of person to make promises I can't keep. Why do we have to keep talking about this?"

Laney's gaze dropped to the table. She knew it was futile to argue with him, but she also had the benefit of hindsight and understood how precious each and every opportunity was. Of course, Ray hadn't lived long enough to cultivate his garden of regrets, but Laney was determined to prevent this one from taking root.

"Do you see all these names?" she asked, waving her fingers over the table. When he nodded, she told him, "None of them have been asked to co-host a colt starting clinic with Mickey Hammond."

"First of all, you don't know that. And secondly, why is Tori on here twice?"

"Raymond, I'm not letting you squander this." Laney's voice teetered on the precipice of desperation. "Call Mickey and tell him you'll do the clinic."

"Why? So he can ruin my reputation, too?"

"He got a little bad press, is all. Mickey turned a terrible accident into an opportunity. People are drawn to that, you know—not the inevitability of failure, but the possibility of hope."

"In that case, I hope we figure out how to comfortably seat a hundred and fifty people," Ray said.

Laney stopped herself short of replying. Her eyes lingered on her godson's face, but his features gave no indication of his misgivings. After a moment, Laney went back to sorting the names, hoping he'd come to his senses in time.

An hour later, Hannah and Ray left Fitzgerald Farms with the tentative seating arrangement tucked into a leather portfolio. As they drove back to the ranch, Hannah tried to picture what a hundred and fifty people looked like crammed into a swelteringly hot church or arranged neatly on white chairs in Jim and Laney's yard. She'd never wanted a huge wedding in the first place, but the thought of so many strangers bearing witness to a moment that would forever define her future with Ray was downright terrifying. Plus, if her mother were here, she'd remind Hannah that there was a clear and direct correlation between how much a wedding cost and its likelihood of ending in divorce. As if Hannah needed any more failure right now.

Ray looked over at the passenger seat. Hannah was toying with her ring again, spinning it round and around on her finger like she always did when she was anxious. He removed his right hand from the wheel and rested it on her thigh until the fidgeting stopped.

"I think Laney's lost her mind," Hannah said bluntly. "We can't afford to feed a hundred and fifty people."

"I know."

"And there's no way she'll have the energy to make the yard wedding-ready when she can barely cook for herself on a good day. It's too much work."

"I know," Ray said again. "Like she said, it's not finalized. We'll probably end up having a smaller wedding anyway, but the planning is giving her something positive to focus on. She needs that right now."

Ray parked in front of the house and turned off the engine. Snowflakes the size of pinheads fell all around them, forming a strange, wintery mist. This was where they'd been sitting the first time Hannah had visited, in the summer that changed everything. As the memory of that day lifted his spirits, Ray smiled and said, "You know, I thought about kissing you."

"What are you talking about?" Hannah asked.

"The day I picked you up from the airport, when you came to stay with us in 2009. We were sitting right here, a little to the left of the front door, and you were looking at me and I was pretending not to notice." At this reminder, Hannah's cheeks turned nearly as pink as the Post-It notes sealed inside the leather case. "And I thought, 'I've waited a whole year to see this girl again, and I don't even know how to make a move.'"

"So, instead, you asked me what kind of chores I wanted to do," Hannah recalled with a grin. "Like I was interviewing for a job or something."

"Well, you did say you wanted to get some work experience."

She leaned her head against the seat. The laugh lines had barely faded from her mouth when she said, "I took the biggest chance of my life coming here. No plan, no goals, just faith that it would all work out, somehow. And it did."

"Were you being serious, when you said your parents might not come to the wedding?"

Hannah nodded. "My mom said it's a long way to travel, and my dad's not in the best shape anymore. I guess that's what happens when you spend your whole life hunched over a computer."

Ray frowned. He'd been expecting his future in-laws to put up a fight about the particulars, like where they chose to get married and who they chose to invite, but he hadn't been prepared for the possibility that they simply wouldn't attend, poor health or not. Hannah was their only child. They'd supported her in good times and in bad times, spent a small fortune on boarding school and anything else they believed would help her achieve happiness. But they wouldn't come to the wedding, and Ray hated that he knew why.

"Is it really because of your dad, or is it because your parents don't want their only daughter marrying a cowboy?" he asked.

Hannah watched the snow form a fine layer on the windshield. Her mom had never overcome her mistrust of Ray, but as time wore on, Hannah had learned to tune out the hurtful jabs toward her fiancé, just as Jeanette had done to her own parents before she'd married Andrew. "A little bit of both, probably."

"They're wrong. I know they think I can't provide for you, but I can and I will."

"I know." As she gathered up her belongings, Hannah said, "I was going to head inside and start making lunch."

"Okay. I'll be in soon."

She leaned across the seat and kissed him. "I love you. Don't worry about my parents, okay?"

As she entered the house, Ray stepped out of the driver's seat and faced the front yard. His feet moved automatically toward the barn, through the snow and along the fence, until he came to the round pen, standing slightly apart from the other enclosures. He braced his arms against the gate and gazed unseeingly at its circular emptiness, remembering the first time his father had invited him in to work with a horse. The round pen, Bernard had explained, symbolized continuous motion. *No corners to hide in.* What Marcus had said was true: Ray *was* a cowboy, just like his dad, granddad, and great-granddad, who'd come to Colorado to give his family a better life. Had it been perfect? No, but it had given them a foundation and a home, and if Hannah's parents couldn't see that, then Ray would just have to find a new way of doing things. A better way.

He reached into one of his pockets for his phone. From the other, he retrieved Mickey's business card.

The phone rang three times. Mickey answered with, "This is the Horse God."

"This is Ray," he replied. "I was just calling to ask if your offer stands."

Ten

After Victor, there were only two other people who believed every word of Adrianna's testimony: her mother, who'd always been able to see through Doug's fake smiles and insincere gestures, and Adrianna's older sister, Heather. Heather had been at the hospital on the night of the attack and held her sister's hand while the doctor went over the x-rays. After Addy had moved back in with her mother, Heather would drop by several times a week to check on her sister and ensure her injuries were healing. And each time, Heather would promise the same thing, often while lying next to Adrianna in the bed she'd outgrown years ago. *We're going to find him, Addy. I promise, he's not going to get away with this.*

Years had passed, and though Adrianna had wrestled with her decision to take Doug to court, Heather's faith in her never wavered. At the wedding, Victor had sworn to protect Adrianna with everything he had, easing Heather's worries about history repeating itself. But as long as Doug remained at large, Heather's guard never came down completely. Somewhere out there was a man who lacked so much self-worth that he had to steal it from someone else. Somewhere out there, Doug was waiting for the perfect opportunity to finish what he started—and if he wasn't afraid of the law, what was to stop him from doing his worst?

"Don't mind the mess," Adrianna said as she and Heather passed through the living room to reach the kitchen. "Victor's been going through the stuff in the basement and trying to organize it all."

"You know, if you ever wanted to rent him out, our spare bedroom is filled with junk from nana's house. He'd have the time of his life going through it."

Adrianna approached the counter, where a trio of mugs sat next to the stove. As she dropped a teabag into each one, she thought of Victor attempting to deal with her neurotic sister and excessively talkative brother-in-law, and shook her head. "Or you could just call 1-800-GOT-JUNK and have them deal with the mess."

"Maybe." Heather dropped onto the sofa and admired the snow swirling outside the window, blanketing the jumble of patio furniture on the deck. "I know I already asked you this, but are you sure you're okay?"

Adrianna smiled indulgently as she poured water over the teabags, releasing the sharp fragrance of mint. "I'm fine. My answer isn't going to change just because you asked me a hundred times."

"Well, *I'm* not fine. This whole trial is wreaking havoc on my digestive system. The doctor says I have a stress ulcer on my stomach."

"Still? I thought you stopped having stomach issues in university."

"My body despises stress. When you found out you got into nursing school, *I* broke out in hives. I mean, how does that even happen?"

Adrianna sighed. "You worry too much. I really am fine, Heather."

"No, you're not. You're strong, but you're not fine."

Adrianna carried two of the mugs into the living room and handed one to her sister. Of course she was strong—she had to be, if she wanted to survive what Doug had put her through—but *fine* was one of those words she'd said so often, she wasn't even sure of its true meaning anymore. She was "fine" living out here with Victor, on a small acreage cushioned by dark evergreens. She was "fine" with being one of Hannah's bridesmaids, even though they hadn't had many opportunities to get to know each other. She was even "fine" with Heather insisting that she wasn't, in fact, fine at all—but she was not "fine" with having to pretend to be okay simply so the rest of the world wouldn't assume the worst about her character.

Heather placed her tea on the coffee table and swept Adrianna's hair back with her fingers.

"You're not fine," she said again, her voice taking on a gentler tone. "You are a *victim*. You're allowed to be angry right now."

"Who says I'm not? Just because I don't have a stress ulcer doesn't mean I'm not stressed."

"Exactly. All I want is for you to acknowledge your pain. Don't hide from it or try to put on a brave face. What Doug did to you was unforgivable, Addy. You deserve some closure."

Adrianna sipped the scalding hot tea. *Closure.* That was what she wanted, wasn't it? To know that justice had prevailed and Doug was behind bars, where he'd never be able to hurt her again? Yes, she thought, closure would be fine.

But it wouldn't be enough.

Heather, who'd been staring down at her phone, said, "Apparently, mom's been cleaning out her basement too. Look, she even found all your old baby stuff." She angled the screen so Adrianna could see the pictures, including that of a plain, wooden crib surrounded by boxes of other junk.

"I'll let Victor know she's planning to do another Goodwill run. We can use his truck to donate the bigger stuff."

"Or," Heather said slowly, "hear me out… you keep the crib."

"What for? Victor and I aren't trying for a baby right now."

"That's what everyone says right before they get pregnant."

"I'm on the pill. And, besides, that crib probably has all kinds of safety issues."

"The pill's good, but it's not a guarantee. And with all this stress around Doug, I wouldn't be surprised if Victor's testosterone levels are through the roof."

Adrianna rolled her eyes. "Shows how much you know about the human body. First of all, stress *decreases* testosterone levels. Secondly, let's not discuss my husband's testosterone ever again."

"Okay. But if you get pregnant, I'm in charge of the baby shower." Heather looked around suddenly. "Speaking of your husband, where is he?"

Gesturing in the direction of the garage, Adrianna replied, "He's been outside all morning, moving stuff around so he can install some shelves. He's a stress cleaner."

"Great. *I* get ulcers, he gets more productive." As Adrianna shrugged, Heather asked, "How's he handling everything?"

"Not well. We went to Vail a couple of weeks ago, but he still couldn't relax. I don't think he will until he knows this mess with Doug is fully behind us."

"Fair enough. Denise gave an excellent testimony. I can't imagine the jury won't convict Doug after hearing all that."

"But what if they still don't believe me? What if they think I'm making all this up?"

"You're not," Heather stated matter-of-factly. "Who even does that?"

"He followed us out to the parking lot," Adrianna went on, staring at her reflection in the tea. The skin under her eyes was the colour of a bruise, dark and murky with overtaxed blood vessels. "He said the press will tear me apart if we lose. I'm afraid he might be right."

"Oh, what does he know? Look, Addy, we know Doug. He's a manipulative liar. He's only bringing up the press because he's trying to scare you into dropping the charges, and he wouldn't be going to such lengths if he didn't have something to hide."

"Maybe… but what if I went to the press first?"

"First? You mean, before they come to you?"

"Exactly. I'll get my story out there. I won't hide from it or try to put on a brave face. I'll tell the world I was a victim, but I'm not going down without a fight."

For a long moment, Heather was silent. Adrianna continued sipping her tea as she imagined herself talking to a reporter, both of them trying to remain emotionally detached from a highly polarizing issue. Who was the public to believe: a man who had everything to lose, or a woman who'd walked away with nothing? It would be easier, Adrianna knew, to let this scenario play out in the courtroom: if Doug was found guilty, he'd never have a normal life again. But to flatter him with privacy when his actions had humiliated her so publicly was an insult to victims everywhere. How could she possibly dream of closure when so many wounds remained open and unhealed?

Then Heather said, "Whatever you want to do, you have my support."

"Really?"

"Yes. Always."

Adrianna stood up and said, "I should take Victor his tea. He'll probably be needing one after working out in the cold for so long."

"Okay. I should go, too."

"Thanks for coming here, even though you didn't have to."

"You're my sister. It's no hardship." Heather placed her empty mug in the sink and slipped into her coat and boots. After exchanging a chilly hug with Adrianna in the doorway, Heather trekked down the driveway to her car and drove through the tunnel of trees toward the road. The forest rose thickly all around the vehicle, quieting the purr of the engine, the distant hum of traffic, and even the constant whir of anxiety inside Adrianna's mind. She breathed in the clean, crisp mountain air, then returned to the kitchen to fetch the third mug.

In the garage, Victor had pushed most of the boxes and totes into one corner, exposing the wall where the new shelves would go. Both Adrianna's SUV and his old grey truck were parked outside the door as if observing his toils with flat, unseeing eyes. Adrianna shuddered at the wintery breeze that swept through the space as Victor shifted a trash can several inches to the left and brushed his hands together.

"It looks great," she enthused.

"Well, we certainly have more room now." He made his way over to her. "How'd it go with Heather?"

"Fine. She's just worried about us. Well, mainly me." Adrianna handed him the tea, and they both sat down on the steps leading to the side door.

Victor took a sip and waited for the rest of her thought. She always came to him when something was bothering her, and it was always under the pretense of a personal favour. Halfway through his tea, she took a deep breath, and he prepared to do what he did best: listening.

"I want to go public with the case," Adrianna began. "It's not really for me, though. I want to show other victims that they don't have to suffer in silence. I want Doug to know what it feels like to be the centre of unwanted attention."

Victor swallowed another mouthful. "What's in it for you?"

"The chance to tell my story. And the chance to help others who may not feel comfortable coming forward."

Victor waited, but Adrianna was staring at something far off in the distance. "Anything else?" he asked.

"That's all." Her gaze cleared. "How's the tea?"

"Perfect. But… are you sure you want to do this? Aren't you worried Doug might retaliate?"

"I am," Adrianna said in reply to both questions, "but I can't let fear hold me back. I've been afraid of him for too long."

Victor stared at his reflection in the tea. He'd always supported her, and this time would be no different. Then again, he'd attended all of Adrianna's hearings, and the attention didn't seem to bother Doug one bit. If anything, he seemed to view the trial as an inconvenience on par with rush hour traffic and broken office printers: a minor impediment to his daily routine that someone else could be paid to fix. As far as Doug was concerned, he'd already won the case; all his lawyer had to do was convince the jury, and Doug could return to his life in the fast lane, free from guilt or accountability.

Adrianna stood up. "By the way, my mom's cleaning out the basement. She might need us to do another Goodwill run soon."

"All right. In that case, I'll see if I can get rid of anything here to make it worth a trip into town." Victor indicated the heap of dusty containers filled with everything from old clothes to broken Christmas ornaments. Going through their belongings was more productive than worrying about what Doug might do next, but his mind had already wandered in that direction by the time his tea break was over.

She held out her hand to accept the mug. As Victor rose to her level, she asked, "How would you feel about keeping my old baby crib?"

"We don't need a crib right now. Besides, we're trying to get rid of stuff."

"I know, but my mom gets attached to these things. Besides, I thought it might be nice to keep it in the family."

Victor raised a brow and cast a pointed glance at her stomach. "How about if we tackle one thing at a time? I don't want to bring a baby into a world where Doug's still a free man."

"I know." Adrianna rolled forward onto the balls of her feet and kissed him lightly, whispering, "Just think about it, okay?" She turned toward the door and retreated to the warmth and safety of the house, clutching the empty mug to her chest.

Eleven

Snow gusted across the road in blinding white sheets. As Ray turned into the driveway of the equine training centre in Boulder, he wondered if he'd been foolish to come out here on a day when drivers were being urged to avoid non-essential travel. But Mickey would never cancel a clinic, and it was too late to turn back now. Ray followed the winding gravel driveway to a large, beige building in the distance. Sure enough, when he got closer, he noticed Mickey's tour bus parked under the trees and several horse trailers lined up near the paddocks. Ray steered his truck around the side of the barn, where the rigid walls promised some shelter from the elements, and reached across the seat for his hat and gloves.

The barn was brightly lit, the aisle crammed with everything from manure carts to grooming caddies and step stools. The stalls were small, but clean, and each of the horses had been provided with hay, fresh water, and a salt lick; a handful poked their heads out as Ray passed. As he neared the end of the aisle, he heard the anxious shuffling of hooves and peered over one of the doors to investigate.

"Hey, you're okay," he said to the smoky grey colt that was weaving back and forth in its stall. "Do you remember me?"

The colt extended its neck to sniff Ray's hand, then quickly returned to its self-soothing behaviour. Just days ago, as Ray and Mickey had walked the stockyard in search of their respective project horses, the grey colt had caught Ray's eye. He'd approached the pen where a clump of horses huddled together for warmth, and watched as the four-legged thunderstorm stamped at the ground and snorted indignantly.

Mickey had leaned on the fence beside him. "If you don't buy him, I will."

"I'm considering it," Ray had replied.

Mickey had looked over at him and smiled. The kid had grit; he liked grit. "Why that one?"

"He's got good bones and clear eyes. Most of the horses here are old, sick, and destined for slaughter. My dad always said 'you gotta start 'em young if you want good results.'"

"You're a real cowboy, Ray. A lot of other guys just pretend. Not you. That's why you're here." Mickey had clapped a hand on his shoulder and turned away from the pen. "Let's go get ourselves a couple of horses."

Leaving the colt to its restless motions, Ray exited the barn, crossed the windy parking lot to the arena, and slipped inside. Mickey's students were lined up along the wall, watching as the Horse God drove his colt around in circles at a steady canter. Using only his hands and his voice, Mickey was able to control the horse's speed, gait, and direction of travel—all while explaining his technique in ways that a mere mortal with no colt starting experience could understand.

"Now, you may be wondering 'why chase a horse away if you want it to bond with you?' Well, I'll tell you why. You see, in a herd, there's a hierarchy. You may not think of yourselves as members of a herd, but when you get a young horse in the ring, that's exactly what you become: its herd leader. That colt will be looking to you for guidance. He'll look to you for safety. And he'll look to you to tell him what to do next."

The students who weren't engrossed in their notetaking nodded. The rest had probably watched Mickey's training videos on YouTube and, like Ray, were waiting to see if his methods held up in real life.

Mickey smiled as he turned in Ray's direction. The young horse was already beginning to show signs of submission: lowering its head, licking its lips, and rounding its back. Granted, Mickey had not chosen the liveliest specimen at the auction, but even Ray had to admit the showman's presence had a calming effect on animals, including the ones with two legs. Ray leaned on the gate, watching as the colt completed one final lap of the arena before stopping to catch its breath.

Mickey spoke more slowly now, his focus trained on the mass of muscle and bone arranged less than twenty feet in front of him. "Now, here's the secret: horses are a lot like humans. The more you push them away, the more they want to stay." His gaze flickered to Ray, who mulled over this crumb of wisdom.

Mickey walked toward the edge of the sand ring, where Ray finally noticed the man with the camera. When Mickey had mentioned a "camera crew," Ray had imagined a throng of reporters covering every angle of the clinic and tripping over one another's equipment, yet this cameraman couldn't have been any older than Ray himself—just another kid Mickey had taken a liking to on his never-ending road to redemption.

As Ray predicted, the moment Mickey retreated, the colt's legs moved in the same direction. He followed Mickey on a meandering path around the sandy enclosure as if led by an invisible string, until Mickey stopped and faced his new partner with a grin.

"There you have it, folks—you give a little, you get a little back. Now that this colt and I have bonded, the next step will be to introduce the saddle—show him there's nothing to be afraid of. But first, there's someone I'd like you all to meet. Ray," Mickey waved his hand for Ray to enter, "why don't you step into the ring with me and tell these fine people a little about yourself?"

Ray's fingers fumbled with the latch on the gate. What was he supposed to tell these people, exactly? That he'd driven all this way to prove to his future in-laws that he was capable of providing a decent life for Hannah? He knew he couldn't do that, so he went with the next best thing: a story from his past that had seemed inconsequential at the time, like most things that formed the building blocks of a person's identity. Ray crossed the arena to where Mickey stood, his favourite cowboy hat pushed back from his forehead, and his eyes, the same dark brown as Ray's, brightening at the sight of him.

"Now, don't be shy," Mickey said as Ray scoped out the crowd. "I call myself the Horse God, but I'm a mere mortal just like everyone else. So, Ray, tell these people how we met... and why I invited you here."

"We met at Wilbur McCullough's place in Aspen," Ray began. "I was working with one of his horses, Supreme Mischief, and you invited me to be a co-host." Mickey stared at him, compelling Ray to add, "You said I knew my way around horses, which is true. I've been a rancher my whole life. When I was a kid, my dad and I found one of our horses tangled up in some old barbed wire. It was hurt pretty bad, and pretty scared."

"What happened next?"

"My dad got off his horse and walked up to this yearling. I remember him being totally calm—just unafraid. That was the first time I'd ever felt nervous around a horse, but my dad said there was nothing to be scared of." Ray trailed off unintentionally, trying to hold on to the memory of his father's reassurance. He pictured his dad crouching next to the injured animal and snipping off a loop of barbed wire as if it posed no risk to his personal safety. Ray eventually finished with, "My dad taught me everything I know—mainly that in order to get a horse to trust you, you have to take away its fear."

"Take away its fear," Mickey repeated. "I like that. It's simple and true."

Ray shrugged. "Horses are prey animals. They go wherever they feel the safest."

"And where is the safest place in a herd?"

"Close to the herd leader, usually."

The Horse God turned to address his students again. Outside the arena, a howling wind whipped up a sheet of snow and ice that battered the windows and bent the trees. For the next three days, Ray would have to call on every ounce of experience to train his colt, calm its fears, and transform it into a creature Laney would be proud to re-home. It wasn't enough time, but it was all the time he had, and Ray was determined to make the most of it—if not for Mickey's sake, then for Hannah, who deserved to have her parents at the wedding. This time, it wasn't just the colt's future Ray would be fighting for, but the future of his marriage as well.

With that, Mickey's three-day colt-starting clinic got underway.

Twelve

Dusk fell on the training centre in a landslide of blue and violet. All through the morning and afternoon, Ray and Mickey had taken turns leading the clinic, teaching the students how to bond with their horses, and making sure no one got hurt. Unfortunately, being so involved in the groundwork meant Ray hadn't had any time to work with his colt. Mickey had seemed to be having considerably more success: by the day's end, his colt had learned to take a saddle and respond to basic verbal cues. And, of course, he'd gotten it all on camera. In a few weeks, when the finished product was uploaded to Mickey's YouTube channel, people would know Ray not as a competent, gifted horseman, but as someone who'd overestimated his abilities and picked a colt that would remain unrideable forever.

Ray was determined to prove Mickey's followers wrong. After the last student had packed up and gone home for the day, he'd retrieved his colt from the barn, along with his ropes and work gloves, and returned to the arena for some peace and quiet.

The creak of the gate's hinges echoed in the dusty air. Ray led the colt to the middle of the ring and breathed deeply, purging the frustration from his body and mind. Right now, it was just him and the horse—no cameras, no rapt audience, and no reason to feel humiliated by his lack of progress.

Ray started with getting the horse acquainted with his touch. He gently massaged the colt's warm, velvety ears before moving his hands down the rest of its face, touching the places a bridle would eventually sit. The colt's nostrils flared as Ray's hands continued their journey over its muzzle, throat, neck, and back. Down the forelegs, then the hindlegs. Across the ribs. Over the rump. By the time he reached the tail, Ray had more or less forgotten about Mickey and the junior horse trainers. So, when the Horse God walked in a few minutes later, his arrival went perfectly unnoticed.

"See? I'm not so bad," Ray said to the colt. He approached its head once more and unfastened the halter, then flicked his rope to send the horse on its way. As the colt broke into a gallop, Ray calmly swung the rope in a circle, reminding the horse of its place in the hierarchy. Dust billowed around him, thick and comforting in its familiarity. In his mind, he pictured the round pen with its non-existent corners and positioned himself at the centre of this imaginary space.

Mickey was still watching their exchange when the colt plunged its head toward the ground and trotted a nervous circle around Ray. It felt almost discourteous to intrude on this join-up, but Mickey was mesmerized by Ray's fluidity and confidence. Sure, you could teach anyone to ride a horse, but some people were just better at speaking their language. If only he hadn't sent his cameraman home so soon. A moment like this could change everything for Ray. It would certainly change everything for the horse.

The colt steered inward toward its handler. Ray raised his hand once more and, with a stern cluck of his tongue, changed the direction of its travel. As the horse continued to run circles around him—this time, to the left instead of the right—Mickey asked, "Why did you turn him away? He wanted to join up."

Ray glanced at the Horse God, but otherwise kept his gaze firmly on his horse.

"I didn't ask him to join up," Ray explained. "He would have run right through me if I hadn't been paying attention. I want to be able to turn my back and not worry about what he's going to do."

"I wish I'd gotten that on camera," Mickey sighed.

Ray kept his shoulder parallel to the colt's. "That's okay. Like I said, the fewer the distractions, the better."

His horse was growing weary. Ray would have made him run all night, if that's what it took to send the message that he was in charge, but after roughly twenty minutes, the colt lowered its head again and licked its lips, imitating a small child concentrating on a difficult task. Ray turned his back, gathered up the rope that had fallen in a pile at his feet, and waited. He couldn't see his colt, but he could hear it breathing heavily behind him. He took a few steps forward, and soon, the colt followed.

Mickey didn't applaud, as he'd done for each of his students that day. Ray knew the reward was in the bond he had with his horse, not in the praise dished out by some celebrity. Still, Mickey couldn't help but say, "I'm glad I took Wilbur's call. He's never wrong about horses or people."

"So I've heard."

"Are you in a hurry to leave?"

"I promised my fiancée I'd call her as soon as I got to the motel. But other than that, no."

Ray slipped the halter back on the colt's head and led it out of the arena. As the group crossed the frozen ground to the barn, Mickey offered, "If you're interested, I can ask Noah to stay after the clinic tomorrow and film you working with your colt. He puts all my videos together. I could ask him to make one for you, too."

"Why would I need a video?"

"For your YouTube channel. Doesn't everyone your age have a channel?"

Ray chuckled and shook his head. "I don't have time for that."

"What about Facebook? Twitter? Instagram? You have to be visible if you want to get your name out there, Ray."

"I have Facebook, but the rest of it seems like…" He stopped himself short of saying *a waste of time*. Clearly, this wasn't the case for Mickey, who boasted thousands of followers and millions of views online. "Something I'm not good at—marketing myself, I mean."

"I can help you with that. All you have to do is focus on the horse."

Ray smiled, shutting the stall door behind the colt as it cut a beeline to its hay pile. "Now *that*, I can do."

A few minutes later, as Ray was heading toward his truck, Mickey pointed to the silhouette of his tour bus. "My home away from home," he stated. "Do you want to see the inside?"

Ray contemplated Mickey's offer. On one hand, he longed for the privacy of his motel room and the sweet sound of Hannah's voice. On the other hand, few people had probably set foot in Mickey Hammond's tour bus. Ray imagined it was filled with leather sofas, cowhide rugs, and a pair of bull horns mounted to the wall above the door to remind the Horse God of his roots. Mickey started toward his portable homestead, and Ray trailed after him, as if he were being led by an invisible string.

As Mickey opened the door, the heady fragrance of hardwood and leather muddled Ray's senses. He climbed the steps, then stood awkwardly in the narrow entryway as his host continued toward the lounge, stripping off his coat as he walked.

"Please, make yourself at home," Mickey urged, discarding his windbreaker on the armrest of the sofa. Picking up a remote, he jabbed it at the flatscreen TV tucked into the corner of the ceiling. Ray had never pictured Mickey as the type of person to watch TV, much less a home makeover show. But it made sense, given the Horse God's affinity for "fixer-uppers." The show went to commercial break, so Ray ventured toward the loveseat and sat down on the nearest cushion.

"I've never liked vinyl floors," Mickey said idly. "Everything is synthetic these days. Soon, there won't be anything natural left in the world." He gazed at the TV a couple seconds longer, then stood up. "How old are you, Ray?"

"Twenty-four."

Mickey bent into the refrigerator, collected two beer cans, and handed the first one to Ray.

"Thanks," Ray replied, wrapping his hands around the beer's cool weight.

"You deserve it. You put on a hell of a clinic today."

"Really? I thought I was kind of... in the way."

Mickey sank into the sofa across from him and knotted his brows. "Why do you say that?" He lifted the metal tab, unleashing a faint spray of the fizzy beverage.

"I didn't get much time to work with my colt. It seemed like every time I had an opportunity, someone would tie their rope incorrectly or ignore their horse's body language. I guess I expected everyone to have more common sense."

Mickey's shoulders rose and fell heavily. "I gave up expecting common sense from people years ago. You'll get used to it."

"My fiancée told me if the distractions became too much, I should just pretend I was in the round pen back home."

"Did it help?"

"It did." Ray cracked the tab on his beer and raised the can to his lips. He scanned the bus again, and his eyes landed on a photograph of a young boy with dark hair, freckles, and a toothy grin. "Is that your son?"

"Yes. Joshua." Mickey set his can on the end table and reclined again, balancing his left ankle on his right knee.

"He's my world," Mickey went on. "There's nothing I wouldn't do for Josh. No mountain I wouldn't move. No ocean I wouldn't swim. The day he got hurt, I thought I was going to die. You won't really understand what I mean until you have a kid of your own. To see something you love suffering so much... well, let's just say I didn't feel like the Horse God that day."

"I bet you miss him when you're on the road."

"I do. His mom and I have a good arrangement though: she takes care of him when I'm on tour, and for the few weeks that I'm back in Montana, he's all mine. I'm living the life of a divorced married man," Mickey added wryly. "But let's talk about you. What made you come around?"

"My fiancée, Hannah. Let's just say she has a complicated relationship with her parents. When I found out they might not come to the wedding, I knew I had to do something to prove I'm ready to take care of her. It's time to be a man, not a cowboy."

Mickey nodded slowly. "You really love this woman, don't you?"

"More than anything."

"Then maybe it's time to think long-term. I see a lot of potential in you, Ray, and I think if you keep working with horses, you might find yourself sitting on a tour bus of your very own one day. It won't be easy, of course. Life on the road isn't as glamourous as it looks on TV, but it has its rewards."

"How long would I be gone?"

"It depends. At first, it'll only be for a few weeks, but as more people hear about you, you'll be stopping in more cities, making more appearances, and booking more clinics. The money's not bad, if that's something you're shy about asking. And of course, I make money every time someone buys my book or DVDs."

Ray took another sip of his beer. He had fame and fortune at his fingertips, and all he could think about was how much he would miss waking up in the morning, getting a lecture from Marcus about leaving toast crumbs on the counter, and heading down to the barn to begin his day. No tour bus could compare to seeing the sun rise over the mountains or watching the way Hannah fixed her coffee. The ranch was his home, and home was nothing without the people he loved.

All the same, he asked, "Where's your next stop?"

"Grand Junction, then it's on to Utah for about three weeks before I begin making my way home." Mickey held out his hand. "I don't need an answer tonight. Go and get some sleep. And tell your fiancée you love her. Life is so damn fragile, and it can change in the blink of an eye."

"I will." Ray rose, his head swimming with questions—including what he ought to do with half a can of beer. Chugging it wasn't an option, and handing it back seemed rude, so instead, he simply stood there, looking to Mickey for direction the way the colt had looked to him.

Mickey indicated the kitchenette. "Dump it down the sink. There's plenty more where that one came from." Once Ray had returned, he said, "By the way, did you give your colt a name yet?"

"No. Should I?"

"It's up to you. It might help you feel more connected."

Heeding this advice, Ray reached for the door and said, "Thanks for the tour."

"Thanks for the company. It's lonely at the top, as they say."

Ray smiled, then stepped outside and commenced the chilly trek back to his truck.

Thirteen

"Do you want the good news first, or the bad news?" Odessa asked over lunch.

Adrianna replied with, "Bad news. I'm used to it by now."

Odessa set down her phone. Whatever she was about to say next, it must've been worse than Adrianna was expecting, since her lawyer never put down her phone for any reason.

Odessa sighed. "Marshall wants you to take a polygraph."

"He *what?*"

"I told him it's too late for that," Odessa assured her, "but it doesn't change the fact that he thinks you're lying."

"Of course he thinks I'm lying. His entire defense is based on the assumption that I'm a vengeful ex-girlfriend out for Doug's money." Adrianna sank back into her chair. Outside the restaurant, tourists were roaming the sidewalks carrying large, paper bags from some of the expensive clothing stores in town. She and Victor had barely been able to afford an attorney, even with Jim and Laney's offer to help, but what choice did they have? What choice did *she* have?

"The good news?" Adrianna prompted.

"The good news is that victims have won before. In fact—" Odessa leaned sideways, opened the portfolio propped against the leg of her chair, and rummaged through the pockets. She straightened and handed a folder across the table to Adrianna, who'd been forcing down a plate of mushroom risotto one sticky grain at a time. "Have a look at this. This is a case from eight years ago. The complainant was a thirty-year-old woman named Ingrid Wilson. She claimed her ex, John Teeter, broke into her apartment late one night and sexually assaulted her in her own bed. Teeter argued that he'd been invited in, and most people believed it because of the couple's long personal history."

"So, what tipped the scales?"

"Ingrid's young daughter witnessed the incident. She'd gotten out of bed to come and ask for a glass of water, and when she arrived in her mother's bedroom, she saw Teeter committing the crime. The daughter told the officers that a strange man was in their apartment, holding her mommy down."

Adrianna's gaze dropped to her lap this time, instead of lingering on the window. *No child should have to see that.* "You said Ingrid won?"

"Yes. She was awarded fifty thousand dollars in damages—enough to relocate to another city far away from Teeter." Odessa hinged forward. "It can be done. I know things seem hopeless right now, but it's always darkest before dawn, right?"

As Odessa relaxed into her chair once more, Adrianna considered her options. No one had witnessed the attack that night—there were no cameras trained on the staff parking lot—and she'd lied to Doug before in the name of self-defense. *Darkest before dawn.* For the women who hadn't survived, there was no sunrise to look forward to, no hope that everything would turn out okay. She and Ingrid had been among the lucky ones. They'd gotten out, gotten away, while countless other victims suffered in silence. How could Adrianna have that on her conscience while also claiming to care so deeply about her patients that she'd cut her own recovery short? Maybe she was a liar, after all.

"We do have a couple more weapons in our arsenal," Odessa was saying now, glancing down at her white shirt to ensure she hadn't dribbled salad dressing on it. Raising her eyes to Adrianna's, she asked, "How would your husband feel about taking the stand?"

A short, sharp laugh burst from Adrianna's lips before she could stop it. "My husband would do anything for me—*except* that."

"His testimony could be instrumental in proving emotional and psychological damage. You said you've woken him up several times with nightmares about Doug. The jury would be all over that like hot fudge on an ice cream sundae."

"My husband has debilitating social anxiety. Putting him on the stand would cause him to have a mental breakdown."

"We need something, Adrianna, or Marshall will insist on a poly."

Adrianna's jaw tightened. "I want to go public with the case. No more hiding in the dark. I want everyone to know who Doug is and what he did to me."

"We are *not* going public with anything."

"Why not? I'm already under scrutiny. Doug's character witness said he doesn't have a violent bone in his body, but I have medical proof to the contrary. If Doug thinks he can hide behind his friends, he's wrong. I want the public to know he's a menace."

"Now you sound hysterical. We are *this* close to swaying the jury, and all because *your* character witness said you were calm and level-headed."

"I can be calm and level-headed and also put up a fight. I may be a victim, but I refuse to act like one."

"You can be Wonder Woman after the trial ends," Odessa argued in a smooth voice. She picked up her phone, took one look at the time, and set her napkin on the table next to her plate, saying, "I'm late to a meeting with another client. Do yourself a favour, Addy: let the experts handle this."

Adrianna opened her mouth, but the words didn't come. She already had every expert she could think of working on this case: doctors, forensic nurses, lawyers, judges. And still the doubt remained. All she wanted was a chance to speak her truth, and if Odessa wasn't willing to help her, then Adrianna would have to take matters into her own hands.

Fourteen

The video turned out better than Ray had expected. It started, as always, with a shot of Mickey, his belt buckle sparkling and his prized Stetson sitting low on his brow. As the camera zoomed in on the Horse God, he smiled and removed one hand from his jeans pocket before resting it on his belt.

"Hello. I'm Mickey Hammond, and if you're looking for a miracle, you've come to the right place."

The camera cut away to a pre-edited montage of video clips: two- and three-second shots of rowdy colts and unrideable rejects interspersed with images of Mickey addressing crowded arenas, or leading small, private clinics like the one Ray had co-hosted. In his voiceover, Mickey said, "I've made my living working with horses, from backyard ponies to Olympic-level competitors. Join me as I show you how to bond with your horse, stay safe, and have fun." The intro ended with Mickey's logo and the words *Performing miracles, one horse at a time* underneath. Then the screen faded to black, and the footage from the clinic began.

"Welcome, and thanks for joining us," Mickey said. "If you're watching this video, then you've probably seen your share of problem horses. My three-day clinics are designed to introduce students to the rough, but rewarding world of professional colt-starting. In this video, I'll show you how to communicate with your colt, how to safely assert your dominance, and, most importantly, how to turn him into a willing and reliable partner. Whether you ride for pleasure, for show, or for business, this step-by-step guide covers everything I talk about in my training DVDs. Best of all—it's absolutely free. But before we begin, there's someone very special I'd like you to meet."

As the Horse God extended his arm, the camera panned left until it captured Ray in the middle of the frame, dressed in jeans, cowboy boots, and the brown coat that had once belonged to his father.

"This is Ray Fisher. Ray and I met when he was working for a friend of mine in Aspen, and he's generously agreed to help me host the clinic you're about to watch." At this time, Mickey adjusted his hat and, flashing a grin at the camera, prompted, "So, Ray, tell us a little about yourself."

"I grew up on a cattle ranch in Aspen, Colorado," he began, minding Mickey's advice to talk directly to the camera. "We still use horses for most of the grunt work, and starting colts is part of the experience."

"And why did you want to come out here?"

"Even though I've been training horses my whole life, I still felt there was more I could learn. This clinic seemed like a good way to test my skills—and impart some wisdom."

Mickey held Ray's gaze, studying him as he would a young horse whose fate hadn't yet been decided. After a moment, the camera panned back to Mickey.

"There you have it, folks. Three days, two hosts, and only one goal: to take the unruliest colts we can find and make them sturdier than a kitchen table. The journey starts now…"

Hannah squeezed Ray's arm. "This is amazing. I can't believe I'm actually watching you on YouTube."

"Neither can I. Can you tell I was nervous?"

"Not really."

"Good, because I felt like I was going to be sick the whole time."

She leaned toward the coffee table and picked up her phone. When it became clear that Ray would need some kind of online presence to support his budding career, she'd reached out to Logan for help. In less than twenty-four hours, Ray had a Twitter account, an Instagram handle, a Facebook page, and his own YouTube channel. Now, he wasn't just some cowboy who'd grown up on a ranch—he was Ray Fisher, the Aspen, Colorado-based horse trainer who'd worked for Wilbur McCullough and co-hosted with Mickey Hammond.

"Logan wants to know if you've thought about having a website," Hannah said.

"Why would I need a website if I have all this?" Ray gestured to the screen.

"She says it'll make it easier for you to book clients and showcase your services."

"Will it help drive more business to the ranch?"

"I'd assume so."

Ray nodded tentatively. Maybe having followers wasn't such a good thing if everyone knew where he lived, but if it kept the roof over their heads and paid for a wedding Hannah's parents might actually attend, he could live with a little less personal space. "All right. Let's set up a website."

His fiancée smiled and turned her attention back to her phone. She'd just hit send on her reply to Logan when the front door opened and Marcus walked in. His truck was parked in front of the house rather than its usual spot down by the barn, and the clothes he was wearing didn't seem suited to spending hours in sub-zero temperatures. When he saw the couple, his face broke into a grin.

"You're in a good mood," Hannah hedged.

"I am."

She made an inquiring gesture with her hands. "Any particular reason why?"

"Let's just say I might've found a solution to your wedding venue problem."

"I thought we were getting married at the church." Hannah's gaze latched on to Ray. The church, and Father Kincaid, seemed like a done deal, even if she did have a few reservations about God and His role in their marriage.

"And I thought you were keeping your options open," Marcus said. "What are you guys watching?"

"Mickey's clinic video. I'm in it," Ray answered.

Marcus removed his keys from his pocket and jingled them impatiently. He hadn't been this excited about anything wedding-related since his fiancée had gotten cold feet two weeks before the big day. In fact, he'd been so staunchly anti-wedding for years that when Ray had announced his engagement to Hannah, Marcus had sworn he wouldn't get involved unless asked—or unless an opportunity came along that was too good to pass up.

Hannah seemed to sense his urgency and stood up. "Are you coming?" she asked, lightly touching Ray's shoulder.

"You guys are going to love this place," Marcus enthused as Ray set the laptop on the table. "It's tucked away in the woods—very private. But it's got plenty of room for Laney's guests, and it overlooks the mountains, which is what Hannah wants."

"And how did you discover it?" Ray asked. He slipped into his coat, then reached to close the door as they followed Marcus out to his truck.

"The way all great things are discovered—by accident."

*

The timing of Marcus's discovery couldn't have been more perfect. Earlier that day, as Hannah was preparing lunch, Jeanette had called to ask when she was coming home, putting a damper on an otherwise peaceful afternoon.

"I don't know," Hannah had answered, going to the fridge for a bottle of salad dressing. "Ray and I still have a lot of wedding stuff to do— venue tours, cake tastings, ring shopping…"

Jeanette had tutted disapprovingly. "You can do most of those things in Canada."

"No, we can't. We already tried it and it didn't work." Hannah had skimmed the nutrition label on the bottle and opted for a light drizzle of balsamic vinegar instead.

"Hannah, you can't hide out at your boyfriend's place forever. There are laws, you know. Sooner or later, you need to come home and face reality. Have you looked into Masters programs yet?"

"Okay, first of all, he's my fiancé. And no, I haven't."

"Well, you should. You've worked so hard for your degree, and I…"

As Jeanette had trailed off, Hannah removed a knife from the block and began slicing a tomato, removing the stem first and flicking it into the trash. "What?"

Her mom had sighed. They'd made so much progress when Hannah was away at university: they'd talked on the phone almost every weekend, and whenever Hannah returned home for the holidays, Jeanette would dig out her family's old recipe box and try to recreate some of her favourite childhood treats. After Hannah had lost her job at CPS, Jeanette had done her best to withhold judgment about her daughter's misstep, but time had proven that people seldom changed. By the fall, the weather hadn't been the only thing cooling down. As she'd added the tomato to the bowl of lettuce, Hannah wondered why she'd answered the phone when she already knew how the conversation would end.

"I don't want you to throw your future away over a boy," Jeanette had finished.

Hannah had shaken her head. "You picked dad over everything," she'd reminded her mother. "Over your own *family*. Or are you going to tell me it was a different time?"

"Hannah, this isn't about me. And what is all that noise? What are you doing?"

"I'm making a salad," Hannah had snapped, taking her anger out on a cucumber. "I want to fit into my wedding dress." As she'd said this, Ray had come down the stairs carrying his laptop. He'd waved her over, then sat down on the couch to watch Noah's latest cinematic masterpiece.

"Mom, I've gotta go," Hannah had said, interrupting Jeanette mid-rant. "I'll talk to you later, maybe."

Jeanette's voice had cut out, and, tucking her phone into her back pocket, Hannah had chomped down a couple slices of cucumber to kill the bitter taste in her mouth.

Now, as Marcus ventured deep into a wooded area where the snow stuck to the sides of the trees, Hannah became caught up in the beauty of her surroundings long enough to forget the conversation with her mother.

"Where are we going?" Ray asked his brother.

"To see a wedding venue. Or were you not listening again?"

"I heard you. But in case you haven't noticed, we've left civilization." Ray nodded at the wall of trees outside his window, their snow-covered bows shimmering in the sun, and seemed to have a change of heart. "It's kind of peaceful. What do you think, babe?"

"I think we could do a lot worse."

Marcus steered into a driveway. At the end of it was a log cabin-style home. Strings of unlit Christmas lights spooled around the thick wooden columns that held up the portico, while a pair of Adirondack chairs faced a stone fire pit, its contents still illuminated by a cluster of fledgling orange embers. The window coverings were seashell white: beyond their modest shade, a glimmer of movement proved they hadn't left civilization after all—only the parts that made living around humans unbearable.

"A house?" Ray said, reaching to remove his seatbelt as Marcus parked the truck.

"We're not here to see the house. We're here to see the woman who owns it."

As they all got out, Hannah looked around and smiled. She could already picture them here, with matching flowers in her bouquet and Ray's lapel, proving that distance didn't matter, that love conquered all. At night, as they lay together as husband and wife, she'd remember the moments leading up to this—a million tiny embers in the dark, glowing with hope. How she'd met a complete stranger at a movie theatre and let her walls crumble. How they'd loved and lost so much together. How the years apart had brought them to this sacred refuge, where they could be joined together forever. This place was perfect, meaning it was probably as far outside of their budget as this house was from the nearest gas station.

Marcus knocked on the door. When it opened, Hannah saw a woman around her age, wearing dark blue jeans and a rust-red vest over a black sweater. The woman's sable hair had been braided into a thick rope that fell over her left shoulder, and her eyes were a deep, earthy brown like Ray's, putting Hannah at ease.

Marcus began, "Eve, I'd like you to meet my brother, Ray, and his fiancée, Hannah. Guys, this is Eve Sparrow. We met in town when I was running errands for Laney."

"Nice to meet you," Ray said. He gestured to his surroundings. "You've got a great setup here."

"It's a real slice of paradise—two hundred acres of rolling hills and woodland. Your brother was telling me you have some land as well," Eve replied.

"We do, but a lot of it is backcountry. I'm not even sure where the boundaries are, to tell you the truth."

"At first we thought we'd have the wedding at home, but we were worried it'd be too disruptive to the livestock. And Laney's no stranger to parties, as I said, but a big reception will be too much for her at this juncture. And that's why we've come all this way to see you," Marcus said with a smirk.

"I'm glad you did. Did you want to take a walk?"

Hannah and Ray both nodded. As Eve shut the door and started down the path into the trees, Marcus fell into step with her. Hannah and Ray trailed behind, soaking up the scenery. The trees had formed a tunnel around them so that the ground was covered in shadows. In the spots where the sunlight broke through, it reflected off the snow like a mirror, bright enough that Hannah was forced to squint.

"So, how did you two meet?" Eve asked, turning to look back at them.

"Through some friends. Hannah was visiting for the summer and we started talking. After she went back to Canada, we decided to keep in touch and, well, here we are."

"You're from Canada?"

"Yes," Hannah replied, dodging a branch that lay twisted across the snowy path.

"How often you come down here?"

"As often as I can. Usually, once a year, but once Ray and I are married, I'll be living here full-time. Ray's planning to take over the ranch and even has his own business training horses."

"And what do you do for a living?"

"I'm planning to get my Masters in Psychology, so I can work with at-risk youths. I used to work for CPS, but that job became… untenable."

As they neared the end of the trail, Eve explained, "When my husband and I bought the property, there was nothing but a little trailer where the house sits. What we didn't know at the time was that there was a barn on the lot as well. Part of the roof had caved in, but it still had good bones. We decided to fix it up, and now…" She waved her arm at a sunny clearing. A classic red barn stood a short distance from the trees, its white trim gleaming and its roof intact. There was even a five-pointed star radiating celestial glory above the doors, and the sight of it took Hannah's breath away. "It looks like this. If you like the outside, you're going to love what's behind those doors."

"It's beautiful," Hannah gushed, unconsciously tightening her hold on Ray's hand.

"It is." He beamed down at her. "I love it already. Maybe even more than the church."

Eve walked toward the doors, pointing out various features along the way. "We attached a swing to that tree over there, and salvaged the wood from some old fence boards to craft that bench next to the pond. When we decided we were going to transform this place into a lover's paradise, we made sure to have lots of places to take pictures. Our ceremonies typically take place behind the barn. See how it slopes up into a hill?" Hannah and Ray nodded at the mound, which at this moment was nothing more than a sparkling white dune. Behind it, a tattered line of rock and trees rose out of the earth to stake their claim on the sky.

"What about seating for guests?" Marcus asked. "Laney's planning to invite a small army. Do you guys provide chairs?"

"We provide everything: chairs, lighting, an altar. You can't really see it from here, but the hill is flat on top—lots of room to seat everyone. Oh, I should have asked if you guys even wanted an outdoor ceremony."

"We do," Ray answered.

"Great. In that case, let me show you the inside of the barn."

As Eve led the way toward the reception site, Marcus swooped in on Ray's left and whispered, "Whatever you do, don't tell Laney about this place."

"Why not?"

"Because then she'll want to come and see it, and I'll never be able to drag her home."

"I think you're more excited about this than we are, Marc," Hannah chided.

"Hey, can't a guy appreciate a nice piece of land?"

She grinned, feeling genuinely happy for the first time that day. As the first door squalled open on its ancient hinges, Hannah's spirits lifted again. Eve crossed to the second door, grasping the metal handle and swinging it in a ceremonious arc. Unlike Ray's barn, this one had been gutted inside, the stalls torn out to make room for a dance floor, stage, and twenty round tables draped in creamy white linens. Globe lights crisscrossed the ceiling, but they were merely supplemental to the main source of illumination: a three-tier chandelier suspended from the roof beam. There was plenty of room for all of Laney's guests, speakers nestled in the rafters, and buffet tables folded and stacked against the wall. Eve and her husband had truly thought of everything, right down to the guestbook propped on an old wooden barrel in the corner, where friends and family could leave messages of love and words of wisdom to guide the newlyweds on their journey. This place, this *slice of paradise*, was everything Hannah had dreamed of—and more.

"First impressions?" Eve prompted.

"It's amazing," Hannah replied. She ran her fingers along the edge of the nearest table, picturing a bouquet of white roses at its centre. Ray's idea for a spray of wild flowers would've worked too, but these were details they could quibble over later.

"How many guests can you fit in here?" Marcus asked.

"Each table seats ten, for a total of two hundred attendees."

"Laney's going to be over the moon," Ray remarked, shooting Hannah a smile. He reached for her hand, then led her toward the middle of the dance floor so they could talk in private.

While Eve and Marcus stood off to the side, exchanging words on the barn's construction, Ray asked, "What do you think?"

Hannah gazed around in wonderment. "I think we're going to be in Marc's debt for the rest of our natural lives."

His face split into a grin. Standing under the chandelier's glow, his skin speckled with the light of a hundred crystal teardrops, he cupped Hannah's shoulders and said, "I'm okay with that. As long as you're happy, I'm happy."

She peered around at the décor again. They could start fresh here, at the intersection of the old and the new. Perhaps they could even borrow some of Laney's decorating ideas, although convincing her to take a backseat in the planning was going to be as tough as handling everything themselves.

Marcus sauntered over to them. In the background, Eve could be seen inspecting one of the chairs for damage while she waited for an answer.

"Well?" Marcus said. "Is this the place?"

Hannah traded a look with Ray. The rational part of her brain knew they should've asked more questions, toured more venues, and consulted with Laney first. But Ray looked so good under that chandelier, so *ready* to take the next step. He raised his brows, and Hannah nodded. "Yes. This is the one."

Having come to a decision about the chair, Eve flitted over to them. She sized up the couple on the dance floor, trying to divine their future together based on the smattering of details they'd provided on the walk here. A psychology major from Canada and a cowboy from Colorado— not the most unusual pairing, but certainly one of the most memorable. She could already see the pictures that would come out of this union, and smiled at how good they'd look on her website.

Marcus took control of the conversation by saying, "I told you they'd love it."

"We really do," Hannah said, keeping an arm around Ray's waist. "Everything about it feels right."

"Tell them the best part," Marcus said to Eve.

"Your brother told me you're planning to get married on July 25th. I checked our calendar, and that date is still available." Eve added, "Now, in order to secure that date, I'm going to need a deposit today. The remaining balance will be due a month before the wedding. The fee does include catering and a live band, but you're more than welcome to bring your own vendors if you prefer. And, of course, the deposit is non-refundable."

Ray's smile drooped. "How much?"

"Fifteen hundred dollars. I accept cash, credit, and debit."

Hannah's grip on Ray's waist slackened. *Of course there'd be a catch.* And since she was an unemployed psychology major, money wasn't exactly something she had in abundance. Another dream, gone.

"Would you excuse us for a minute?" she asked, taking Ray's hand. He followed her to the place where the dance floor met the stage and ran a hand through his hair. He'd already cashed Wilbur's cheque and spent most of the money on upgrades to the ranch and his truck. Whatever was left over had gone toward paying off his outstanding hospital debt. Was this what life was going to be like for them from now on—a financial rollercoaster?

Hannah lowered her voice. "What do you want to do?"

"I don't know." He scanned their surroundings. "I love this place, but can we really afford it?"

She didn't speak, mainly because they already knew the answer.

Ray leaned down to capture her gaze. "We'll keep looking. I'm sure there are tons of venues out there that are just as nice as this one."

"I know." Hannah sighed.

Marcus made his way toward them, stuffing something in his pocket as he walked. At the far end of the barn, Eve could be seen pulling one of the doors closed to prevent the wind and snow from doing further damage to her chairs and sound system. Her silhouette puttered industriously around the space, preserving its beauty for whichever couple was lucky enough to afford it.

"Well, thanks for getting our hopes up," Ray said to his brother, "we might as well tell Laney to start decorating the backyard now."

"Why? You're not having the wedding in her backyard."

"We don't have fifteen hundred dollars on us, Marc."

"No, but I do." In response to Ray's quizzical frown, Marcus said, "I just paid your deposit. You're welcome."

"You mean—"

"I talked to Jim and Laney before I dragged you guys out here. We agreed I'd pay the deposit and they'd pay seventy-five percent of the venue fee, leaving you and Hannah to pay the remaining twenty-five percent. Congratulations—you officially have a venue."

Hannah stared at him, speechless. They had a venue—*this* venue, full of rustic charm and elegant accoutrements. Beside her, Ray had finally stopped gaping and started grinning instead.

Marcus boasted, "They don't call me the 'best man' for nothing, you know."

Fifteen

"Are you sure you want to do this?" Victor asked. "I'm sure people would understand if you stayed home a little longer, given the circumstances."

Adrianna continued to pack her lunch, giving her an excuse to avoid looking at him. He meant well, but sitting at home all day twiddling her thumbs wasn't doing either of them any good.

As she plucked a tangerine out of the fruit bowl, she said, "I can't bring myself to regret what I did, and I can't let the fear of what other people think stop me from working." She raised her gaze at last. Across the counter, Victor was dressed in dark grey jeans, a black toque, and wore an orange safety vest over his sweater. Like her, he couldn't afford any more days off, but he'd stuck around a little longer this morning so she wouldn't have to eat breakfast alone. "I'll be fine," she said.

"I worry."

"Well, don't." Adrianna set her jaw. She hadn't meant to snap at him, but the echo of her voice lingered, forming an invisible wall between them. She placed her palms flat on the counter and fanned her fingers over the cool slab of stone to calm herself. "This is my choice. I *want* to go to work."

He stayed silent. There was nothing he could say to persuade her: even as teenagers, his attempts to keep her safe had always been met with anger or denial. Eventually, these feelings had settled and taken root in him—how dare she push him away now, when he'd believed her all along?

Adrianna zipped up her lunch bag. "I'm sorry. I need to get out of my head. I've been obsessing over the trial for weeks, and I just can't sit around and let everyone else handle it. I know you understand, Victor."

He removed his arms from the counter, his jaw stiffening. "I have to get to work."

Victor reached for his keys and headed for the front door. As Adrianna lost sight of his truck, she took a deep breath, lifted her lunch off the counter, and prepared to face the consequences of her actions.

When she got to the hospital, she crossed the entryway at a brisk pace and stepped into the first available elevator. It didn't matter what anyone thought, she reminded herself. This was *her* fight. Her choice. But even as she tried desperately to block out the doubt, her phone quivered with endless notifications at the bottom of her bag. For most of the morning, old friends and total strangers had been commenting on her post, either praising her courage or punishing her honesty. She hadn't considered what would happen if her post got back to Doug, but now that the thought was in her head, she couldn't ignore it. Would he retaliate, like Victor had suggested? Or would he try and preserve whatever remained of his reputation, and let his lawyer throw the punches in the courtroom?

The elevator bumped to a stop, and Adrianna got off. She walked past the nurses station and disappeared into the breakroom, where she took a few minutes to collect herself before starting her shift.

"I didn't think I'd see you back so soon," Rachel said from the doorway.

Adrianna removed her coat and hung it on one of the pegs. "I got tired of sitting at home. Has it been busy around here?"

"It always is. Wes is on his fourth twelve-hour shift this week." Rachel threw a glimpse down the hall before entering the room. Even though they were alone, she lowered her voice, causing a lump to form in Adrianna's throat. "I know we need to keep things professional here, but I saw your post on Facebook and…" Rachel trailed off, studying the floor. "I believe you. I can't believe you decided to post it online, but I've met Doug, and the red flags were pretty obvious."

"Everything seems obvious in hindsight."

"True."

"You don't think I should've written what I did?"

"I didn't say that. I said I think you shouldn't have posted it on a very public forum where anyone can see it." Rachel gave a tiny shrug. "Some things should stay private is all."

Adrianna gathered her hair into a bun and crossed to the door. "Keeping things private is what got me into this mess. It's called 'suffering in silence' for a reason—abusers count on the doors staying closed."

As she took a seat at one of the computers, Wes approached the counter. Rachel had gone back to her workstation, but Adrianna heard the soft squeak of her chair as she turned to listen. *So much for keeping things professional*, Adrianna thought.

"Welcome back," Wes said.

Adrianna smiled politely. "Thanks. I hear you've been busy."

"Just picking up the slack." He tried to hold her gaze, but Adrianna focused on a wrinkle in his shirt instead. "So. How are you?"

"I'm fine. Glad to be back."

He nodded. "I read your post. I'm not sure if this is something we should be discussing at work, but let me know if there's anything I can do to help."

"I will. Thanks."

Adrianna breathed a sigh of relief as Wes left to answer a patient's call bell. She'd forgotten she'd added him on Facebook, along with a number of Doug's friends, back when he still permitted her to socialize freely. That morning, she'd woken up to a scathing message from one of Doug's drinking buddies, calling her a liar and worse. Still, Adrianna refused to take down her post: nothing his friends could do would compare to what he'd already done.

Then Justina appeared.

"Addy." As she raised her eyes, Justina curled a finger at her. "Let's go."

Adrianna swallowed a cold pill of panic. She fell into step with the charge nurse as she led the way down the hall, passing patient rooms and supply closets without deviating from her course. Soon, Justina veered into a room occupied not by a bed or other medical equipment, but a boardroom table and eight black chairs. Three of them were filled with hospital administrators, their faces somber and their clothes dry cleaned to a wrinkle-free shine. The nearest one, a woman, met Adrianna's gaze with stinging apathy.

Justina urged Adrianna to take a seat and closed the door.

"Thank you for joining us, Ms. Bishop," the man directly across from her said. Like Marshall Newman, he was well groomed, smartly dressed, and counting on a dry smile to ease the tension between them. "I trust you know why you're here."

"Actually, I don't. This is my first day back after taking a personal leave of absence, so you'll forgive me if I'm not yet caught up on the latest hospital gossip."

He held her gaze momentarily, then directed his attention down at a folder on the table. He flipped it open with his thumb and handed her the contents—a printout of the post she'd made on Facebook. "Could you confirm if this is your account?" he asked.

Adrianna glimpsed the profile picture in the upper left hand corner of the page. "Yes, that's my personal account."

Returning the printout to the folder, the man stated, "Ms. Bishop, the board has expressed some concern over the content of your post. As you know, nothing on the Internet is private... not even if it's posted via a personal account." When Adrianna nodded to indicate she understood, he said, "Therefore, the board has decided that disciplinary action must be taken."

"Disciplinary action?"

The woman chimed in, "The board is looking into whether your post constitutes defamation. If it does, the case may go to court."

"Defamation?" Adrianna exclaimed. "What, because I used my *personal* account to tell my story?"

"You tagged the hospital's page. Now, we're forced to do damage control. We can't have the public or members of the staff thinking that hospital property isn't safe."

"But it isn't. There are no security cameras trained on the staff parking lot, or my attacker would be behind bars by now. The hospital should consider itself lucky I didn't sue."

"Ms. Bishop." Adrianna shifted her gaze back to the man, who said, "I realize you're upset. And perhaps you thought you were only venting to your friends when you decided to post this…story." He waved his hand over the folder. "However, none of these considerations negate the damage done to the hospital's reputation, now or in the future. For this reason, I've put in a request for your immediate removal unless you agree to make reparations."

"I won't apologize. What happened to me was terrifying and traumatic. Besides, nothing I said was false. How can victims of violence possibly expect justice when they're scared into silence for the sake of saving face?"

For several seconds, no one spoke. Adrianna had never heard her own heartbeat so clearly, as loud as footsteps in an empty stairwell. Under the table, she grasped her fingers in her hand in a feeble effort to warm them up.

At last, the third administrator, a half-bald man around fifty, spoke for the first time since Adrianna had sat down. "I agree. Justice must prevail."

Her spirits lifted. *Finally, a dash of common sense.*

"And," he continued, "if you feel strongly about this cause, you're encouraged to pursue it in your own time—something you will have plenty of by the conclusion of this meeting."

Adrianna pushed her chair back from the table. "I'll be sure to. Now, if you don't mind, I need to get back to my patients."

"That won't be necessary."

"I assure you it is."

"Addy." Justina leaned toward her, placing one hand on the table between them. "You're fired."

"But—"

"You will be escorted out of the building. Justina will accompany you to collect your belongings, and you will be asked to surrender your ID badge. We're terribly sorry, Ms. Bishop. We wouldn't have done this if we'd had any other choice…"

All the way back to the nurses station, Adrianna kept a straight face. *Fired.* What was she supposed to tell Victor? He'd understand—of course he'd understand, but he'd still worry. Adrianna swallowed the urge to scream. Would she ever be free of Doug?

Justina stood in the doorway as Adrianna emptied her locker, taking down the thank-you cards from patients and letters of gratitude from their families. She slipped the pictures from last year's Christmas party into her bag and threw out the newspaper clipping from a story in which her department had been recognized for their diligence. When the space lay bare, Adrianna shut the door and turned toward Justina, who held out her hand to accept the badge.

Adrianna strode past the nurses station to the elevators. As she stepped inside, she turned to see Justina standing outside the doors, holding Adrianna's badge in one hand.

"You had a choice, Addy. I'm sorry to see you go."

Then the doors closed, and Adrianna was alone.

Sixteen

Adrianna spent the next week in near total darkness. The curtains stayed closed, the bed covers had been pulled up to the headboard, and she kept her phone in the drawer of her nightstand, where sleep masks and reading material muffled Heather's attempts to reach her. With the trial dragging on, her job had been a refuge, and she'd looked forward to the days when she could make a difference in someone's life. And now, she didn't even have that.

From down the hall, Victor's approaching footsteps roused Adrianna from her semi-slumbering state. He sat down on the edge of the bed and leaned over the pillow, where a sprout of blonde hair proved there was indeed life in this room, despite the stale emptiness that consumed it.

He gently peeled back the covers. "Addy?"

At the sound of his voice, Adrianna snuggled deeper into the bed until no part of her was visible.

Victor leaned back. He knew how it felt to need space, but nothing good came from shutting out the world. His mother had been proof of this, although he'd refrained from mentioning her out of fear that it would exacerbate Adrianna's fragile mental state.

"Are you hungry? Maybe I can make you some breakfast before I go to work."

"I'm not hungry," she mumbled.

"At least have some coffee. It'll help with the headaches." Victor sighed. "Addy, you need to meet me halfway. I know it seems impossible now, but things will only get worse if you stay in this bed."

She sat up. Her eyes were swollen and bloodshot, and a patch of raw, pink skin ringed her nose. Bringing her knees to her chest, she wrapped her arms around her legs and stared at the crack in the curtains, laying a line of light across the floor: on one half, the dresser and bathroom; on the other, everything her world had been reduced to, including her bed, her husband, and a phone she refused to answer.

"How could things get worse?" she asked in a washboard voice. "I lost my job."

"I know."

"I *loved* my job."

"I know," Victor repeated, placing a hand on her arm. "It's going to be okay. Your skills are always in demand, so I'm sure you'll find work soon. In the meantime, we can file for EI."

She blew some hair out of her eyes and looked at the curtains again. "I don't want to go on EI."

"I know, but we need the money." Victor stood up and made his way to the window. As he swept the curtains aside, Adrianna dove beneath the covers once more. Strawberry light broke through the trees and filled the room. It was shaping up to be a beautiful, clear morning, one Victor hoped would be the start of an upward climb toward better days.

He turned to stare at the heap of covers. They'd been through so much together, but this was the lowest he'd ever seen her, and the most helpless he'd ever felt. With another glance at the sparkling horizon, he crossed the room, planted a kiss on her head, and whispered, "I love you. I'll pick up dinner on my way home."

"Okay." Adrianna stayed buried in the bed's warmth until she heard the front door close. Before long, silence filled the house. It sat heavy in her ears, calling attention back to the ticking of her heart and the pointlessness of her existence. She had no job to go to, no patients in need of cleaning or turning, no coworkers in need of pens or a listening ear. Why did she have to be so careless? To get back at Doug? To prove she was *a survivor*? Or was it just in her nature to put herself in situations where she knew she could get hurt? Adrianna let the questions torture her until she felt like she couldn't breathe, then tossed the covers aside and sat up, gulping down the cool air that rushed toward her face. Victor was right: she couldn't stay here. She had to get up. She had to fight. But for what?

While she contemplated whether coffee would be worth leaving the comfort of her bed, Adrianna opened the nightstand drawer and pulled out her phone. Hundreds of Facebook notifications awaited her, along with a text from Heather asking when she could come over. Adrianna replied to her sister first ("Another time"), then took a deep breath before delving into the quagmire of her ruined reputation.

The comments ranged from sympathetic to sinister. She hadn't expected her post to be seen by anyone outside of her online circle, but thanks to a handful of people who felt compelled to "Share" her story, her career-ending rant had amassed thousands of likes and comments. The nastiest ones sat near the top, condemning her honesty as an act of petty revenge. Total strangers labeled her a whore, a slut, a homewrecker. The same insults she'd heard in high school when everyone found out about her unplanned pregnancy. Somehow, the blame always fell on the people most likely to be crushed by it.

Adrianna scrolled through the latest additions to the growing pile-on. She was just about to put her phone away when she received a message request from a woman named Sylvie Blanchard. She accepted it with some reluctance, then leaned back against the headboard to read.

Hi Adrianna,

You don't know me. My name is Sylvie Blanchard. I recently came across your heartfelt Facebook post about taking your abuser to court, and I just wanted you to know: you're not alone. I, too, am a victim of abuse.

My abuser was relentless. We met at work, and at first, he seemed like the nicest guy (I'm sure you know too well how this one ends). We became friends, which led to getting drinks after work. But soon, he got nasty. It started with an insult and escalated to physical abuse. I told myself it was my fault for trusting him too soon. Up until I met my abuser, I considered myself a strong, confident woman with an exciting social life. Needless to say, that all changed in the blink of an eye.

The longer the abuse went on, the less I recognized myself. He was so clever, he even had me believing that my friends weren't really my friends. Pieces of my life that had been there for years were quickly ripped away. I thought I was going crazy, but isn't that what they say love is supposed to feel like—a rollercoaster?

To tell the truth, I don't really know what drove me to reach out to you. For all I know, you could be lying. But our stories are so similar, and I would never lie about being abused (if I ever had the courage to admit that's what it was). If you're not too busy, I'd like to meet you. I think it will help both of us heal.

Yours respectfully,

Sylvie Blanchard

Adrianna read the message again. Who was this Sylvie Blanchard anyway? People could pretend to be anyone on the Internet. How could she be sure "Sylvie" was even a real person, and not one of Doug's friends trying to lure her into a trap? The thought turned her stomach, despite its emptiness. Still her thumbs typed, the words flowing out of her like blood.

Hi Sylvie,

Thanks for trusting me with your story. I know it wasn't an easy one to share.

I'd be willing to meet with you in a public place during the day. My husband will be nearby. I'm sure you can understand the need for these precautions, given the nature of the trial.

Sincerely yours,

Adrianna

She hit "Send," then placed her phone on the nightstand and went to the kitchen for a much-needed cup of coffee.

Seventeen

"Are you sure this is going to work?" Hannah asked. She was holding her cell phone horizontally in front of her, but it was hard to see anything for the glare on the screen.

"Why wouldn't it work? I'm just doing what Mickey said. Are you recording this?"

"Not yet." Hannah pressed the red button, triggering the video camera. Then she nodded to Ray.

"Hi. Um…" Ray's eyes flickered from Hannah's face to the phone. *Act naturally*, he thought as Mickey's voice echoed through his memories. But acting didn't come naturally to him at all, and after a couple of seconds, he shook his head. "I'm not good at this. It was a stupid idea—"

"What if you just started working with him, and I'll start recording when you feel more comfortable?"

His muscles relaxed somewhat. Standing next to him in the round pen was Laney's gelding. While not yet fully recovered from his ordeal, he'd gained enough weight to make his ribs virtually invisible. In working with the horse, which he'd named 'Red', Ray had discovered that he could take a saddle, and responded to simple verbal cues like "walk on" and "whoa." Today, his mission was to determine whether Red was actually rideable. If not, at least they could laugh at the video later.

"Hey, Red. You ready to show everyone your good side?" Ray slid his hand up the middle of Red's face until the gelding leaned in to his touch. "I'll take that as a yes."

Hannah smiled. So what if Ray had forgotten his lines? He was still a cowboy, and Red was proof he knew his way around horses. Ray completed a simple desensitization exercise that included rubbing the horse's body with his hands, beginning with its ears and ending with both hooves on the rear legs.

Hannah prompted, "Maybe you could explain what you're doing for people who don't know much about training horses. Just pretend you're talking to me."

"Okay. Well, what I'm doing is looking for places where he's sensitive. Horses can become sensitive if they've had a bad experience with something."

Moving to Red's other side, Ray repeated the process from head to toe. With every inch he covered, he became increasingly concerned that Laney had lost her ability to gauge a horse's temperament. He concluded his assessment by saying, "So far, so good. But you can't get a proper sense of what a horse is like from the ground, so it's time to get the saddle."

Ray led the gelding toward the edge of the ring, where his saddle was draped over the fence along with a black foam saddle pad. He took down the pad first and positioned it on Red's back, then slung the saddle on top, rocking it back and forth a couple of times until he was satisfied with its placement.

As if suddenly remembering the camera, Ray turned to Hannah and said, "Normally I go a little slower with the saddle, but he doesn't seem bothered by it."

"He looks really calm," Hannah agreed, "for a horse that was abandoned."

"I don't like to think it was intentional. Truth is, we don't know anything about this horse. All I know is that he's here now, and it's my job to help him."

Ray drew up the cinch. He'd just finished attaching the bridle when Marcus sauntered over and leaned on the fence next to Hannah. Propping a boot on the bottom rail, he watched Ray in a blend of curiosity and irritation, his mouth drawing in tightly at the corners in a tense smile.

"What are you doing?" he asked.

"Making a video," Hannah replied.

"I can see that, just like I can see neither of you are helping me move hay."

"It's for Ray's YouTube channel," she explained. "I told him he should do something with Red, since he was abandoned and most likely to need the help."

Marcus smirked. "Nice of you to take the blame for your fiancé, even though we both know Ray's the one slacking off."

"I heard that," Ray muttered as he rode past them at a walk.

"Good. By the way, I thought Laney said he was unrideable."

"So did I."

"Do either of you know anything about video editing?" Marcus asked, waving a hand between the couple.

"No, but my friend, Logan, is an expert. She set up Ray's website."

"He has a website now, too? What for?"

"For getting you to shut up about not having any customers." Ray lifted the reins and issued a curt "whoa." Red stopped.

Stepping back from the pen, Marcus brushed off Ray's jab as if it were a harmless piece of debris. He'd have to look at the website later, once the real work around here was done. "Don't let all that fame go to your head," Marcus warned as he walked away.

As Hannah faced Ray again, she squinted, her eyes catching on a strange sight. "Is that… a brand?"

"Where?"

"On his off-side hindquarter."

Ray twisted around and traced the faint marking with his right hand. He shook his head. "No. It feels like an old scar."

"A scar from what? A whip?"

"Maybe. Or something in the barn. It doesn't seem to bother him when I touch it."

Hannah studied the shape a minute longer. It zigzagged along the horse's hip, rising out of the fiery red hair like smoke. The original injury must have been excruciating to leave such a distinctive mark—a terrible accident, or further proof of humanity's viciousness. Hannah decided that sometimes, it was better not to know.

"Anything else you want to say to your adoring fans?" she asked.

Ray considered his response, and smiled.

"That's how we do it on a working ranch. We take away the fear, one horse at a time."

*

A week later, when Logan sent her the link to the edited video, Hannah watched Ray as if it were her first time seeing him. On screen, he was careful and competent as he guided Red around the round pen, clearly in his element despite the rocky start. Toward the end, right before Ray delivered his sign-off, he lightly traced the grey line of Red's unattributed scar. The short video concluded with a black screen overlaid with Ray's contact information and the ranch's address. If this was the closest Hannah and Logan got to being friends, then it was good enough for her.

Hannah had just hit replay on the video when Ray walked in from outside. His dark green sweater had become a magnet for dust and hay, and his jeans were splattered with mud. He rounded the corner and stepped into the kitchen, where he bent into the fridge for a bottle of water, cracked off the cap, and took a long drink.

"Looks like Marc's keeping you busy out there," Hannah said.

Ray nodded. "We'll probably end up working through dinner. We need to tear down part of the fence in the isolation paddock and replace the rotted boards. And there's still a lot of hay to move out of the shed." He tossed the empty bottle in the recycle bin and faced the living room, where Hannah was sitting.

She pinched her bottom lip between her teeth. "I see."

"Is that a problem?"

"No, it's just that I thought we were going to look over the menu tonight." Hannah waited, but the confusion didn't clear from Ray's eyes. "You know, for the wedding."

"Oh." He shook his head. "Right. The menu."

Rising from the couch, Hannah proceeded to the kitchen, where her laptop sat on the table. These days, the wedding plans progressed slowly, and Hannah often wondered if it wouldn't just be easier to elope, like Victor and Adrianna had done. As the screen's glow illuminated the darkening room, Ray peeled himself away from the counter and leaned on the back of her chair.

"So, the menu's pretty standard," Hannah explained. "Guests can choose either chicken, beef, or vegetarian. A buffet style dinner would be cheaper, but I don't know how popular that would be for a wedding. Otherwise, we pay by the plate."

"How much is a plate?"

"Fifty dollars."

Ray's eyes widened. "Please tell me that includes the cost of the food *on* the plate."

"I know it seems like a lot, but bear in mind that not everyone who's invited is actually going to come. And Jim and Laney *are* paying half of the catering bill."

"That's still a lot of money. I know it's our wedding, but fifty bucks a plate is too much."

Hannah's smile leveled out. Deep down, she knew he was right, but she feared that if they didn't make a decision now, they wouldn't get another opportunity to discuss it until after the spring calves had dropped and the paddock repairs were complete. Yes, Hannah thought glumly, she'd chosen the perfect time to plan a wedding with a career cowboy.

"What's wrong?" Ray asked, seeing the frown that twitched over her face.

"I'm worried about running out of time. Our wedding is in four months, and we don't have a caterer lined up."

"What am I supposed to say? I told you, this is a working ranch. I wish I had more free time, but I don't—especially now that I'm booking client horses and working for Wilbur."

Hannah closed her computer and moved to stand beside the table, directly across from Ray. Not many people got to see this side of him: dusty and disheveled, his dark eyes encircled by even darker bags. Over his shoulder, Marcus could be seen dismantling the warped fence. He'd be expecting Ray back soon, and Hannah didn't want to be the cause of their inevitable bickering.

"You're right—you did say that." She smiled and stepped toward him, placing both hands on his chest. His heart thumped against her palm at regular intervals, briefly synchronizing with the arcing motions of Marcus's hammer swings. "I just want everything to be perfect."

Ray's hands settled on her waist and drew her against the sturdy warmth of his body. "Why do you think I'm doing all this?" he asked with a nod at the round pen behind him. "Was Logan able to work with the footage we shot?"

"Yes. In fact, it turned out better than I'd hoped."

"Good. I look forward to seeing it later." Ray smoothed her hair back from her eyes and smiled. When he leaned in to kiss her, she was overcome by the familiar musk of hay, horse sweat, and something that was distinctly Ray.

As his hands dropped from her face, he turned and headed for the front door. She tracked him across the yard as a cool breeze pressed his sweater against the side of his body, then returned to the living room to watch the video again.

Eighteen

Sylvie was late. Adrianna sat at a table near the coffee shop's window, where she had an unimpeded view of the door and, if necessary, an escape route. Scattered around the disposable cup that held her non-fat latte were thin ribbons of paper from the napkin she'd been shredding, along with a few crystals of sugar left behind by the previous patron. *Coming here was pure foolishness*, Adrianna thought as another paper curl fell into the detritus. She didn't even know what Sylvie looked like, wouldn't have recognized her if they passed each other on the street. And maybe that was why Adrianna had agreed to meet her in the first place: this wasn't about what had happened with Doug, but about what went on behind other people's doors. The other victims. She owed it to Sylvie to be here. To believe her.

Adrianna picked up her phone to check the time, then darted a nervous glance at a table in the corner, where Victor was also watching the door with a tense expression. A brittle smile quirked his lips as their eyes met. He wasn't exactly sure what his plan was if Sylvie turned out to be one of Doug's friends—or worse, Doug himself. But Adrianna had been immovable in her resolve, dauntless in the face of the vile comments thrown her way, so Victor had agreed to come. He took a sip of his coffee as his gaze migrated across the busy café, seeking a distraction from the worries buzzing around his brain.

Adrianna flicked her eyes at the door again. *Fifteen minutes late.* Maybe Sylvie had changed her mind. Or she didn't really exist. Adrianna suppressed her annoyance with a sigh, then lifted her cup and pulled in a deep sip. It was only when she lowered her drink that she noticed the woman by the door, wrapped in a leather jacket with matching gloves. She reached behind her head and yanked out her hair tie; her chocolate brown hair tumbled down her back in a silky cascade that ended at her hips. Her pale, round face sported a dusting of pink freckles, although she'd tried to draw attention away from them with a swipe of blood-red lipstick. The woman panned her gaze over her surroundings. When it landed on Adrianna, the stranger's ruby lips curled into a smile.

She approached Adrianna's table, her mousy voice struggling to penetrate the din of mid-morning caffeine seekers. "Adrianna?"

"Sylvie?" Adrianna answered back. This wasn't the image she'd had in mind when Sylvie reached out to her. On Facebook, she was merely a white head in a blue frame—another face in the virtual crowd.

Sylvie slid into the seat across from Adrianna and lifted her bag over her head to place it on the table.

"Sorry I'm late," she began. "Motorcycle was acting up."

"That explains the leather jacket. Did you want to order something?" Adrianna asked.

"That's okay. I'm not a coffee drinker."

Adrianna smiled. She liked Sylvie already, and not just because they were both survivors. She motioned toward one of the tables and caught the glimmer of surprise that flitted over Victor's face. "By the way, that's my husband over there. He's been extremely supportive of me during all this… trouble."

"Does he believe you?"

"Of course."

"You're lucky." Sylvie cast her eyes down at the table. Her finger cleared a path through the sprinkle of sugar as she added, "My own *father* thinks I'm making everything up. Men have a harder time believing these things happen—like they've all taken a vow of silence on the matter. My dad says it's because they're 'vulnerable' now."

"Vulnerable?"

"You know, to accusations of sexual harassment." Sylvie shrugged. "Their game, their rules, right?"

A light chatter blanketed the coffee shop. At a nearby table, a man in a suit was talking on his phone about his company's latest merger. Behind him, hunched over a laptop, a male college student was working on a paper. *What about him? Or him?* Had these men ever said something they knew was inappropriate and laughed it off as harmless locker room banter? Had any of them ever used their position in society to ensure their choices didn't come back to haunt them, as Doug had done countless times before?

Sylvie asked, "Why did you decide to post your story on Facebook? Would it not have been easier to take your story directly to the press?"

"I honestly don't know. The truth is, I was so angry and I just wanted people to listen. I wasn't thinking about the consequences at the time, and I certainly didn't expect my story to reach so many people." Adrianna cupped her hands around her coffee and stared at the traffic streaking past the window. "I lost my job. I was a nurse. I really thought they would help me, you know, being a hospital and all. But all they cared about was their reputation."

"You should sue."

"I've thought about it. One trial is enough."

Sylvie exhaled. "How's it going?"

"Well, to tell you the truth, I'm afraid we won't win. Doug's lawyer is Marshall Newman—one of the best defense attorneys in the state."

"I've seen his billboards. He looks like a prick."

"He is. I mean, how can any normal person sit there and listen to a victim pour their heart out, then turn around and call them a liar?"

"Because he's a man. He plays for their team." Brushing the sugar off her hands, Sylvie continued, "You wouldn't believe the things my abuser said. If he flew into a rage and broke the TV remote, it was because I *provoked* him. If I stood up for myself, I was a bitch. And," she said, dropping her voice to a whisper, "he accused me of fucking just about everyone I made eye contact with—especially when he was drunk."

"Yes," Adrianna said firmly, her skin tightening with goosebumps. "No accountability. No remorse. Just ego. That's how these men are—all of them."

Sylvie nodded somberly. "You're lucky you got out. A lot of girls don't."

"I know." Adrianna leaned across the table. "If I can take my abuser to court, so can you. It's time for both of us to get the justice we deserve, don't you think?"

As she said this, Sylvie crossed her arms and stared down at her lap. The creases in her forehead smoothed away, and she was so pale that her freckles stood in stark contrast to her cheeks. Adrianna observed Sylvie's hands as they crumpled the sleeves of her sweater, stretching the material so thin that her skin was visible through the woolen mesh.

"I can't do that," Sylvie said, "as much as I would love to, it's not my fight."

"Of course it is. You have every right to live free in this world, without worrying about what your abuser is going to do next."

Sylvie raised her eyes to the woman across the table. She'd thought about skipping this meeting a hundred times, but Adrianna deserved to know the truth about why she was here.

Sylvie cleared her throat and said, "I think you misunderstand me. I wasn't just another victim... I was one of Doug's victims."

One of Doug's victims. Adrianna swallowed, but the invisible vice around her throat didn't ease up. *Victims,* plural. She wondered if there were more, and why she even wanted to know. No, she didn't. She didn't.

She stood up, and her knees wobbled under her. Out of the corner of her eye, she spotted Victor—he was halfway out of his seat, ready to come to her rescue once again. She gave him what she hoped was a reassuring smile, then looked at Sylvie and croaked, "Would you excuse me for a minute?"

Adrianna angled in the direction of the restrooms, hoping she'd make it before the coffee reversed its journey through her digestive system.

As she darted past him, Victor scraped back his chair and followed her into the hallway behind the registers. The way Addy had looked right before she fled told him everything he needed to know, and then some. Sylvie's words had shattered her, just like Doug's fist.

Adrianna shut the door to the ladies' room and turned the lock. This single, handicap stall was the perfect size for a mental breakdown. She staggered toward the sink, registered her bloodless reflection in the mirror, then sat down on the lid of the toilet as her head began to swim. Her relationship with Doug had always been a masquerade, but there'd been enough good moments to make her forget most of his transgressions. At times, he was downright delightful... and she had loved him once, hadn't she? And all this time, there'd been other women—when? When they were still together, lying in bed after making up for the thousandth time? When he was feeling slighted and screaming obscenities at her? After she'd finally plucked up the courage to leave him, had he turned to Sylvie for comfort? It didn't make anything better, but Adrianna went with this scenario to soften the blow of her shock.

A soft knock at the door brought Victor's voice. "Addy? Are you okay?"

Of course not, she almost snapped. Instead, Adrianna took a deep breath and relaxed her fists. Once she was composed enough to speak, she said, "This is harder than I thought it was going to be."

"Do you want me to take you home?"

Adrianna weighed her choices in silence: go home and hide from her humiliation, or go back out to the coffee shop, where Sylvie was waiting for her? In the end, she picked Sylvie for one simple reason: they were on the same team.

She stood up, washed her hands, and patted her face with a damp paper towel. When she emerged from the bathroom, Victor was leaning against the opposite wall.

Adrianna began, "Doug abused Sylvie, too. There might be others. I want to talk to Odessa about having Sylvie testify."

He nodded slowly. "Whatever you feel is best."

"I don't know what I feel. Numb, I guess." She looked away. "How could I have been so stupid?"

"You're not stupid. You're a good person, and good people see the best in others. But there's nothing good in Doug—nothing you need to protect." Placing an arm around her shoulder, he guided her back to the dining area and sat down to finish his coffee.

As Adrianna returned to her seat, Sylvie gazed at her expectantly. This woman held more power than she realized, Adrianna thought. Her story could tip the scales, sway the jury in ways an emotional ex-girlfriend could only dream. Sometimes, the best ally was a total stranger.

"How would you feel about taking the stand?" Adrianna asked.

"I don't think I can. Believe me, I want closure just as much as you do, but going to court—"

"Please, Sylvie. I know you're scared. I was terrified to face Doug. But I think we can win, with your testimony. I think if the jury sees how much damage Doug has done, they'll decide not to let him walk away. Right now, the trial is looking like a garden variety domestic dispute. But it's not—it's far bigger than that. This fight is about equality. It's about leveling the playing field. We need you."

Sylvie blinked, trying to process everything Adrianna had said. After a moment or two, her red lips curled into a smile.

"In that case, tell me what I have to say."

Nineteen

"Nervous" didn't begin to describe Adrianna's mental state. She was immobilized by terror, content to spend all day in her chair at the prosecution's table if it meant Odessa did all the talking. After the backlash caused by her ill-considered Facebook post, Adrianna had practically begged her lawyer to listen to Sylvie's testimony. But she had listened, and now, she'd have to hear it all again, in front of Marshall, Judge McKay, and a dozen local strangers representing the greater good.

Everyone rose as Judge McKay conducted himself to the bench and sat down.

"Be seated," he said. There was a ruckus as bodies sank into chairs. The trial had been dragging on for weeks, and each time it reconvened, Adrianna swore the judge's hair was turning greyer. At the adjacent table, Marshall wore his usual slate suit and unctuous smile. Beside him, Doug was leaning back in his chair with his hands joined loosely in his lap. Adrianna wasn't surprised to see that he hadn't bothered to shave or dry-clean his outfit—in fact, she'd been expecting this, since these details fit with Marshall's carefully-crafted image of a man ruined by a love gone wrong. Doug looked over at her, set his jaw, and revived his vacant stare a second later.

Judge McKay began, "Thank you for coming, everyone. I promise, we're in the homestretch. Now, before we get underway, I believe the Crown has something it would like to say."

"That's correct, Your Honour." Odessa stood up. Her paperwork sat in a neat pile on the table, with pertinent information highlighted in yellow. "There is one more witness that we believe should be given an opportunity to testify."

Marshall sprang to his feet, pinching his jacket closed with a curt twist of the button. "Your Honour, I object to this last-minute change of plans. All the witnesses have already provided their testimonies. I believe there is sufficient evidence to proceed with jury deliberations."

"Your Honour," Odessa resumed, unfazed by the interruption, "for the sake of my client's safety, I'd ask that the court please allow this exception."

Marshall stiffened, his eyes trained on Judge McKay. Adrianna scanned the room discreetly, tallying the reactions to Odessa's request, then took a deep breath and let whatever was going to happen, happen.

At last, Judge McKay nodded, wrinkling the leathery skin around his neck. "I'll allow it."

Popping his button, Marshall planted himself back in his seat. He'd just leaned sideways to whisper something in Doug's ear when Odessa announced, "The prosecution calls Sylvia Blanchard to the stand."

Adrianna turned her head. At the sound of Sylvie's name, Doug sat bolt upright, his eyes widening. A blend of emotions chaffed in Adrianna's throat. He wasn't just scared—he was terrified, knowing what awaited him on the other side of that door.

When it opened, Sylvie appeared. She had her hair pulled back and her lips were as naked as the truth she was about to tell. As she made her way to the stand, Adrianna maintained a neutral appearance to hide her relief. Sylvie was her last hope—her only chance to beat Doug at his own game. Their eyes met briefly before Sylvie raised her right hand and took an oath that might just save them both.

"Prosecution may begin the examination," Judge McKay droned. With his permission, Odessa approached the witness.

"Ms. Blanchard, thank you for coming. Could you please start by telling the court how you know the defendant?"

"Mr. Alderman and I worked together at a car dealership. I'm a mechanic by trade, and we would often talk over lunch—mostly about cars, but occasionally about our lives outside of work."

"I see. And at the time that you and Mr. Alderman worked together, was he having relations with Ms. Bishop?"

"Yes," Sylvie said firmly, "but I didn't know it at the time. He told me he was 'frustrated' with women, but that I seemed different from the rest."

"Could you elaborate on that conversation?"

"The defendant asked me—several times—if I was seeing anyone. When I told him I was single, he said he couldn't believe it since I was, in his words, 'A sexy lady.'"

"And how did that make you feel?"

"I felt it was inappropriate for the workplace, but I wasn't offended by it."

"Why not?" Odessa asked.

"Because I've heard comments like that my entire adult life. You can get used to anything if you're exposed to it long enough."

Odessa nodded thoughtfully. "Now, this next question may be a bit more difficult to answer." She paused. "Did you and the defendant ever have relations?"

"Yes, we did."

"While he was engaged?"

"Yes, but again, I didn't know he was engaged until certain details of the case started coming out and I began comparing timelines. As I said, he often complained about women, but he seemed to like me. And I didn't mind the attention, if I'm being honest."

"So, what made you want to testify? From everything you've said, it seems like you and Mr. Alderman were fond of each other."

"I'm here because of..." Sylvie faltered, her breath hitching. Adrianna glanced at Sylvie's clamped hands, where the skin was bone-white and ice-cold. "Because of what happened in March of 2010, around the time that Ms. Bishop was attacked."

Odessa pressed her lips together and dipped her chin. Sylvie continued.

"It was a rainy night. I was working late when Doug—Mr. Alderman—walked in. Right away, I could tell he'd been drinking, which wasn't uncommon for him. But he also seemed upset, so I suggested we step into the office to talk."

"What was said during that conversation?"

"He told me about the problems he was having in his personal life, specifically with his relationship. He said he'd been trying to 'make things work' with his ex-girlfriend, but that she'd rejected him. That she was tormenting him."

"Tormenting him," Odessa repeated. Right away, Adrianna could tell that they hadn't discussed this beforehand; a hint of panic feathered over her lawyer's face. "Are you absolutely certain that was what he said?"

"Yes—it stood out to me. We talked some more, and that was when Mr. Alderman revealed that he and Ms. Bishop had, well, *had relations* earlier in the evening." Although Odessa hadn't asked for clarification, Sylvie added, "He said he'd had sex with her before coming to see me."

"Right. And how did this make you feel?"

"I felt… uneasy." Sylvie nodded, looking down at her hands. Her voice softened. "He was so drunk. And angry. And I wondered if…"

As her silence blanketed the courtroom, Odessa proceeded with caution. "What did you wonder, Ms. Blanchard?"

Sylvie bit her lip and swallowed. She looked up at the Judge, who nodded, then over at Adrianna, who didn't dare move a muscle.

"I wondered if she was okay," Sylvie said at last. "I had this horrible feeling that there was something Doug wasn't telling me, but I was scared of what might happen if I knew the truth. So, I stayed quiet. But that feeling followed me for years. It made me paranoid."

Odessa smiled. "Thank you. No further questions, Your Honour."

Marshall wasted no time in getting to his feet. In his haste, his suit remained unbuttoned at the chest. Adrianna stared at the empty slot, her mind filled with static as he approached the witness stand.

"Ms. Blanchard, approximately how long after this conversation did you and Mr. Alderman keep in touch?"

"About four months."

"And why did you and Mr. Alderman cease contact?"

"I quit my job at the dealership to open my own garage. Doug said he wanted to keep in touch with me, but I never took any of his calls after that."

"So, you knew something horrible had happened in March, but you didn't think it would be prudent to alert the relevant authorities?"

"I didn't say I knew what happened. All I knew was that Doug was drunk that night."

"And that he'd had relations with Ms. Bishop."

"Correct."

"That doesn't answer my question, though: why did you wait this long to speak up?"

"Because I feared for my safety. Doug knew where I lived and where my garage was located, and I was scared that if I spoke up about our conversation that night, he'd make me pay for it." Sylvie added, her voice strained, "When I saw Ms. Bishop's Facebook post, I knew she was talking about Doug, even though she hadn't used his name. I knew she was the 'crazy ex-girlfriend' he always ranted about, and she didn't seem crazy at all. Doug abused me, too. He broke me down, one insult at a time.

"I've never admitted any of this to anyone. Not only was I allowing someone I loved to hurt me, but in staying with him I was hurting someone else. I guess that's why I'm here—to apologize for not coming forward sooner." This time, she stared directly at Adrianna when she spoke. "He's a monster. And he doesn't deserve his freedom."

Marshall sighed. "No further questions."

Adrianna reminded herself to breathe. *He's a monster.* Doug had been drunk that night and unable to control himself, like a rabid dog snapping at anyone who dared to get too close. To set him free was to unleash a dangerous predator on society—and what honest juror wanted that on their conscience?

"If there are no other last-minute requests, I will now ask both parties to deliver their closing arguments," Judge McKay said, in the same dry tone he'd been using to narrate the rest of the proceedings. "After that, the jury may begin deliberation."

The room turned its focus back to Odessa.

"What have we learned from this trial?" she asked as she approached the jury box. Though no one answered, she could see the different reactions to her question flickering on their faces. "To start with, we've learned that being a victim is to be vulnerable to scrutiny. We've seen that, when given the opportunity to speak up, other parties would prefer us to remain silent. The time for silence is over. During the course of this trial, you have been presented with copious evidence that the defendant is indeed guilty of the crime for which he is being charged. You have heard from witnesses who have corroborated my client's assertion that Mr. Alderman is a dangerous individual and a repeat offender. Ask yourselves: What would it mean for other women if this man is allowed to walk free? What does it mean for women *in general* when we, as a society, side with the offender?

"You will recall that early in the proceedings, I asked Ms. Bishop to read the results of her forensic exam. The results were conclusive, and the DNA collected on the night of the attack tied Mr. Alderman to the crime. Now, Mr. Newman would like you to forget about all of that. His argument is about consent. But my client did not consent to any of the defendant's advances. By letting the defendant go free, we risk letting this relentless harassment continue. We render meaningless all language around consent and boundaries. We jeopardize the right to safety that every victim should feel when they leave their home or walk down the street. We teach our children that bodily autonomy is only as good as our ability to defend those who cannot defend themselves... This trial has never been a lover's quarrel or a cash grab. It's a fight for equality. It's one small drop in an ocean of injustice, and it is my sincerest hope that your verdict will turn the tide in the victim's favour. In every victim's favour." Odessa nodded. "Thank you."

As she returned to her seat, Marshall rose to take her place. As he passed their table, his gaze ricocheted off Adrianna's face. She could only imagine the things Doug had told him: about her, about their relationship, and about the attack itself. Adrianna felt the heat rising in her face as Doug made eye contact with her. His pupils were enlarged, just as they had been that night in the parking lot, when the foul stink of gin had overwhelmed her senses.

He was drunk, then and now. If the jury sided with him, he'd be sent to rehab, not jail—and in a few years, he'd be out roaming the streets again. Looking for her.

"Ladies and gentlemen of the jury, I think it's very clear what's really going on here," Marshall began. Adrianna tore her eyes from Doug's and stared at the attorney standing directly in front of their table, blocking her view of the star-spangled banner behind him. "This trial is a smear campaign—nothing more. Before the proceedings began, my client was a productive, well-liked member of society. His character witnesses described him as a good friend, an excellent employee, and a man who could do no wrong. He had a successful career and a vivacious social life. At one point, he even had a fiancée. Then, by some terrible misunderstanding, he lost everything. And here we are."

Marshall took a step back from the jury box and motioned to Odessa.

"Ms. Hanson here talked quite a bit about being a victim. By definition, a victim is an individual subjected to undue hardship. Well, I think we can all agree that Mr. Alderman has been victimized. The Crown will try and convince you that he is a dangerous offender, a felon, a convict—labels that can, and do, ruin many people's lives. And for what? So that Ms. Bishop here can walk away a few thousand dollars richer? What exactly has been accomplished, aside from complete and total defamation of the accused's reputation? Ladies and gentlemen, we've all behaved in ways we're not proud of, and we all deserve a chance to learn from our mistakes. And I think it's safe to say we've all been in the wrong place at the wrong time, as Mr. Alderman was on the night of the so-called 'attack.' Does that make him guilty? Are we really willing to rob ordinary citizens of their freedom for the sake of some feminist agenda?

"When Ms. Blanchard took the stand, she admitted that Mr. Alderman's remarks did not bother her—so why does Ms. Bishop want him put away? Are we content to live in a world where something as benign as a compliment could result in incarceration? Cases such as this one are becoming increasingly common. So I ask you: at what point does enough become enough? I'll let you be the judge of that." Marshall locked eyes with Adrianna once again. From the darkest recesses of her mind, she thought of every insult she could and hurled them silently in his direction.

"Ladies and gentlemen of the jury, we are *all* innocent until proven guilty under the law of the land. May your quest for justice free this man from a life of undue hardship. Thank you, and Godspeed."

"Godspeed?" Adrianna whispered, darting a look at Odessa. Her lawyer merely raised her brows and shrugged.

As Marshall strutted back to his table, Judge McKay shuffled his papers and took a moment to digest the latest round of debate. Marshall Newman and Odessa Hanson were both capable and competent attorneys who'd argued their stances to the fullest, but only one could win, and their victory would have far-reaching implications both in the courtroom and outside of it. The judge's shoulders sagged, and soon, he turned to address the jury.

"Ladies and gentlemen of the jury, you have now heard all the evidence in the case. You will be given a copy of the instructions to take with you into the deliberation room, but while you're still present, I'd like to remind you that as jurors, you have a duty to remain unbiased and impartial. As your verdict will determine the outcome of this case, you must do your best to arrive at a unanimous decision. You must consider all the evidence and testimonies presented in the case, and are encouraged to use your best judgment as it relates to both the defendant and the complainant. Having said all that, the court will now break for deliberations, and will reconvene once you've made your decision."

The judge banged his gavel. Its wooden echo jolted through Adrianna's bones, but she couldn't bring herself to join the exodus flooding toward the doors. Instead, she watched as the jury was herded off in the opposite direction, into a room behind the bench, where her future would be written one way or another.

Odessa turned to her and smiled. "Come on. You look like you could use some fresh air."

Twenty

It was too cold to go outside, so Adrianna and her lawyer sat in the chairs by the courthouse doors, sipping coffee from paper cups in silence. Men and women donning heavy black coats drifted in every direction; Adrianna fixed her gaze on the sea of solemn faces and tried to lose herself in the rhythm of their footsteps. Somewhere upstairs, a group of strangers was rehashing her ordeal and quibbling over the evidence. Adrianna stared at her hand wrapped around the cup: the blood had drained from her knuckles, leaving the skin cold and tight. She pressed the back of her other hand against her cheek, feeling the sting of her own icy flesh under her left eye, and hoped the years-old scar from Doug's watchband wouldn't surface on her pallid face.

"How are you feeling?" Odessa asked.

Adrianna lowered her hand. "Cold."

"Do you want to sit somewhere else?"

"That's okay. It's only anxiety." Adrianna took a sip of her coffee. "How long do the deliberations take?"

"Depends. Hours, maybe days."

"Days?"

"Lengthier trials demand longer deliberation. But the court is expecting this jury to reach a verdict swiftly." Odessa dropped her empty cup into the waste receptacle. "Listen, however this one ends, you put up a hell of a fight."

"I hope it ends with my abuser behind bars and my husband and I able to live our lives in peace."

"Me too."

"This was never about revenge," Adrianna continued. "I never *wanted* to hurt Doug. I only wanted him to understand that he can't keep treating people as anything less than people."

A smile flitted across Odessa's face. She leaned sideways to pull her phone out of her pocket, and Adrianna went back to observing the crowd, her thoughts going in as many directions as there were hallways.

"The jury's reached a verdict," Odessa announced, returning the device to her pocket. She stood up, brushed the creases out of her pantsuit, and waited for Adrianna to fall into step with her.

They started down a hallway and stepped into an elevator. All the way to their destination, Adrianna avoided her reflection in the mirrored walls. Her hands, folded in front of the blue jacket she'd worn on her first day in court, shook with a primal urge to flee this steel cage. When the door opened, she pressed her jaws together and followed Odessa down the hallway to the courtroom. Everyone else had already arrived. Victor sat at the back of the room alongside Heather and her mother. Adrianna stepped through the partition with Odessa at the same time that Marshall and Doug appeared and took their places at the neighbouring table.

Odessa sat down first. As Adrianna sank into the adjacent seat, she smoothed down the hair behind her head and squared her shoulders. The jury was escorted in. Like the faces in the lobby, they moved mechanically toward their respective seats, their shoes scuffing the carpet, their eyes trained on nothing in particular. Adrianna scanned the jurors closest to the prosecution's table, but their tired, grey faces gave no indication of their feelings. They were exactly as Judge McKay had instructed them to be: unbiased and impartial. She felt relieved. And terrified.

"All rise."

Judge McKay entered the courtroom. He took his place behind the bench and sat down, but Adrianna's legs were stone beneath her body. The warm flush of Odessa's hand brought her back to herself, and she lowered herself into the wooden chair with her hands clasped under the table.

"Has the jury reached a decision?" Judge McKay asked.

A man at the front of the jury box replied, "We have, Your Honour." He handed the decision to the clerk.

Adrianna closed her eyes, listened to her heart tolling in her chest, and squeezed her fingers together.

"We, the jury, find the defendant, Douglas Wade Alderman... guilty on all charges..."

She heard a gasp and looked over at Doug. His eyes were wide and glowing white at the edges. The tendons in his neck practically split the skin. As the blood drained from his face, Adrianna saw more clearly the rash of stubble tracing his jawline, its barrenness reminding her of a forest that had been razed to the ground.

Marshall requested the jury be polled. All twelve of its members agreed with the verdict. A unanimous decision.

Judge McKay brought the court to order again. As the jury was rounded up and returned to the deliberation room one last time, he said, "That concludes the case of Bishop v. Alderman. Counsellors, I appreciate your cooperation over these past several weeks. You will be notified when a date for a sentencing hearing is set."

He picked up his gavel, and as it fell, Adrianna burst into tears.

*

It was nearly noon by the time Hannah dragged herself out of bed, her head pounding. Ray had kept the curtains closed, save for a narrow slit in the fabric where blinding white sunlight knifed through. On the nightstand, he'd left a bottle of ibuprofen, a glass of water, and a note that proved he hadn't forgotten how much she hated waking up alone. Hannah shook two of the pain relievers into her hand, washed them down with the water, and picked up the slip of paper. Her memories of the previous night were foggy, although she vaguely recalled walking down a country road in the dark, her hands and face burning from the icy wind, and seeing the flood of stars overhead—a million silver-blue specks that looked just as lost as she was. And, she remembered Ray's voice somewhere behind her, growing faint as the distance between them widened.

Hannah squinted at the note:

Take these and meet me downstairs. - Ray

She carefully refolded the note and set it down beside her alarm clock. Her body felt warm despite the chill seeping through the windows and floors, and when she attempted to stand up, she found it impossible to move her legs. Hannah flicked her eyes at the curt directive on the nightstand. She couldn't remember coming home, much less what they'd talked about before bed. *Unless we didn't exactly talk*, Hannah thought uneasily. Steeling herself, she pulled on the sweater draped over the chair in the corner and opened the bedroom door, swallowing the uncomfortable fullness in her throat as she headed downstairs.

"He's looking a lot better," she heard Ray say. As Hannah neared the bottom step, she saw the cordless phone tucked against his shoulder and figured that the listener was Laney, since no one else ever called the house. "You should come and see him sometime—if your arthritis isn't bothering you, of course."

He finished stirring the pancake batter and shifted a couple of steps to his right, where a cast iron pan sat on the stove. Ray poured three large circles of the viscous mixture into the hot pan and reached for the flipper as Hannah wandered into his periphery.

Ray glanced back at her and smiled. Hannah frowned. Wasn't he supposed to be angry at her? His note certainly gave that impression, and then there was that whole part about her storming off in a rage the night before…

"Anyway, Hannah's awake, so I've gotta go. Love to you and Jim." Ray hung up the call and set the phone back in its cradle, a smile lingering in his voice. "Laney says hi."

"Thanks."

Ray checked the progress of one of the pancakes before turning away from the stove and leaning back against the counter. His gaze swept over her slowly. "How are you feeling?"

"I don't know." Hannah rubbed her forehead as if to speed up the healing process. "Am I… what happened last night?"

His brows shot up in surprise. "You don't remember?"

"I'm trying."

Ray pulled out a chair for her at the kitchen table. The throbbing in her head, the hot flush of her skin, and the temporary amnesia could only be explained by one thing: she'd lost control again, fallen back into her old ways. Ray appeared considerably more sober, so maybe it wasn't all bad—or maybe it was worse than she thought.

Taking down a mug from the cupboard, Ray filled it with coffee and set it in front of his fiancée, whose face was buried in her hands to block out the light. "Did you get my note?" he asked.

Hannah nodded. "I thought we were supposed to be fighting."

"No, we already did that. Last night."

She groaned. "Of course we did."

Ray flipped the pancakes. The golden-brown rounds filled the kitchen with the comforting scent of home, although Hannah was sure she was too nauseous to eat. As Ray slid into the chair across from her, she wrapped her hands around the mug and brought it to her lips. The coffee was scorching; its heat stung her tongue, making her mouth numb.

He dropped his gaze to the table, where he crushed a toast crumb under his index finger. "So, about last night…"

"I don't remember anything," Hannah said, pushing her hair back from her eyes. "Well, that's not true. I remember a few things… I was kind of hoping you'd fill me in on the rest."

Ray leaned forward, folded his arms on the table, and glanced at the window. The light was everywhere, blazing off the blanket of snow covering the ground and the thick cords of ice dangling from the trees. He considered closing the curtains on the kitchen window, but they were the papery white kind—hardly effective in mitigating the effects of a hangover.

"Russ threw us an engagement party," he began. "He and Tori invited a few of their friends, and we all went to The Kicking Mule."

"The Kicking Mule?"

"Some pub Addy recommended. Anyway, we had some drinks, ordered some food, and around ten o'clock, I suggested heading out. But you wanted to stay, so, we stayed."

"What did I order? To drink, I mean."

"A couple glasses of red wine."

Hannah furrowed her brows, then quickly relaxed them again as pain spiked behind her eyes. "That's not a lot. When I lived with Jo, I often drank wine and I *never* woke up like this."

Ray pursed his lips and shifted his gaze to the calendar. "Then it was probably the tequila shots that did you in. I've never seen you take *one* shot, much less three in close succession. Oh, and you finished my beer."

The blood drained from Hannah's face. She'd done shots in university, but back then, she used to stay out all night, dancing under neon strobe lights with her roommates until she'd sweated out every last drop of poor judgment.

"Why didn't you cut me off?" she asked.

"I tried," Ray replied, "but you got belligerent. And when I told the bartender not to serve you anymore, you stormed out."

The memory of the frigid wind cut into Hannah's skin anew. She pictured the deserted road lit by a blushing moon, and wondered how far she would have gotten if Ray hadn't been right behind her every step of the way.

"You didn't get very far," he said with a shrug. "When I caught up to you, you said something about how the stars were... wrong." Ray's forehead creased. "Honestly, you were pretty drunk, so I didn't think much of it until we came home."

"And then we had our fight," Hannah said resignedly.

"You remember that?"

"No, just guessing." She swallowed. Her mind was clearing, and she didn't like what she saw. "Ray, what did I say to you last night?"

A frown bent the corners of his mouth toward the table. He couldn't look at her, so he focused on rounding up the toast crumbs instead, telling himself that she hadn't meant to hurt him.

"You said you wanted to call off the wedding," he whispered.

Hannah's eyes widened. "I did?"

"Among other things."

"Ray, you know I didn't mean it. I was intoxicated. I love you. You know that."

"I know."

"And I don't want to call off the wedding. I don't even know why I would've said something like that."

"I don't either." Ray's lips lifted at the corners, though he wasn't smiling per se. The crumbs sat in a neat little pile on the table, waiting to be swept into the trash. "Marcus once said there are only two times when a person is totally honest: when they're drunk, and when they're dying."

"Yeah, well, people have been known to ramble incoherently under both conditions," Hannah returned. Out of the corner of her eye, she caught a glimmer of movement as a white Jeep Cherokee drove past the house and down to the barn, crumbling the snow under its shiny black tires. "Who's that?"

"Our vet, Dr. Bardwell. I asked him to come take a look at Red."

Ray stood and crossed to the stove. He stacked the pancakes on a plate and drizzled a spiral of syrup on top before placing the breakfast in front of Hannah. "You should eat something. Fill up your stomach."

She nodded, unable to take her eyes off the sweet blobs of syrup that dripped from the flapjacks' edges. "Thank you."

"And take a hot shower. You'll sober up faster." Ray bent to kiss her head. "I'll be outside if you need me." The front door opened and closed, and Ray followed the Jeep's tracks to their destination. Hannah forced herself to eat the pancakes between sips of coffee, but she felt empty in a way food couldn't cure.

Half an hour later, with her damp hair tucked under a dark blue toque and her headache reduced to a dull ache behind her brows, Hannah made the trek down to the barn. Dr. Bardwell was a sturdy-looking man around sixty-five who had a tendency to interrupt himself mid-sentence. His hair was a monochrome of greys that faded into a white fringe, and his moustache was thick enough to obscure his entire upper lip and a considerable portion of his lower one.

Hannah peeked into the back of the Jeep, where Dr. Bardwell kept all his veterinary equipment, including a portable x-ray machine and several rolls of poultice wrap. Ray was standing in the aisle, running his hand over Red's ribcage and hip bones. Though still visible, the horse's skeleton was less pronounced than it had been last winter, when Laney had gone on one of her infamous rescue missions.

"He eating much?" Dr. Bardwell asked, giving the gelding a shot of some sort.

"Alfalfa with a bit of timothy hay mixed in. I've been keeping track of his feeding schedule." Ray ducked under the crosstie and walked toward the storage room, where he selected a book from the shelf above the workbench. He handed the dusty jotter to Dr. Bardwell.

"Just keep doing that," the vet said after a quick perusal of Ray's notes. "I'll make sure he's up to date on shots and de-wormer. There's— I'm sure I still have some, in my Jeep."

"Great." Ray turned his attention to Hannah. "There you are."

"Here I am," she replied, tucking her hands in her coat pockets. As Ray stuck the notebook back on the shelf, she asked, "Is there anything I can help with?"

His eyes darted back to the gelding. He'd already mucked out the stalls, swept the aisle, and put down fresh hay for the horses and cattle, all while Hannah was asleep.

"I don't think so," Ray said, looking past her to the sand ring. "Dr. Bardwell's going to check up on a few of the mares, then I'm going to head up to the bunkhouse with Marc so we can figure out what needs to be fixed."

Hannah nodded, clamping her teeth around her bottom lip. Turning away from him, she trekked across the patch of snow toward the paddock. Piles of greenish-grey hay littered the ground, and small groups of horses were gathered around each one. Hannah was leaning on the fence, observing the subtle changes in their body language as they feuded over turf, when Ray appeared beside her.

He indicated the bay mare with a nod. "Blaze is moving up in the world," he said as she pinned her ears at a yearling that had wandered too close to her pile.

A smile flickered across Hannah's mouth. Turning to him, she lowered her voice and asked, "Are we okay?"

Ray didn't speak right away, being more concerned about whether he should have put down more hay to reduce friction in the herd. After a minute, he smiled. "Yeah, of course."

"Are you sure? Because I don't want what happened last night to change things between us." Hannah added, "All that stuff I said—it didn't mean anything."

Ray's mouth pulled into a frown. He didn't feel like having this fight right now, but how could she say it meant nothing when her words had cut him to the bone?

"If you say so," he said at length.

As Hannah thought of saying more, Marcus's truck rumbled down the driveway toward them. In the bed of it were a couple dozen planks of wood and an assortment of tools he'd borrowed from Jim. Since Victor had moved out, the bunkhouse had fallen into a state of disrepair both inside and out. If they could get the place fixed up by the spring, then it could be rented out for passive income or serve as lodging for hired help.

Marcus rolled down the passenger window to address Ray. "You ready?"

"Almost."

Hannah fixed a smile on her face. "Good morning."

Marcus scowled. "Is it still morning?"

"Marc, don't be an asshole," Ray said.

"Why not? You heard what she said to me last night." His blue eyes switched back to Hannah momentarily, and he set his jaw. "Get in," he ordered with a glance at his brother.

Ray nodded once, then set a hand on Hannah's shoulder. "We're fine," he told her, a smile hinging on his voice. Then he approached the truck, opened the passenger door, and climbed inside. The tires squeaked on the snow as they pulled away, disappearing through a break in the trees that barely concealed the path to the bunkhouse.

Twenty-one

Victor could hear the assortment of tools rattling in the toolbox as he turned into the driveway of his former home. The trial was over, and Odessa was expecting Judge McKay to hand Doug a harsh sentence—lengthy imprisonment with zero chance of parole. *God willing,* Victor thought, though a real God would've never let this happen. Still, he saw no reason to be in a sour mood about it. Justice had prevailed, and he and Adrianna were officially free to live their lives... just as soon as Victor helped Marcus renovate the bunkhouse.

The melting snow had revealed the path through the trees. At the end of it was the small, cozy cabin, with its wood stove, mini fridge, and all-natural pine-wood floors. Marcus's truck was parked beside the firepit, with various cords and scraps of building material spilling out of the bed. A pair of sawhorses had been set up on the porch, with a sheet of plywood laid on top to imitate a table (or a bar, judging by the beer bottles). Victor parked his truck on the bunkhouse's opposite side and got out, breathing in the fresh air mingled with the scent of mud and sawdust. An unexpected smile caught on his lips as he walked around to the door.

"For the last time, we're not ripping that out. We're only fixing the things that don't work. Does 'building code' mean nothing to you?" Victor heard Marcus say.

Ray replied, "But it's hideous."

"*You're* hideous." Marcus emerged from the bunkhouse shaking his head. When he noticed Victor, he said, "Took you long enough to get here."

"Addy had a job interview to go to, and I had to help her find her keys. What does Ray want to rip out?"

"Marc's jugular," Ray joked. He leaned in the doorway, his face half-lit by the afternoon sun as he squinted at Victor. "Where's Addy interviewing?"

"Some women's shelter downtown called Helping Hands."

"I hope she gets the job."

"Me too. So, what have I missed?" As he said this, Victor gazed around at the scraps of wood littering the ground, the bent nails, and the dusty chunks of drywall. In all the time he'd occupied the bunkhouse, he'd never noticed any of its issues, but then again, he wasn't the one who'd spent a year working for Jim in his teens.

Marcus answered, "The usual—Ray not listening to me, and me cleaning up his messes." He ducked back into the cabin and returned a moment later with a bottle, which he handed to Victor.

"Thanks."

"It's about time you visited. I haven't seen you since Christmas." Marcus approached the plywood table, where a level, a hammer, and two glass bottles pinned down the corners of several building plans.

"I'm not going to apologize for putting my wife first. That's the whole point of getting married."

"I'm not asking you to. I'm just saying it would be nice if you didn't avoid this place so much."

Victor nodded, twisting the cap off his beer. "I'm sorry. Now that the trial's behind us, I'll see if I can come here more often." But Marcus, as expected, did not get his hopes up.

They got to work, with Marcus delegating small tasks to Ray and pointing out the areas, both inside and out, that needed to be changed or repaired to Victor. The first argument came when Marcus claimed that the roof needed to be re-shingled. Later, in talking about the insulation around the windows, Victor found himself growing frustrated with Marcus's know-it-all attitude and stepped outside to cool down, where Ray was picking pieces of fiberglass out of the grass.

"What's going on?" Ray asked.

Victor sank down on the step and picked up his beer. "The usual," he muttered, putting the bottle to his lips. "I thought we'd just be making a few small fixes, but what Marc's talking about doing is way beyond my expertise."

161

Ray nodded understandingly.

"Where's Hannah?" Victor asked.

"She went out for a trail ride—said she needed to clear her head." Ray went back to scavenging for bits of drywall. "She's been off these past few weeks. Russ threw us an engagement party and she stormed out, got a bad hangover, and now she keeps asking me if we're okay."

"Jeez."

"I know. She said she wanted to call off the wedding, but she was drunk when she said it, so I'm not sure if I should believe her…"

Ray rested his elbows on his knees and stared at his hands in thought. It had been a long winter, and, admittedly, he hadn't spent as much time with Hannah as he would've liked—but it was only because he'd been trying to prove himself to her family. Hannah didn't seem to get this. And what did "okay" even mean?

"I know it's not my place to say," Victor hedged as Ray looked up at him, "but maybe you guys should talk to someone before you get married, just to be sure that you're emotionally prepared to take on such a big commitment."

"That's what Hannah said, too. I don't know if I feel comfortable talking to a complete stranger about our relationship though."

"Addy and I did it. There was a lot of baggage to unpack, between the baby and Doug and my feelings about mom and dad."

"Yeah, but Hannah and I don't have baggage."

Victor raised a brow at Ray's naivety. "Are you sure? You guys don't have any dead ex-boyfriends or parental abandonment issues to confront?"

"Okay, so we have a bit of baggage. But I'm still not talking to a shrink." Ray lowered his gaze and went back to collecting the small, white pebbles like seashells.

Marcus had finally finished his assessment of the bathroom and now stood behind Victor in the doorway. His gaze jumped from one brother to the other and landed on Ray in a blend of shock and exasperation.

"How many times do I have to tell you not to handle fiberglass with your bare hands?"

"I don't know, but I'm almost done, so it doesn't matter."

Marcus reached into his back pocket, pulled out a pair of work gloves, and chucked them at Ray's face. Startled, he staggered and fell backwards from his crouched position, landing in a patch of damp, shiny mud with a growl of irritation.

"Come on! I just washed these," Ray said, brushing mud from the back of his jeans.

"That ass is not riding in my truck," Marcus told him.

"You did that on purpose."

Marcus picked up his beer bottle. "Should've listened to me," he called over his shoulder as he disappeared into the bunkhouse.

*

A week later, Hannah awoke in the middle of the night to a faint crunching noise. When she lifted her head from the pillow, she saw nothing out of the ordinary—just the pitch-black silhouettes of the furniture and the hazy glow of the numbers on the digital clock. Whatever she'd heard, it hadn't been loud enough to wake Ray. Hannah lay down again, tucked the covers under her chin, and closed her eyes, comforted by the deep, steady tempo of his breathing in the dark.

Moments later, right as she was about to drift off again, she heard another sound. A clang, like that of a door being closed, followed by the irregular tones of a human voice.

Hannah stared at the window. The curtain, swaying gently above the air vent, blocked most of her view. Raising herself onto her elbow, she peeled back the covers and stood up, shivering as she abandoned the warmth of the bed. Hannah reached for the edge of the curtain and shifted it a couple of inches to the left, just enough to peer out into the front yard without being seen from below. There was a pickup truck in the driveway, and bright red taillights breaking through the trees. She watched as a black figure exited the vehicle and walked toward the barn.

As it disappeared inside, her heart surged into her throat, choking her. She spun back to the bed and shook Ray awake.

"Ray," she whispered, "there's someone outside."

He turned onto his back, squinting up at her. "What?"

"Someone just pulled in. In a truck."

All at once, the fog of sleep lifted and Ray bounded out of bed. In a few steps, he'd crossed the room to the window and was standing in front of the glass, motionless except for the frantic beating of his heart.

He turned away suddenly, his voice strained. "They're towing a trailer." His hand fell on the doorknob and gave it a brisk twist.

As he vanished into the darkness, Hannah went to the window again. That was when she noticed the silver attachment stretching out behind the truck: a large gooseneck trailer with a black stripe along its side, and a decal, possibly a logo, near the top.

In the hall, she heard Marcus's voice.

"You're sure it's a trailer?" he asked.

"Yes."

"Shit." Marcus pulled a sweater over his head, tousling his hair in the process.

Hannah folded her arms over her chest. Her hands were ice-cold through the sleeves of her shirt. "What's going on?"

"Someone's about to learn why you don't mess with a man's livelihood," Ray said darkly. The murky pools of his eyes settled on her. "I want you to stay here. Marc and I are going to go deal with this."

A shiver ran up Hannah's spine. "What? No—we need to call the police."

"They won't get here in time. We need to do something *now*."

"Then I'm coming with you guys," Hannah insisted.

"No."

"Why not?"

164

"Because it might be dangerous."

She scowled. "Then why are *you* going?"

"Hannah, just… stay here, okay?" Ray's features softened. "I love you."

"Don't say that," Hannah replied with a flush of indignation, "don't say it like—"

"Ray, we've got to go." Ignoring Hannah's pleas, Marcus led the way downstairs and quickly disappeared from sight.

Ray turned back to her, his expression half apologetic, half deranged with fear. "I'm sorry." Then he spun away and followed his brother into the dark.

Hannah returned to the bedroom in time to see them climb into Marcus's truck. A second later, the headlights flashed on, illuminating the light drizzle that fell across the golden beams. He backed away from the house, then peeled off in the direction of the fields until Hannah lost sight of the bobbing red lights.

*

"Where are these bastards?" Marcus blew through the open gate and into the main paddock. There was no moon tonight, a fact made more apparent by the suddenness with which the trees seemed to lurch out of the darkness at them.

"I don't get it. Who'd want to steal our horses?"

"I don't know, but they clearly had a plan. I'll bet they know the layout of our house, too."

Ray's mouth went dry. He'd left Hannah back at the house thinking it would be safer for her there, but couldn't stomach the idea of her being alone and totally unprotected if anyone else decided to show up. "Maybe we should go back."

"We can't. We need to see who these people are."

"But what about Hannah?"

"She's smart enough to not draw attention to herself," Marcus assured him as they crested the hill. "Don't worry—she'll be fine."

Ray turned his focus back to their present crisis and tried to ignore the icy sweat collecting in his armpits. The main paddock was large and geographically diverse, populated with trees and carved by the natural course of the river running through it. At night, the horses moved about cautiously, using their heightened sense of smell to avoid the usual perils. But tonight was not a night for caution, and even before he'd gotten out of the truck, Ray heard their thunderous stampeding as they charged along the fence, seeking an escape.

The truck with the trailer had parked down in the valley. Its headlights were beaming into the abyss, and the pale green eyes of the herd were gazing back, manic with terror. The horses jostled and shoved, slamming against the fence boards and each other with audible force. Then a silhouette came around the rear of the trailer with its arms raised, and the horses at the front of the crush staggered back, only to find themselves cornered by a second figure wielding a long, narrow rod.

Marcus hadn't even stopped the truck when Ray threw open the passenger door and jumped out. What had Laney said that one time? *Who you are is defined by the choices you make.* What did *this* choice say about him? That he was stupid beyond belief—he'd abandoned Hannah in favour of protecting his horses. But he couldn't stand by and watch his family's legacy be ripped away like this. He had to do something.

"Ray—" Marcus leapt out of the driver's seat behind him.

"They have a cattle prod. It's looking bad." *Way to state the obvious, Ray,* he thought.

"Maybe we should—"

And that was the last thing Ray heard before he saw a flash, and a gunshot rang out in the dark.

Twenty-two

Ray awoke to the sound of beeping machines and murmured voices. He was in a room of some sort, with two green curtains flanking his bed and a bevy of medical equipment huddled around him. His limbs felt heavy, but as far as Ray could tell, he wasn't in any pain. As his vision recovered, he pried his gaze from the ceiling and peered down at his left shoulder, where a thick, white bandage extended from a spot under his collarbone to the outside of his arm. He let his head fall back against the pillow, his eyes flicking to the curtain as a nurse entered the room.

"Welcome back," he said, pushing a couple of buttons on one of the machines tracking Ray's vitals. "You're in post-op. Dr. Carell said you got lucky—the bullet managed to miss all your major arteries."

"I don't feel lucky," Ray admitted. He felt lethargic, disoriented, and anxious to know how many of his horses had been taken. His mind jolted to Hannah, then Marcus. Were they okay? Were they here?

"Your family's been waiting for hours to see you. I'll go let them know you're awake."

Ray nodded, a wave of relief washing over him. Bit by bit, his memories of the shooting returned. He saw himself now in the shimmering haze of post-traumatic recollection, skidding down the muddy hill in the dark, his bare hands burning from the cold. Across the field, a man in black clothing had been overseeing the late-night roundup. His hat sat low on his brow, and the bottom half of his face had been covered by some kind of material, leaving only the shadowy almonds of his eyes visible.

There'd been a flash, and a burning pain had exploded from Ray's shoulder. Marcus had driven him to the hospital, saying nothing about the blood on the truck's leather seats. They'd collected Hannah from the house, and Ray had suffered the trip into town with an old plaid shirt knotted around his left shoulder, the fabric turning black from the seepage. Over and over again, he'd replayed the shooting in his mind, and been tormented by the shrouded face of his attacker. Who would want to steal his horses? He had no idea. Nauseous and dizzy from the pain, Ray had concentrated on the warmth of Hannah's fingers wrapped around his hand. This wasn't an accident—someone had wanted to hurt him, and they'd succeeded. Or maybe, Ray had thought, right as they'd pulled up to the front doors of the hospital, the worst was yet to come.

The curtains swayed, and Hannah appeared first, followed by Marcus. Ray couldn't tell which of them looked worse.

Hannah moved around to the left-hand side of the bed and took his hand.

"Hey," she said, "I'm glad to see you're awake."

"Barely," Ray mumbled, catching Marcus's eyes. "You look terrible."

"So do you."

Hannah skimmed her fingers over the rough patch of gauze padding Ray's shoulder. "Does it hurt?"

"No. I'm trying to enjoy it while it lasts." Ray struggled to sit up, his movements slow and stilted. Maybe it was the morphine blunting his emotions, but seeing his family didn't offer the comfort he'd been expecting. How was he supposed to feel elated at their arrival knowing that someone out there wanted him dead?

Marcus began, "So, there's a lot we need to talk about. The first priority, obviously, is getting you healed up. I talked to Dr. Carell, and he said you should be out of here in a few days, barring any post-op complications."

"Okay. Then what?"

"Then," Marcus continued, tucking his hands in his pockets, "we need to fix the damage they caused. Victor said he'd come over to help me."

"Everyone's been really supportive," Hannah added. "I know it doesn't seem this way now, but things are going to be okay."

Marcus stared at his brother, and his demeanour went instantly frigid. "How could you be so stupid? Getting out of the truck like that—what were you trying to prove?"

168

"I don't know."

"All I wanted to do was see what was going on, and maybe get some pictures. But you just had to—"

"What, protect our home?"

Marcus looked away. His face was a sickly blend of grey and purple, with one particular vein near his temple noticeably more swollen than the rest. Hannah continued to clutch Ray's hand as silence filled the small, cramped room. Eventually, the magenta tint of apoplexy faded from Marcus's cheeks and the engorged vessel shrank to a nearly-invisible thread above his brow.

Ray rasped, "I had to do it. You know that."

Marcus pried his gaze from the floor and nodded. "I know." He leveled his gaze with Hannah's. "Are you okay?"

"I'm fine."

They fell into a sort of mute understanding. Outside the hospital, morning was beginning to unfold in a sharp orange banner along the horizon, setting one side of the sky on fire. The activity in the hallways had picked up slightly in the hours since Hannah and Marcus had been moved to a different waiting room, one with no magazines or TV to pass the time. Strangely, she hadn't felt as hopeless as she had on the night of Cameron's accident—possibly because she knew another day would come. And now that it had, there was an even heavier cloud hanging over her: dread mixed with her fear of the unknown.

It wasn't long before the nurse reappeared. He stepped into the room behind Marcus, frowned at Ray, and said, "The police are here. They'd like to talk to you about what happened tonight."

All the colour went out of Ray's face. He didn't have much experience in dealing with police, aside from the handful of times Marcus had gotten too rowdy in his teens and been dropped off on Jim and Laney's doorstep. All the same, he nodded. Hannah's hand tightened on his fingers as the nurse left to fetch them.

"It's going to be okay," she whispered, "you didn't do anything wrong."

When the curtain moved again, Ray saw two people, a man and a woman, standing near the foot of his bed. Both were wearing dark blue uniforms, their names engraved on small metal plates adorning their right breast pockets. Marcus visibly stiffened at their arrival, then made up some excuse about needing to call Jim and Laney before ducking out of the room.

The female officer, P. Moore, turned her attention back to Ray. "Are you Ray Fisher?"

He gave a small nod.

"I'm Officer Moore. This is my partner, Officer Lee. Would you be willing to answer a few questions?"

"Sure," Ray replied, even though his shoulder was starting to hurt again. He focused on Officer Moore's notepad and tried to ignore the gnawing ache under his collarbone.

Officer Lee indicated Hannah and said, "Unfortunately, we'll need you to step out of the room for a few minutes. But we'd like to speak to you afterwards, so don't go too far."

Hannah let go of Ray's hand. When she was out of sight, Officer Lee shut the curtain, then stood at the end of the bed with his hands clasped in front of his body.

"To start with, could you tell us what happened?" Officer Moore prompted.

"Hannah woke me up and said there was someone outside. I got out of bed, looked out the window, and that's when I saw the truck and trailer."

"Did you recognize the vehicle?"

"No."

"What happened next?"

"I went down the hall and woke my brother. He got dressed and we headed out."

"How soon after you located the driver would you say you got shot?"

"Less than ten minutes."

"Did you get a look at their face?"

"No, but I'm pretty sure it was a man that shot me."

"Old, young…?"

Ray shrugged. "Middle aged, I guess? I couldn't see very well."

Officer Moore added these details to her notes, then faced Ray with a look he felt was more accusatory than sympathetic. "Do you have any idea who might've wanted to hurt you?"

Ray's mind reeled and came up empty after a few seconds. Sure, he'd had a couple of bad sales in the past, like the day Bill McQuaid had ripped up the cheque, but he'd always done his best to smooth over any problems. Even now, with all the interest around his horse training videos, he'd never received a vitriolic comment or threatening message. He'd built his relationships with people the same way he'd built them with horses: using trust and understanding.

"No," Ray replied, staring at the sheet draped over his lap, "I don't."

She closed the notepad and slipped it back into her pocket. "Thanks for your time. We'll be in touch."

Ray watched as the officers exited the room. The morphine was wearing off, leaving behind the dull, throbbing pain it had temporarily masked. A strange blend of fear, anger, and hopelessness sat like a brick in his stomach. Ray imagined it was tethered to him by a long rope, and that he was sinking into some kind of abyss. Until now, he'd never anticipated being a target for anything. He was just Ray Fisher—a nobody. Clearly, not everyone saw it that way.

*

"There are a couple of things you need to know before you start learning how to rope," Marcus explained, waving his hand at the metal

171

drum he'd borrowed from the Fitzgeralds. "First, a real steer is not going to stand still so you can rope it. Second, they're a lot stronger than they look. I hope you're not too attached to your right arm."

Hannah cracked a smile. "Seems pretty straightforward so far." She measured out a length of rope and gave it a practice swing. How hard could it really be to throw a lasso around something?

Amusement sparked in Marcus's gaze. For a moment, it looked like he was back to his old, insouciant self, but when he faced the drum again to demonstrate the proper throwing technique, a dark cloud of preoccupation transcended his features. With branding season approaching, and Ray unable to help on account of his healing shoulder, Hannah had volunteered to take his place. The only problem was, she'd never roped a steer in her life, much less while mounted on horseback.

Calling on a lifetime of experience, Marcus took up the rope in his left hand, spun it over his head to build momentum, cast a wide loop around the neck of the barrel, and snapped it tight. Hannah raised her brows as he smirked, clearly expecting some kind of adulation.

"Impressive," she said, wondering how on earth she was supposed to keep up with the rest of the crew tomorrow. As Marcus lifted the lariat off the barrel and recoiled it, she asked, "Doesn't it seem a little cruel though? I mean, they're just baby cows."

"It's not cruel. It's business, and cattle are a product. The calves we'll be branding tomorrow are a little older and, as I said, heavy enough to put up a decent fight. Your turn."

Holding the excess rope in her left hand, she raised the loop in her right hand and attempted to twirl it over her head. Instead, it flopped uselessly around her shoulders, ensnaring her in its rough weight.

"Are you trying to rope an elephant?" Marcus chided.

"No," Hannah fired back. Freeing herself, she threw the lasso on the ground and recoiled it again. Her next loop was smaller, but still felt awkward in her grasp.

Marcus cut in, "You're holding your rope too tight."

"I'm holding it the way you showed me."

"I definitely didn't show you *that*," Marcus said, shaking his head. "Let's start over. Your rope—"

"I know!" Hannah sighed curtly. Closing her eyes, she took a couple of calming breaths before facing him. "Sorry. I'm just worried about… everything, I guess."

"Me too." Marcus's voice softened. "Think of your rope as a living thing. If you try too hard to control it, it'll never do what you want it to do."

She nodded and relaxed her shoulders. The drum sat about eight feet away, its edges rusty and dented from years of use. It wasn't the best target, being both too tall and too wide to imitate a six-week-old calf's neck, but for today, it would have to do.

Minding Marcus's advice, Hannah let the rope glide through her hands like thread through a needle. The calf-sized loop whooshed past her ears, caught the lip of the barrel, and slipped to the ground.

"Are you seriously taking roping lessons from Marc?"

Hannah turned around and found Ray leaning on the outside of the round pen. His left arm had been placed in a dark blue sling to limit its movement. Under the collar of his shirt, the corner of the bandage was plainly visible, triggering what felt like a hot lump of coal in Hannah's throat.

"Yes, she is," Marcus replied, twisting in Ray's direction. "For your information, she's doing really well."

"Do you mean that?" Hannah asked.

"I do," Marcus said, switching his focus back to her. "Don't let it go to your head though. You still need a lot of practice. If you can't rope from the ground, you won't be able to do it on a horse. I'd let you practice on Abby, but that's not possible right now…"

Hannah nodded somberly. Abby, Marcus's beloved raven mare, had been rounded up on the night of the shooting, along with Ray's sorrel gelding and four other horses. So far, the police had no leads, even with Laney's expansive network on the lookout.

Another fifteen minutes passed before Marcus suggested taking a break, although Hannah suspected it had more to do with his feelings over Abby's disappearance than her abysmal roping skills. She gathered her lariat and set it on top of the drum, then pulled off her gloves and crossed the ring to where Ray was standing.

"How's your shoulder?" she asked.

"Still sore."

Hannah unlatched the gate to let herself out. "Did you take the pain medication the doctor prescribed?"

"I don't need it. It's not that bad."

"Ray."

His smile wavered and he looked away. "I'm fine," he said after a short pause. "I'm more worried about the horses, you know? And Marc—he can't handle all this work by himself."

"I know, that's why I'm helping him."

They headed back to the house. Following surgery to remove the bullet, Ray had spent just two days in the hospital. On the first day, he'd mostly slept, but his grogginess was soon replaced by a near-constant state of agitation over the welfare of his horses. Even before he'd been given the all-clear to go home, Hannah had started preparing for the inevitable backlog of work by watching calf roping videos on YouTube, cleaning the house, and perfecting Laney's chili recipe, which would keep their freezer stocked for at least two weeks. Having a plan again, even just for the short-term, had been the ideal antidote to her anxiety. Still, she wondered what would happen once she returned to Canada. A gunshot wound could take weeks, even months, to heal properly, and Ray wasn't in the habit of listening to Marcus as it was.

"It smells good in here," Ray remarked as they walked through the front door. He squinted at the Crock Pot. "Is that Laney's chili?"

"Yup. Her recipe feeds twenty, so we have lots of leftovers." As Ray went to the cupboard for a bowl, she caught a hint of a smile on his lips and asked, "What? Is that bad?"

"No. It's just really cool to see you getting so involved around here." He indicated the window, which overlooked the round pen and lone, metal drum. "Are you actually going to help with the branding tomorrow?"

"Too late to back out now. Plus, Russ is going to be there, and I thought it might be a good way to smooth things over after all the trouble I caused at the engagement party."

"You didn't cause any trouble. You were just scared."

"Not as scared as I was when I heard that gunshot." She watched Ray spoon the hearty mixture into a bowl. "You were so out of it in the truck—mumbling, shaking. I've never felt so helpless."

Ray kept stirring the chili until most of the heat had escaped into the surrounding air. "I was in a lot of pain. I could feel the blood running down my arm and it made me feel like I was covered in hot tar. Uncomfortable. Like my skin wasn't really my skin." He let the spoon rest against the side of the bowl and braced his hand against the counter. "I know it sounds weird, but I didn't worry about dying. I mean, I did at first, when I realized the bullet had hit me, but when I was in Marc's truck, I felt safe. I think maybe it's not death we're afraid of, but being alone."

"I'm afraid of being alone," Hannah whispered.

"I know." Ray reached out his right arm and pulled her against his body. Despite the unusual placement of his left arm, she settled into his familiar warmth, listening to the undaunted tempo of his heartbeat. Her gaze drifted to the window. Every time she glanced outside, she pictured the truck and trailer parked in front of the barn, a rangy silhouette snooping around, and leaves fluttering on the trees. Someone had known where they lived and where they kept their horses—details that could only be gleaned through careful observation.

"Do you think those guys will come back?" Hannah wondered.

Ray carried his bowl to the table and sat down. He took a bite, swallowed, then said, "No. Lightning never strikes twice, as they say."

"But they know where we live. Doesn't that worry you?"

"It does, but I think they're smart enough to keep a low-profile. At least, I hope they are." He spooned some more chili into his mouth. "I'm trying not to think about it. The thought that someone actually wanted to hurt me—or you..." Ray shook his head. Laney's chili was the one thing that always made him feel better, but it was hard to have an appetite when there were still so many unknowns. "I'm just glad you're okay."

Before Hannah could speak, Marcus popped his head around the corner.

"Break's over," he announced. "I saddled one of the geldings so you can practice roping off of him. Tomorrow's going to be a long day—sunup to sundown. Think you can handle it?"

Hannah nodded. "I'll be right there." To Ray, she said, "I'm glad you're okay, too."

"More or less." Ray smirked. "You should go. He gets cranky if you make him wait."

Twenty-three

Hannah hadn't requested a wake-up call, but she got one anyway.

"Rise and shine," Marcus called through the door. 4:00AM darkness greeted Hannah's bleary eyes as she lifted her head from the pillow. "I'm going to go get the horses ready. Meet me outside in fifteen minutes."

"Okay," she returned in a scratchy voice. It wasn't even light out yet, and she was still drunk on sleep and the warmth of Ray's bed.

Hannah allowed herself another ten seconds of glorious slumber, then swept back the covers and stood up. The floors were ice-cold beneath her feet, with tiny dimples in the hardwood that she could feel as she rushed to pull on a pair of wool socks. After dressing in jeans, a long-sleeved shirt, and the sweater she always wore around the barn, she brushed her hair and tucked it into a messy bun. Hannah was just about to reach for the door when she heard a groan, and turned to see Ray propped on his right elbow.

"I'm here," Hannah whispered, taking a seat on the edge of the bed. "I was trying not to wake you."

"You didn't," Ray replied dryly. He let out a breath and stared disdainfully at the sling cradling his arm, locking his elbow joint at an uncomfortable angle.

"Do you want me to get another pillow?"

Shaking his head, Ray told her, "I've had enough of lying around. I'm coming with you guys."

"No, you're not. You're going to stay here and let your body heal."

"I didn't say I was going to help with the branding. But I can't stay inside all day. I'll find something else to do."

"Marc said we have all the help we need," Hannah assured him. "Your only job right now is to get better, okay? You can help with the fall branding."

Despite her less-than-satisfactory answer, Ray smiled mildly. He'd only been awake for a couple of minutes, and already he could feel a dull ache seeping through his muscles like a waterlogged book, each layer slowly dissolving into the next. At Hannah's gentle urging, he lowered himself into a horizontal position once more.

"Do you need anything before I go?" Hannah asked.

"No. I'll probably sleep as long as I can, and try to forget why I'm here."

"Just take it easy today. And if your shoulder starts to bother you, take the pain meds the doctor prescribed."

Ray motioned to the door. "You should go. Long day ahead of you."

Hannah did. Ten minutes later, she was crossing the yard to the barn just as Marcus was leading a pair of horses to the trailer.

"We're not riding them out to the field?" she asked. The horses were already saddled, and clearly more awake than she was.

"The cows are a few miles north of here. No sense wasting the horses' energy before the day's even started." Marcus stepped into the trailer with a gelding in each hand. After securing them both, he descended the ramp and bolted the door. As the light from the barn fell across his face, he looked Hannah over and said, "Last chance to change your mind."

She threw a glance at the house behind her, then looked forward, in the direction of the frosted peaks. "I can't."

Marcus hooked a thumb at the truck. "Hop in."

Hannah walked around to the passenger side. As she climbed inside, all she could smell was the lingering scent of cleaner wafting from the backseat, where Ray's blood had stained the beige leather. She stared straight ahead, watching as the sky brightened to a soft lilac in the distance. Soon, the driver's door opened and Marcus slid behind the wheel. If he noticed the insidious smell, he didn't mention it.

"The guys said they'd meet us there. We've got two hundred and seventy-eight cows and their calves to process and only one day to do it, so everyone's expected to participate." Marcus turned over the engine.

The headlights beamed off the fence posts as they drove through the gate and along the edge of the field, where a rudimentary path would take them directly to the branding station in the foothills. Hannah fought to keep her eyes open as the truck's swaying motions threatened to lull her back to sleep. "Typically, you'd have a few people on horseback, separating the cows from their calves, and a couple more people on the ground, handling the branding. Once the calves are sorted out, we vaccinate them and castrate the bulls—that's Russ's job, usually. Then we mark the ones that have been treated and reunite them with their mothers. It sounds easy, but it requires a lot of coordination."

"What do you normally do?" Hannah asked.

"Well, it's my ranch, so I brand them. It's nice to put your name on something, you know?"

"I'm not sure the calves would agree."

Marcus smirked. "Just do what I tell you. That's the only thing you have to worry about today."

*

By mid-morning, the north pasture was teeming with activity. Six pickup trucks and a handful of trailers had been parked near the trees, where the shade from the spring blooms promised to keep them from overheating. A rectangular pen had been erected in the middle of the grassy plateau: on one half, a thick carpet of black Angus cattle and their calves jostled for breathing room. On the other, several members of the crew were crowded around a writhing calf. One of the ranchers, an older man named Micah, had captured the six-week-old bull and dragged it away from its mother, and now stood over it on his horse, keeping the rope around its neck taut. At the same time that a cowboy was administering shots, Russ was at the other end, removing the calf's testicles. Marcus applied the brand to the animal's left shoulder, and Hannah shuddered at the likeness to Ray's injury—burning metal on bare skin, the mark of human cruelty. She forced her mind to expel this thought in time to see the calf stagger back to the herd, where she quickly lost sight of it in the frenzy of legs and tails.

"How are we doing so far?" Marcus asked the man who'd been tasked with tallying the day's numbers.

"We've branded forty-one calves so far. Castrated twenty-two."

"We're behind schedule," Marcus said, mostly to himself. He scanned the herd, then yelled, "Hey, Hannah. Grab that little one at the front."

For the most part, the calves stuck close to their mothers, but one calf in particular had failed to heed this age-old wisdom and was standing on the cusp of the herd. Hannah readied her rope and nudged the gelding on at a walk. The sun was beating down on the back of her neck, and her hair stuck to the sweat on her forehead and chin. Very slowly, she approached the calf and cast her rope, only for the animal to scamper back to the herd with its tail flying out behind it.

"That's okay," Marcus said, and made a circling motion with his hand, "just round him up again and Micah will bring him over."

Hannah hated this part—wading into the herd. It felt like being back in university, stuck in a noisy, crowded bar and fending off drunk idiots wanting to sleep with her. She squeezed the gelding's sides and weaved through the chaos, feeling the heat from the broad, black bodies pushing and shoving around her. Their sharp, tangy stench was overpowering: as it worked its way into Hannah's nostrils, she soon forgot about the smell of Marcus's truck and the real reason she was out here, covered in dust, sweat, and bug bites the size of pennies.

The calf was alone again, so she walked straight up to it and clucked her tongue. When that didn't work, she used her rope to swat the calf on its hide. As it gave chase, she spurred the gelding into a trot and drove the young bull toward the edge of the herd, where Micah waited to collect it.

"Don't look so guilty," he said upon seeing her face, "sometimes you gotta be a bit mean—show 'em who's boss."

"I thought Marc was the boss," Hannah replied.

Micah chuckled, then hauled the calf to the branding station. Even after several hours of this savagery, Hannah still had to look away as the calf was immobilized and stripped of its dignity.

When the team eventually broke for lunch, she slipped from the saddle and tied her gelding alongside the others. She was stiff from the waist down, especially along her inner thighs and tailbone, which had suffered the brunt of the horse's choppy movements. Hannah made her way over to the group, where Russ was serving sandwiches and pop cans out of a cooler in the back of his truck.

"Are the police having any luck?" one of the cowboys asked.

Marcus raised the can of Coke to his lips and pulled in a sip, shaking his head.

"How's Ray?"

"He's okay. His shoulder's pretty banged up, but we're hoping there's no long-term damage to his arm." Seeing Hannah hovering off to the side with a ham and cheese sandwich and a can of Sprite, Marcus added, "She's been taking care of him since he came home. I'm just not sure what's going to happen once she leaves. There's no way I can look after Ray *and* work while also taking care of Laney. We'll have no help around the ranch."

Hannah pretended not to hear him. Instead, she focused on the one thing she could still control: her hunger. The sandwich was plain, but fresh, and she relished the cool fizz of the Sprite on her tongue. As she stood in the shade of the trees, alternating bites of food with sips of pop, one of the crew members looked over at her and cracked a grin.

"Hard to believe a skinny girl like you could have such an appetite," he said, tearing off a hunk of his sandwich.

Hannah glowered. "Excuse me?"

"I'm just saying, you can barely rope a calf, yet you're eating like you've been in the woods for a week."

"What is your problem?" she barked. "I know I'm not good at roping anything, but that doesn't mean I'm not hungry."

Micah chuckled at her sharp retort, his moustache twitching. "That time of the month, eh, sweetheart?"

Blood rushed to Hannah's face—anger, not embarrassment. Her gaze shot to Marcus, who hung his head in a poor attempt at disguising his smirk. Struck mute by her fury, Hannah could only watch as the crew went back to their banter, as oblivious to her discomfort as she was to the stories behind their inside jokes.

Lunch ended a few minutes later. Rejuvenated by their conversation and refreshments, the cowboys headed back to the pen. Their horses stood by the fence, right next to the branding iron Marcus had set aside to cool. Hannah scanned the field for him, and found her future brother-in-law sitting in the driver's seat of his truck.

As she approached the open door, she said, "Thanks for sticking up for me back there."

"It's not my job to stick up for you," Marcus reminded her without looking up from his paperwork. "My job is to oversee the branding. Besides, the guys were just having a bit of fun."

"*Fun?* They were acting completely obnoxious—or did you not hear the horrible, sexist things they were saying to me?"

Marcus set down his papers and stepped out of the vehicle, slamming the door behind him. "I heard. They were just teasing you a bit. If Ray were here, we'd be doing the same thing to him."

"I find that hard to believe, considering he's a man and I'm not."

Marcus's expression hardened. Taking her by the arm, he led her behind the trailer. He might've been the boss, and he might've even had a point about the teasing, but Hannah wasn't about to be treated like some kind of animal. She twisted her arm free, then glared at him with all the venom she could muster.

He lowered his voice. "Listen to me. This is a working ranch, and those men out there are cowboys to their core. Did Micah take it a step too far with that time-of-the-month joke? Yes, but you have to understand that he comes from a different time."

"That doesn't make it right! My body doesn't exist for your amusement."

"I know it doesn't, but *you* wanted to do this. *You* volunteered to take Ray's place, and now *you* have to deal with the consequences of that decision… I'm not going to go easy on you just because you're a woman. If you want to cut it in this world, then you have to be just as tough, if not tougher, than them." Marcus jabbed a finger in the direction of the corral. "Ray and I aren't always going to be there to stick up for you, so you need to learn to fight back."

Hannah shook her head. "I can't. I'm not mean."

"No? You get pretty mean when you're drunk." Marcus smothered her with a knowing look until Hannah was forced to look away. "I'm sorry that they made you uncomfortable. But I know what you're made of, and I think you can handle a little locker room talk."

"Can, yes. *Should*… no."

"I know they can be a bit old-school, but trust me—they didn't mean any of that." Marcus turned away from her, pushing his cowboy hat down onto his head. "I've got to get back to work. Feel free to join us whenever you're ready to act like an adult."

Hannah lingered in the shade, letting the cool breeze wick the excess heat from her face and arms. She felt tears forming in her eyes and quickly swept them away using the back of her hand. If her psychology degree had taught her anything, it was that anger was a complicated, tangled mess of emotions with multiple sources. Ever since the shooting, she'd been haunted by fear, uncertainty, and grief—feelings that were too big to handle on her own, so she channeled her rage at a harmless comment instead.

She took another minute to collect herself, then pulled her cap down over her eyes and stepped out from behind the trailer.

Hannah had been in Colorado for nearly six months when Laney called her with some exciting news.

"The wedding invitations just arrived. They're sitting in a box on our dining room table as we speak," Laney chirped.

"That's great," Hannah replied, trying to match Laney's enthusiasm. At the mention of her impending nuptials, a rush of emotions filled her chest, making it difficult to breathe.

"It is. I'll admit, I was a little worried they wouldn't come in time, but God works in mysterious ways. Anyway, I figured you and Raymond would like to mail them out yourselves, but if that's too much trouble, I'm more than happy to help. You know, when Marcus was engaged, I personally stuffed and addressed over two hundred envelopes. But, of course, my arthritis was nowhere near as bad as it is now…"

Hannah's attention drifted to the window. The trees were bursting with velvety green buds and a warm breeze jingled the wind chimes. Even if Ray hadn't been shot, she doubted he'd want to spend such a beautiful day penning names on envelopes. As it was, he'd gone down to the barn to help Marcus deworm the horses, leaving Hannah to pack for her trip alone.

She faded back into the conversation in time to hear Laney ask, "You're still getting married in July, yes?"

"Yes," Hannah said, closing her eyes momentarily. "So, when did you want me to pick up the invitations?"

"Well, I assumed you would want to do it as soon as possible. I'm home this afternoon."

"Sounds great. I'll see you then." Hannah hung up the call, then placed the phone back in its cradle and reached for the front door. Within moments of stepping outside, her boots were covered in a thin coating of dust. The heaviness in her chest lifted, although she could still feel the icy dregs of grief scattered between each breath. With marriage came a new life and a new family: already Hannah felt like an entirely different person, changed in ways she couldn't have imagined last winter. She knew how to rope a steer and brand a calf, along with some more practical skills like how to stretch her meagre savings. Colorado was home to her now, and the only reason she was going back to Canada was because American laws wouldn't permit her to stay longer than six months without a visa.

In the barn, Ray was standing in the aisle, holding the halter of a young bay gelding while Marcus fiddled with the syringe of medicated paste.

"Hey," Ray said, brightening as Hannah came into view. "Did you come to help us out?"

"Kind of, but not in the way you might think." Hannah gestured to the horse. "Who's this handsome boy?"

"This is Biscuit. Unfortunately, he's not the biggest fan of taking his medicine."

"Poor guy." Hannah scratched Biscuit's muzzle.

As Marcus walked over to them, he asked her, "What did you mean by 'not in the way you might think'?"

"I just got a call from Laney. She said we can pick up the wedding invitations this afternoon."

"Huh." Ray looked around as if "we" might have included someone other than himself. "I'm kind of busy helping with the horses, but maybe we can go over tomorrow."

"Tomorrow's no good. We have the insurance company coming to look at the damaged fence. Hold him still," Marcus said.

"I am." As Marcus injected the syringe into the corner of Biscuit's mouth and gently squeezed the plunger, Ray turned back to Hannah and shrugged. "She'll understand if we can't get over there right away."

"Actually, I was thinking I'd go over by myself. Where are your keys?"

Ray looked surprised. He passed Biscuit's lead rope to his brother and, reaching into his pocket, dropped the Chevy's keys into Hannah's hand.

"Thanks," she replied. "I'll be back soon."

"Take all the time you need. If every horse is like Biscuit, we're going to be here for a while."

Marcus withdrew the now empty tube of de-wormer and tossed it into the garbage. "Make sure Laney takes her new arthritis pills. She insists she doesn't need them, but I think she only says that so I won't worry."

Hannah nodded. "I'll tell her she needs to help us address the invitations. She'd never say no to wedding planning."

"Now you're thinking like a Fisher," Marcus said, smirking.

Hannah smiled and headed for Ray's truck, trying her new name on for fit. Mrs. Hannah Fisher. It felt awkward at first, like brand new boots. But after a few more steps, she couldn't imagine taking it off.

*

The wedding invitations were beautiful. They came in an elegant white box with a red ribbon and a paper tag that said *For the future Mr. and Mrs.* tucked into the bow. Inside the box were a hundred and fifty cream-coloured sheets of paper glowing with gold letters. It was this tiny detail that solidified the wedding in Hannah's mind, even more than the venue or the magazines from Adrianna.

"What do you think?" Laney asked.

Hannah traced Ray's full name—Raymond Matthew Fisher—and smiled.

"It feels real now," she replied, setting the invitation back in its box. "If that makes sense."

Laney nodded. "The written word has that power. The envelopes are down at the bottom. I have a few nice pens you can take with you to write the addresses."

"That would be great." As Hannah put the lid back on the box, she said, "I've been meaning to ask: how's your arthritis?"

"Oh, it's never the same from one day to the next. Right now, it's manageable."

"That's good. It's just… Marc worries."

Laney scoffed into her coffee, a hint of her usual stubbornness crossing her wizened face. "You tell Marcus to stay in his lane, and I will stay in mine." She leaned back in her chair and smiled defiantly. Heeding this playful warning, Hannah took her leave.

She drove home slowly, letting the warm, sweet air flood through the open windows. The box of invitations occupied the passenger seat, its ribbon fluttering gaily as she steered onto the main road, leaving the choppy, gravel one in the dust. Once she'd gotten used to the controls, Hannah found she preferred the Chevy's lean toughness to the more sophisticated vehicles she was used to back home. There was nothing simple or automatic about Ray's truck, just like there was nothing simple or automatic about his way of life. There was only hard work and harder roads, and Hannah felt the echoes of every long day and sleepless night pulsing through the tires and into the steering wheel. His life, her life. His truck, her truck. Once they were married, it would all blur into one.

The highway slithered left and right, dodging the thick tangle of trees and rocky outcroppings. As she came around the corner, a long line of taillights appeared in front of her. Hannah lifted her chin slightly, hoping to spot the cause of the delay, then sank back against the driver's seat with one hand still curled around the wheel.

Up ahead, a police officer in a neon-yellow vest strolled along the road. As he neared the Chevy, he smiled, so Hannah asked, "What's going on, officer?"

He leaned toward the window, waving his hand in the direction of the holdup.

"Looks like we've got a bit of a landslide. It might take some time to clear the debris from the road, so we're advising drivers to turn around."

"Right," Hannah agreed, wishing she were more familiar with the backroads.

The officer straightened and moved to the next vehicle. "You drive safely now, ma'am."

"I will." Her eyes flickered to the side mirror, and the accumulation of cars stretching out behind her. Reaching across the seat, Hannah withdrew her phone from her bag, clicked on the GPS app, and typed in the ranch's address. The Chevy may have had character, but there was something to be said for built-in navigation systems. Hannah set the phone down beside her, then flipped on her turn signal and circled back toward Fitzgerald Farms, letting the flashing blue dot on her phone screen be her guide.

Before long, the GPS directed her down a gravel road enclosed by stout pine trees. Small stones pinged against the truck's metal body while dust rose in a chalky cloud around the windows. If it weren't for the mailboxes scattered along the shoulder, Hannah would've assumed no one ever came this way. Of course, her GPS couldn't tell the difference: roads were roads, and some were just creepier than others.

She glanced at the screen. When she looked up again, she saw a streak of white in the corner of her eye, too large to be an animal and too bright to go unnoticed. She shifted her foot to the brake, bringing the Chevy to a grinding halt.

Hannah put the truck in reverse. The sighting had been so brief, her mind couldn't even begin to fill in the gaps. An overgrown driveway poked out of the trees, with no mailbox nearby to alert anyone to its presence. Stopping the Chevy again, Hannah leaned toward the mud-specked passenger window, and her heart gave a little kick when she realized what she was looking at: a horse trailer, loosely covered by a blue tarp to conceal any distinguishing features. As the wind flicked back one of the unanchored corners, Hannah saw the black stripe along the side, and the logo, near the top, partly hidden by the crackling cobalt sheet. It was the same trailer she'd seen on the night of the shooting—the trailer that had taken Ray's horses.

She put the truck in park and got out, slipping her phone into her pocket as she closed the door. As she started down the path into the trees, a squat, white house came into view, hunkered down behind reddish-brown mounds of scrap metal and wiry tufts of grass. The property appeared to be abandoned: the shingles were peeling and littered with yellow pine needles, and a sheet of plywood had been nailed over one of the windows. Hannah picked her way through the curved shards of glass. Clearly, 'abandoned' wasn't the right word—if the broken beer bottles and trailer were anything to go by, someone had been here quite recently. But the home was definitely uninhabitable, so she didn't think twice about walking around the back of it and over to the trailer.

The front end had been propped on a couple of cinderblocks. Hannah approached the massive, metal shell and ran her hand along the side, her heart pounding under her collarbone. Reaching for the tarp, she ripped it back to expose the door at the trailer's rear, then, swallowing her trepidation, slid back the bolt and peered inside.

The trailer was empty, save for the musty odour of soggy hay and horse manure. Mixed in with her relief at finding no trapped horses was a needling sense of dread—where were they? Had they been sold, slaughtered, or set free? It was impossible to tell from the blue-tinted air and lingering musk.

Hannah retreated. Her gaze gravitated back to the house, with its dirty windows and crooked shutters. There might've been more clues inside, but then, unexpectedly, she thought of Bexley, her old roommate from boarding school, whose boyfriend had fallen through the floor of an abandoned house and broken his leg. *No one would ever think to look for me here*, Hannah thought. But no one would think to look for the horses here either.

She looked toward the barn. It was an unsightly thing, its wooden walls grey and warped, and its roof sagging in the middle. There were no windows that she could see, and the foundation appeared to be sinking into a quagmire of mud and manure, rising thickly around the rusted door. Encircling the crumbling structure was a fence—not a sturdy wooden fence like the ones that made up Ray's paddocks, but something more flimsy, rotted boards cobbled together to create a barrier. Not that anyone in their right mind would dream of entering the barn. But maybe Hannah wasn't in her right mind in this moment.

She scanned her surroundings again, then grasped the top board and climbed over the fence. When she landed on the opposite side, her shoes got sucked into the ground. She struggled toward the barn, placing her feet wherever the mud-and-manure soup seemed the thinnest. There must've been fifty horses here at one point, crammed cheek by jowl in this makeshift pen, unable to move or graze or even breathe. In many ways, it reminded her of the homes she used to visit when she worked for CPS—dark, dingy hovels where the air was heavy and the floors impossible to tread. *Haunted houses*, Hannah thought as she reached the barn door—places haunted not by death, but by life.

With a grunt of effort, Hannah slid back the door, grating and squealing on its overhead track. What awaited her on the other side was nothing but pure blackness and that heavy, caustic smell of ammonia and rot. She reached into her back pocket and pulled out her phone. As she turned on the flashlight, a hazy white circle beamed onto the floor. More dirt and manure. And hoofprints.

She stepped inside. The barn was tall, but narrow: the stalls occupied only one side of the aisle, with doors that dangled off their tracks. A faint squeaking noise attracted Hannah's attention. She looked down, startling when her phone's light fell on the pale grey shape of a mouse darting deftly around her foot. *What are they eating?* There were no grain bins as far as she could tell. No haybales tucked into a corner. No water anywhere at all.

From deep within the darkness, Hannah heard a snuffle. She panned her phone left, her heart jumping through her sweat-soaked shirt, and her light fell on the long, sleek, black head that poked out of the stall to greet her.

"Abby," Hannah whispered. Abby blinked, dazed by the harsh glow, her hooves squelching noisily in the muck of her stall. Her ears pricked forward as Hannah approached, reaching out to stroke the mare's silken nose. "It's okay. I'm here now."

She directed her light at the remaining stalls. One by one, the other horses emerged from the shadows, drawn by Hannah's familiar scent. They were all here, as far as she could tell. The light reflected off the green discs of their eyes, faces floating in the dark like ghosts.

Her mind reeled with potential solutions. She had a truck—she could hook it up to the trailer and take them home. She could call Ray or Marc. But the horses had to get out of this place *now*. If she rode Abby home, would the other horses follow her?

"It's okay," she said again, petting Abby's neck, "I'm going to get you out. I just need a plan…"

"What the hell are you doing here?"

A chill scurried up Hannah's spine. It was a male voice, rough, deep, and yet clear enough to carry through a crowded arena. She whirled around, and found Don, Wilbur's other trainer, standing in the doorway. His hair was sticking out from under his grimy beige ballcap and he smelled pungent, like stale cigarettes and alcohol.

"I asked you a question, girl," Don went on, his voice even. Hannah swallowed, but couldn't get the words out. Her eyes had finally adjusted to the darkness, so she could see the boots he wore were covered in mud as he came toward her.

At last, she replied, "I saw the trailer. These are Ray Fisher's horses."

His eyes skipped to the stalls, then back to her. "This is private property."

"And these horses are *stolen* property," Hannah shot back.

"Funny that you should be so concerned with stolen horses when you're marrying a horse thief."

She shook her head. "What are you *talking* about?"

Don pointed to Ray's gelding, two stalls down. "See that sorrel? I used to have one just like him—here." Don gestured to the ground. "Then someone came in one day and snatched him up. All for some fucking YouTube video."

Hannah's eyes widened in comprehension. "Red is *your* horse?"

"Yes. And I want him back."

"You abandoned him. He was skin and bones when he arrived at the ranch. I'm not going to let you starve these horses too."

As Hannah stepped to the side, Don's arm shot out in front of her, blocking her escape. She backed against the door as he leaned toward her. Her breathing was shallow and tight, and she kept her eyes on his face, trying to reconcile this disheveled version of Don with the more put-together one she'd encountered at Windreach six months ago.

Don cocked his head. "Does Ray know where you are?"

Hannah didn't answer.

Don slammed his hand against the door, his face contorting in anger over her silence. The sharp blow jolted Hannah from her terror. She suddenly became aware of her phone in her back pocket and pulled it out.

"I'm calling the cops," Hannah told him, pulling up the keypad. The second she looked down, Don lunged. He grabbed her wrists, making her drop the phone, and shoved her back against the door. One of the boards hit her lower back, sending a dart of pain through her hips. As Hannah struggled against the damp weight of Don's breath, she felt her heartbeat in every cell of her body—a million tiny explosions across her skin. No one knew she was here. As her phone hit the ground, she screamed as loud as she could, hoping one of the neighbours might be home to hear it.

Fear turned Hannah's stomach to acid. Don's hands were still locked around her arms. She imagined Ray coming here days from now and finding her phone, the battery dead and the screen cracked. But then she thought of something else, something Marcus had said during the branding. Hannah heard his voice at the back of her mind, not so much as a memory, but a command. *Fight back.*

Hannah raised her knee and drove it into Don's groin. A bark of pain and surprise burst from his lips. Stunned by the attack, his hands tore free and he staggered back, unpinning her from the stall door. Hannah left her phone on the floor and sprinted out into the pen. Once she'd climbed over the fence, she felt light as air again, racing across the backyard, past the house, and up the driveway to the truck. Without even doing up her seatbelt, Hannah put the truck in drive and hit the accelerator, speeding down the gravel road until all she could see was a plume of dust billowing out behind her.

Twenty-five

"You're sure you're okay?" Ray asked again, leaning forward a little as he said it.

Hannah avoided his strained gaze. The coffee cup on the table was still mostly full, its contents lukewarm at best. She'd been waiting until her fingers stopped shaking to take another sip.

"I'm fine," she answered, "I'm just a bit shaken up."

"Then you're not fine," Marcus cut in rather brusquely. Hannah saw his hands working in his pockets, like they always did before he decided to take action about something. A nervous tic. "He didn't hurt you, did he?"

"He grabbed my wrists, and he pushed me back against the door, but he didn't do what Doug did to Addy."

Marcus's upper lip stiffened, his eyes darting to Ray. "You know we have to tell Wilbur."

"I know."

"I remember the place Hannah's talking about—the barn where we found Red," Marcus went on. "I'll call Officer Moore and ask her to meet me there. We can take Russ's trailer—it's big enough for all the horses."

"Okay. What do you want me to do?" Ray asked.

"I want you to stay here. Hannah needs you."

"I said I'm fine, Marc."

"Don's already hurt both of you. Russ and I can take care of this." Marcus straightened, then headed for the door. His boots rang on the porch steps, followed shortly by the clanging of the driver's door and the sputter of the truck's engine. And then he was gone.

Ray faced Hannah again, but didn't speak. He'd been in the process of helping Marcus contain one of the fillies when he'd seen his Chevy, engulfed in a cloud of dust, peeling down the driveway. Moments later, Hannah had leapt out of the truck. When she'd hugged him, Ray had felt every nerve in her body vibrating under her skin and her heart thundering against his chest. He'd stood there holding her for a minute, letting her calm down. And then she'd told him everything.

Hannah drew a breath, pulling him out of his memories. "I lost my phone."

"Where?"

"At Don's place." She slid a lock of hair behind her ear, revealing the high arch of her cheekbone. "I dropped it when he grabbed me. I was so scared I didn't even think about picking it up—just ran as fast as I could back to the truck."

Ray rested a hand on her thigh. "You did the right thing."

"So, what happens now? I mean, Marc's going to go pick up the horses obviously… then what? We carry on as if nothing happened?" Her eyes drifted to his face, then roamed to his left shoulder. Ray had done away with the sling a couple of days ago, claiming it interfered with his need to feel useful. Beneath the bandages, he could feel the tightness of his sutures and the prickling of his skin as it struggled to adjust to its new shape.

Ray subconsciously rubbed the patch of gauze. *What now?* It was the kind of question that could only be answered with a plan—and he'd never been particularly good at charting a course.

"I guess… you go back to packing for your trip," he ventured, "and I'll wait and see what Marc says. I don't really know what to say. Don is one of Wilbur's employees… to think he could be behind this, especially when he and Laney are so close…"

Hannah offered him a sympathetic smile and laced her fingers with his.

"Maybe he doesn't know," she postulated, "you know Laney would never do anything to hurt you, and Wilbur's been so good to you."

Ray smiled, pulling them both off the couch as he stood. A sharp jab radiated down his left arm, but he set his jaw and looked away before the discomfort could migrate to his face. He didn't want Hannah to see him in pain: as far as she was concerned, he was on the mend, what with abandoning his sling and assisting Marcus around the barn. But recovery was rarely linear. Even when he didn't notice the pain at all, his body still remembered the damage the bullet had caused when it ripped into him. He hadn't told Hannah about the nightmares, or how he'd slip away to the bathroom because the blood from a medium rare steak was causing his throat to close up until he couldn't breathe. As they climbed the stairs, Ray tightened his grip on her hand in hopes it would prevent him from getting swept away by thoughts of Don and what he had or hadn't done.

Hannah touched his arm. "Are you okay?"

"What? I'm fine."

"You winced."

Ray relaxed his fingers. They were in his room, standing between the door and his bed, where Hannah's clothes had been sorted into piles. The mattress groaned as he sat down, and pulled her back against his chest so that she was loosely straddling his knee. It was easier to talk to her this way. Easier to be honest, when he couldn't see the pain his words were causing.

"I don't want you to leave," he whispered, spooning his chin in her shoulder.

Hannah cinched his arms around her waist. "I don't want to leave either, but I have to. I'll be back in a few weeks—and then I won't have to leave ever again."

"But you still might," he went on, "you might want to see your family."

"They'll be your family, too." He nodded awkwardly. She inhaled, closing what little space remained between them. "Ray, I want to go to Toronto."

"Toronto?"

Hannah turned her upper body toward him. Highlighting his bewildered gaze was a hint of sunburn, which added a distinct rosiness to his copper complexion. His arms loosened momentarily, then reconnected to prevent her from sliding off his lap.

"I want to see her," Hannah said softly. "Sam and Terry said we could. It was a semi-open adoption and… I want to see our daughter. And I want you to come with me, as my husband."

At first, Ray didn't speak. He knew Hannah still kept in touch with Samantha and Terry Varchuk, the hip, young couple who'd adopted their daughter five years ago, and indulged the occasional update about Denver/Kyleigh's development. Maybe Hannah found that comforting, but he didn't. Like his father, Ray treated goodbye as a permanent thing—case closed, end of story. Hannah was the only exception to this rule, and for now, that was how he wanted to keep it.

He swallowed, annoyed by the way his throat ached like a pulled muscle. "I guess."

"You don't want to see your own daughter?"

"She's not my daughter. She's Sam and Terry's responsibility. We said we didn't want to be parents."

"But she's your flesh and blood. And if I'm going to be a part of you, and she's a part of me, then she's a part of you too." Hannah rose to face him, and Ray faltered. There was no hiding the pain when she was standing less than a foot away from him, holding his face in her hands. He felt the emotions bubbling under his skin, and his heat pushing forward into her fingers. Tears rushed to fill his eyes, but he couldn't look away in time.

"Talk to me," Hannah prompted.

"I can't. Nothing makes sense."

A smile quirked on her lips. "That's okay. It doesn't make sense to me either." She shook her head. "Nothing makes sense, not adulthood or the shooting or why weddings cost so much. I thought growing up would mean I suddenly understood everything, but I feel more like a kid than I ever did when I was little."

"Do you think everyone feels that way—lost?"

"Probably."

Ray slipped his left hand behind Hannah's head and drew her to him, pain be damned. She was right: nothing made sense, and life had a way of hurting more than it should. He leaned back on the bed, his body supported in various places by the bundles of clothing, and let Hannah's weight cover him at the hips.

"Are you sure you should be doing this, in your condition?" she asked.

"No, but I'm not sure about anything at this point." Balancing himself on his right elbow, Ray sat up, kissing her once, then twice. He then rested his forehead against her collarbone, giving in to the feeling of vulnerability at last. "Okay."

"Okay?"

"I'll come to Toronto with you."

Reaching her hand under his shirt, Hannah lifted the thin fabric away from his stomach and over his head. He was strong and soft, scarred and sunburned. She tossed the shirt into one of the piles, then leaned down and kissed his bandaged shoulder first.

*

Marcus wasn't sure why he hadn't thought to look here first: the house was set back from the road, conveniently concealed by a thick tangle of trees and waist-high grass. Russ had backed his trailer in; it sat by the barn with its ramp lowered, ready to load the horses as soon as Officer Moore cleared the area. Her squad car occupied the narrow strip of gravel next to the house, directly on the path Hannah had taken to reach the barn.

Marcus picked his way through the detritus of rusty cars, wooden pallets, and other junk, not looking for anything so much as watching where his feet fell. He doubted anyone actually lived here, but if Don was desperate enough, he might've been squatting in the house, or using the property as a place to conduct shady business transactions—like selling stolen horses. Marcus rounded the back corner of the house just as Officer Moore completed her walkthrough of the hovel.

"Find anything?" Marcus asked her.

"Nothing incriminating," she reported, hooking her thumbs through her belt loops. She nodded at the barn, where the horses were still waiting to be extracted from their filthy prison. "Did you get a chance to look them over?"

Leading her in that direction, Marcus said, "From what I could tell, Abby's got a pretty nasty cut on her leg—it looks fresh, too. And they're all pretty dehydrated. I gave our vet a call, and he agreed to come out and examine them once they're back on our property." He faced the officer and frowned. "So, you didn't find anything in the house?"

"Nope. Nothing."

"But he had a gun. He shot Ray."

"We don't know for certain that the gun was Don's, or that he's the one who shot Ray," Officer Moore explained. "He might've been the accomplice. Not that that's any better." She paused, holding Marcus's gaze. "Any idea who Don might've been working with?"

Marcus hesitated to say the first name that came to mind, though the possibilities had been eating at him all day. A man of Wilbur's caliber wouldn't have been stupid enough to get caught up in some horse-rustling scheme, but if his reputation was on the line, he might've hired someone else to do his dirty work.

"Could've been anyone, really," Marcus said. Out of the corner of his eye, he spotted a grey pickup truck creeping down the hill toward them. "For now, I just want to get the horses home."

She nodded, then turned her attention to their visitor.

"I'm sorry, sir, but this area is off-limits to visitors right now," Officer Moore said as Victor got out of the truck.

Marcus stepped forward. "It's okay. That's my brother. I called him because he's always been good with the horses, and I thought he might be able to help."

"All right. I'll be in my car if you need me." Officer Moore started back up the knoll toward her vehicle, where the crackle of the police scanner trumped the dull chatter of insects buzzing around it.

Victor approached his twin. On the dashboard of Victor's truck, Marcus saw the fluorescent orange shape of his reflective vest, the kind construction workers wore to make themselves more visible on dark, country roads. Unsurprisingly, Victor loved the job, which got him outside and away from people. But when Marcus had called to say they'd found the horses, Victor had driven straight from the job site without even changing out of his steel-toe boots.

Marcus smiled a little, relieved to see a familiar face. "I didn't think you'd be here so quickly."

"I wasn't that far away."

They started toward the paddock, where Russ was in the process of cutting the lock off the chain that was threaded through the gate.

"Abby's got a cut on her leg. She got her tetanus shot a few months ago, but I'll ask Dr. Bardwell to give her another dose when he comes to check all the horses tomorrow," Marcus explained. "The ground is almost pure manure. Don must've had a lot of horses here at one point, like he was trying to run some backwoods stockyard or something."

"Who?" Victor asked.

"Don Mallen. One of Wilbur's employees."

They turned their attention to Russ. The bolt cutters he normally kept in his truck had proven inadequate for the size of the lock, and he'd switched to an angle grinder soon after. Either Hannah had not noticed the lock in the first place, or Don had affixed it to the gate after she'd fled, fearing another imminent loss of livestock.

The grinder whirred to a stop, allowing Russ to remove the severed padlock. He unwound the chain from around the post, then cast it aside, where it landed in the grass at Victor's feet.

"You want me to try and move the trailer closer?" Russ asked, returning the grinder to the toolbox he'd brought.

"That's okay. The ground's too soft here—you might end up getting stuck. Victor and I are going to lead them out one at a time." Russ nodded, then, picking up the box, carried it back to his truck. As Marcus led the way to the barn, he said to Victor, "I have a lot of thoughts about this situation. I don't know much about this Don guy, except that he works for Wilbur. And if Red really was his horse, and he found out that Laney had rescued him, why come after Ray?"

"Do you think Wilbur's behind it?" Victor asked, stepping carefully around a large, brown puddle.

"I don't know. I mean, he could be, if he thought any of this could get back to him." They'd managed to reach the barn, and Marcus could hear the horses shuffling inside, plus the groaning of the timbers as the wind pushed against the wooden walls. He gazed down at his boots and muttered, "Only one way to find out."

They went from stall to stall, inspecting each of the horses more closely for signs of trauma. As Marcus turned away from Abby's stall, the light from the doorway fell across the floor and caught the corner of a shiny, black rectangle. He bent down and picked it up.

"Whose phone is that?" Victor asked.

"I'm guessing it's Hannah's. She must've dropped it when she ran." Marcus tucked it into his back pocket and reached for the lead rope, fashioning it into a loop. This he guided over Abby's head before leading her out of the stall. In the light of day, he could see more clearly the injury she'd sustained on her right foreleg: the gash was about four inches long, cutting diagonally across her knee, with raised edges surrounding a glowing pink fissure. Abby hobbled after him, encouraged by the comforting tone of his voice.

The men fell into a simple rhythm, with Russ manning the gate, Marcus completing a cursory check of each horse's vitals, and Victor transporting them to the trailer. It was late afternoon, and as the sun melted behind the trees, a general weariness, brought on by emotional distress and physical exertion, was beginning to settle into everyone's bones. As Marcus handed the sixth and final horse off to Victor, he thought he might've had some inkling of Wilbur's motives for getting involved—if he was, in fact, an accomplice. Only the police could really prove anything, but that didn't mean Marcus couldn't conduct an investigation of his own, with Victor's help and without Officer Moore's knowledge.

Russ closed the trailer door and bolted it. Turning to Marcus, he said, "I'll take them straight to your place and unload them in that little paddock out front. I'll make sure they have water too."

"Good man. Thanks, bud." Marcus saw him off as Russ climbed behind the wheel and started the engine. The truck's headlights blazed a wide, yellow path through the trees as it started forward, hauling the trailer behind it.

"What are you thinking?" Victor asked, glimpsing Marcus's face. Not one to sit around and wait for help, Marcus always insisted on defending those who needed it, whether it meant sticking up for Adrianna in high school or confronting Wilbur over Don's crimes.

Marcus blinked a couple of times. "I'm thinking that I need to go to Windreach and talk to Wilbur, and if I go alone, I might just beat him to death." He faced his twin. "You have to come with me—for my protection."

"Okay. But if things start to go sideways, we're both leaving."

Marcus nodded, his eyes dark. As the temptation to inflict harm on Wilbur passed, he said, "I got a ride here with Russ, so I'm going to need you to take me home."

"Now?"

"Yes. And with any luck, I won't be back here again."

Twenty-six

Show season was a busy time of year for any equine establishment, but especially a place like Windreach. As Marcus steered into the driveway, he saw the pristine white trailers parked by the barn and a small crowd of people gathered around one of the outdoor sand rings. A handful of Wilbur's employees looked up from their work as Marcus parked his truck in the gravel lot next to the barn and killed the engine.

"So, what's the plan?" Victor asked, turning toward the driver's seat.

Marcus removed his sunglasses and set them on the dashboard. He'd considered stopping at the house, but a man like Wilbur would never pass up an opportunity to glad-hand with his guests. No, he'd probably be somewhere nearby, keeping an eye out for anyone who didn't belong in his shiny little bubble.

After a moment, Marcus stated, "We find Wilbur, ask him if he knows what Don's been up to."

"He'll say no. They always do."

"Fine. Then we go to Plan B." Marcus nodded to himself, a look of grim certainty stirring in his gaze.

"Whatever Plan B is, it better not involve me bailing you out of jail," Victor intoned.

"It won't. Just trust me, okay?" With that, Marcus reached for the door and got out.

There were people everywhere, some dressed in leather chaps and cowboy hats, and others wearing jeans and light blue polo shirts. The polo-shirt-wearers moved like fireflies around the barn, appearing in brief flashes out of the corner of Marcus's eye as he and Victor made their way down the aisle. One of them, a girl with a blonde ponytail, was talking to a man in a white Stetson and leather boots. Marcus walked directly toward them, fighting back the urge to let fly every curse word and insult he could think of.

"You Wilbur McCullough?" was all he managed to get past his clenched teeth.

"Who's asking?" Wilbur replied. He dismissed the girl with a nod and turned to give his visitors his full attention.

"I'm Marcus. This is Victor. I think you know our brother, Ray."

Wilbur's gaze waffled between them, as if trying to decide which sibling posed the greater threat. It eventually settled on Marcus, toying with the insides of his pockets.

"I know Ray," Wilbur said evenly. "What's this about?"

"I think you know."

"I don't. As you can see, I'm quite busy running this place." Spreading his arms, Wilbur indicated the activity simmering around them, dozens of bodies in endless motion.

"Yes, I can see that," Marcus returned. "What I don't see is Don. Where is he?"

"I don't need to tell you anything."

"The way I see it, you have two choices. One, you tell me what I want to know about Don, or two, I beat your head in right now and we call it even."

"Marc," Victor warned.

"Fine," Wilbur relented, "I'll tell you about Don. But not here. Let's go up to the house."

The house was a modest bungalow, with a porch that wrapped around its north and east sides. Flower planters snuggled under the windows, while a stone walkway granted access to a short flight of stairs constructed from the same material. The front entrance, flanked on both sides by outdoor vases bursting with sprays of feather reed, had two layers: a framed-in screen to keep the bugs out, and a solid, blue door with a circular window near the top that could be locked from the inside. Marcus exchanged a look with Victor, then followed Wilbur into the house.

Plastered on the living room walls were dozens of photographs of Wilbur's past and current champions, posing in dusty arenas all over the country. An assortment of trophies populated a glass case in the corner of the living room, with prestigious titles like *NRHA All-around Champion* carved into their wooden bases. The kitchen, located on the left, appeared almost barren compared to the living room, but Marcus didn't get a chance to scope out its décor before Wilbur offered him a seat on one of the sofas.

"So, you want to know about Don," Wilbur said dryly, lowering himself into the armchair across from Marcus. "I can't imagine why."

"Really? You can't imagine?"

Wilbur cocked his head. "Are you making fun of me, son? I don't like it when people mock me."

"I'm not making fun of you. I just find it hard to believe that you're ignorant to what Don's been up to." Marcus pretended to crack his knuckles as Wilbur stared at him, his eyes narrow and watery. "You know, it's interesting that you haven't asked about Ray, considering he's been working with your best horse."

"How is Ray?"

"He's pretty banged up," Marcus said, watching Wilbur's face for any hint of culpability. "Took a gunshot to the shoulder a couple of weeks ago. Weird, right?"

"I heard. Laney said there was no major damage."

No major damage. What an odd way of phrasing it, Marcus thought. Almost like Wilbur was disappointed.

But he was getting ahead of himself here.

"Yeah, he's… very lucky." Marcus glanced at the window, through which he could scarcely make out the sand ring beyond the wooden blinds. "Is Don around?"

"He has the day off."

"What does he normally do, when he's not here?"

"I wouldn't know. I can't even guess why *you* would want to know."

"Hannah was out running some errands the other day, and on her way home, she saw his trailer parked on an abandoned lot. She could've sworn it was the same trailer that came to our ranch the night Ray was shot. Anyway, she decided to investigate, and that was when she found our horses. Don showed up a few minutes later."

"What would Don be doing with your horses?" Wilbur asked, his bushy brows nearly touching as his forehead puckered suspiciously.

"That's what we were wondering. And that's why we came to you." Marcus leaned forward, planting his elbows on his knees. "Why was one of *your* employees on our property at two o'clock in the morning with a *gun*?"

"That's a hell of an accusation you're making," Wilbur said hotly, "for all you know, some other crook was on your property, and Don was merely keeping your horses safe until you could pick them up."

"Well, then, Don better have a damn good alibi, 'cause I'm not buying that for a second." Marcus stood up, too incensed to remain seated. "Here's another fun fact about that property: it's the same one where Laney rescued that gelding. Red. That's the name we gave him. Anyway, a couple of hikers said they found him locked in the barn. But I suppose it's possible that Don was 'keeping him safe' until his owners could be contacted."

"Don would never abuse a horse."

"Are you sure? Because Red didn't look particularly well when I picked him up. In fact, he looked like he'd been neglected for weeks." Marcus went on, "I didn't think much about Laney wanting to rescue Red, but then I thought… isn't it just a little coincidental that you happened to pay her an overdue visit on the exact same day that Red arrived at our ranch? Windreach and Fitzgerald Farms are practically neighbours, yet you hadn't talked to Laney in years."

"Whatever happened between Laney and myself is our business. You know as well as I do that she's not in the proper condition to entertain people these days. Frankly, I'm appalled that you'd even hold this over my head."

"You know what? You're absolutely right. It's not my place to comment on your affairs." Marcus cleared his throat and made a face like he'd swallowed something unpleasant. "I'm actually feeling a little parched. Could I please have a glass of water?"

Wilbur lifted his head from his hand and, sighing, rose from the armchair. As he made his way into the kitchen, Marcus took a seat next to Victor, where they could converse in whispers.

"What are you doing?" Victor asked.

Marcus watched as Wilbur took down a glass from the cupboard and set it on the counter next to the sink. From the fridge, he retrieved a pitcher of water.

"He's pouring with his left hand," Marcus murmured.

"And?"

Marcus's eyes switched to Victor's face. "Whoever shot Ray was left-handed." A look of understanding passed between them and quickly vanished as Wilbur reappeared, extending the glass as if he found the contents repulsive.

"Thank you," Marcus said, reaching out to accept it. He brought the glass to his lips and took several deep drinks, his throat moving visibly with each swallow. When the glass was nearly empty, he set it on the coffee table and continued with his line of thought, reinforced by the observations he'd made seconds before.

"As I was saying—" Marcus began, only to be interrupted by the arrival of a slender woman with platinum blonde hair and a familiar, sashaying walk. If he hadn't looked up to see the visitor's face, he would've sworn it was Laney. Or her twin, if she had one.

"Oh, hello," the lady twittered, as surprised to see her guests as they were to see her. "Wilbur, I didn't know we were expecting company."

Wilbur gestured to the sofa. "Neither did I. Anita, meet Marcus and Victor—Ray's brothers."

"Oh," Anita said, more slowly this time. Even though she was smiling, her voice was cold, especially when directed at her husband. "You should've offered them refreshments."

"I just did." Wilbur indicated the water glass. "I trust your thirst has been quenched?" he asked, meeting Marcus's steely blue gaze.

Marcus made a show of bowing graciously toward his host, a smile stretched across his face. "It has, thank you."

"Honey, why don't you go see how they're doing down at the barn? I'll come join you in a few minutes." Wilbur tore his attention from Anita and rested it, almost uncomfortably, on the two figures across from him. As Anita departed without comment, Marcus pulled himself upright again, letting his smile fade.

"You were saying something about minding your own business," Wilbur prompted.

"I'd love to, but when someone hurts a member of my family, I can't help but get involved." Marcus scratched his cheek. "I—*we*—went to Don's place a few days ago. I don't know if you've seen it, but that barn looks like it's about to collapse at any second. And there isn't nearly enough acreage for the kind of business he's conducting."

"Oh, really? And what business would that be?"

"Some kind of unlicensed stockyard, from the looks of it. We're thinking he planned to sell the horses he stole. And judging by how sick Red was when he came to us, I'm guessing that deal fell through. It's not like Don could return him to his owners, so Red wasted away in that barn for weeks. That is, until Laney caught wind of what was going on.

"Everyone in this town knows Laney—I'll bet Don does, too. And when he saw her breaking Red out of that barn, he came to you. He couldn't report Red missing, or the police would know he'd been stolen."

"Stolen," Wilbur scoffed. "The horse wasn't stolen—Don bought him at an auction. He was malnourished when Don got there, so don't you dare try to pin the blame on him."

Marcus furrowed his brows. "And what did Don do to try and nurse Red back to health?"

"Do you have any idea how long it takes to put weight back on an underfed horse? You can't just shove grain down its throat and pray for a miracle."

"I'm aware of that, but it doesn't answer my question: what did Don *do*? Did he call a vet? Report the stockyard?"

"I don't know!" Wilbur bellowed.

The lines in Marcus's forehead ironed out. "I think you do. I think you know a lot more than you're letting on."

"Son, you're about to cross a very dangerous line with me," Wilbur warned. His cheeks burned red, though he didn't raise his voice or even rise from his armchair. But Marcus had been a rancher long enough to know that it was the quiet animals that posed the greatest threat: the rattlesnake coiled in the grass, or the mountain lion perfectly camouflaged against the rocks, both with their yellow eyes stalking his every move.

"I know that," Marcus said without effect, "that's why I suspected your involvement immediately. And forgive me for jumping to conclusions here, but the only reason you didn't report Don's venture is because he promised you a cut of the profit. Didn't he?" Wilbur glared at him. "Now the question is, on the night of the shooting, were you trying to hurt Ray… or Laney? I'm guessing you didn't like her meddling in your business. And to think you two were so close when you were younger. She told me that the two of you almost went into business together, but she backed out when you wouldn't tell her where you got the startup capital—"

Wilbur shot to his feet, causing the armchair to spring backwards. Marcus was on his feet too, along with Victor, who couldn't decide between dragging his brother out of here now, or letting Marcus finish what he started.

"Listen to me," Wilbur growled, inches from Marcus's face, "if you think for one god damn second that I'm afraid of someone like you—"

"You should be. *I* have nothing to lose. Face it: you helped Don cover up the mess with Red because you knew that if this got out, your career would be over. You know what that makes you? An accomplice."

"What's going on?" The question came from Anita, who'd entered the house through a back door after several minutes passed without any appearances from Wilbur. Her eyes were wide as they lingered on her husband, whose face was a deadly shade of persimmon down to his neck.

"I want you out of my house, before I call the cops," Wilbur said, ignoring his wife.

"I've already been in contact with them. In fact, when the officers asked me who I thought might've wanted to hurt Ray, you were the first person I thought of."

"Wilbur, what's going on?" Anita asked again. She was tiny like Laney; with her shoulders hunched, she looked as fragile as a sparrow, hovering at the edge of the room where she could take flight on a moment's notice. "What happened to Ray?"

"Anita, please go wait for me at the barn," Wilbur said in a measured tone, not quite looking in her direction. His eyes swam back to Marcus, who merely raised his brows. "Get out."

Marcus stepped back, and the glass of water quivered as his knee knocked against the coffee table. He glanced down at it, then back up at Wilbur, saying, "You might want to hire a good lawyer."

"Out!"

Marcus smirked. With Victor practically dragging him out the door, he let his shoulders relax and his fists unfurl. They walked through the screen and down the steps, beating a hasty retreat back to the truck. Between them, the silence was both impenetrably thick and sizzling with the rawest of emotions. They'd nearly reached their vehicle when Victor decided to speak up.

"How'd you figure it out?" he asked.

Marcus opened the driver's door, but didn't get in. His gaze roamed over the faces in the crowd, wondering what would become of Windreach if Wilbur was found guilty.

"Just asked the right questions, I guess. I hope I'm wrong and Wilbur had nothing to do with any of this, but I can't ignore my instincts."

"Well, your instincts are better than mine. Now let's go home. I'm sure Ray will want to hear all of this."

Twenty-seven

Hannah's room was unrecognizable. In January, Jeanette had finally decided to get serious about her health and purchased a treadmill. But a few weeks later, she became disillusioned with her fitness ambitions, and the monstrous machine went into storage—in this case, the corner of Hannah's bedroom. At first, she'd balked at the attack on her personal space. Then she'd seen it as an opportunity.

Music blasted through Hannah's earbuds. She'd been running for approximately thirty minutes, losing herself in the mindless momentum until her muscles grew heavy and her lungs burned. She stared at the garment bag on the back of her door, inside which was her wedding gown. For the past few weeks, she'd made a point of sticking to an exercise routine and watched the extra pounds she'd gained over the winter melt away. The positive effect on her mental health was just icing on the cake.

A knock sounded at the door, and Andrew popped his head inside.

"How's the training going?" he asked.

Hannah dialed back the treadmill's speed, bringing some relief to her legs.

"I'm not training for anything. I'm trying to avoid looking like a human marshmallow on my wedding day," she explained, indicating the garment bag.

"You won't. You're beautiful exactly the way you are."

She smiled and reached for her bottle of water. "That's Ray's line, dad, not yours."

"What? I can't give my daughter a compliment anymore?" Andrew patted the treadmill. "It's great to see you're getting some use out of this baby. Your mom had high hopes for it, but not as high as her career, evidently."

"Her career has always been important to her. Which is a good thing, I guess, but sometimes I worry that she's using work as a distraction from internal conflict, specifically a lack of control over other areas of her life."

Andrew wagged a finger at her biting insight. "I'm glad all that money you spent on a psychology degree didn't go to waste."

"Except for the part where I lost my job."

His expression softened. Taking a seat on the bed, he gestured for Hannah to join him and laced his fingers together in his lap. Ever since she was little, whenever there was a life lesson in need of teaching, Andrew would sit with her on the bed and they'd talk about what she'd done wrong, without judgment or consternation. In that moment, it occurred to him that this might be one of the last opportunities to impart his wisdom in such a fashion.

"Jobs are like boys—they come and go," Andrew began. Hannah raised her brows, but didn't interrupt. "Did you know I got fired from my very first job out of university?"

"No. What happened?"

"I was new to the job and I thought I had a pretty solid idea of how the market behaved. I advised a client to take a greater risk than they were comfortable with, and they lost everything. Even my boss tried to warn me that this wasn't a sensible move, and I ignored him."

"Why?"

"Well, I guess a big part of it was that I thought I knew everything—being young makes you arrogant sometimes." He licked his lips. "Anyway, all that to say that losing a job isn't the end of the world. The trick is to take what you learned from the first job and use it to do better in the next one."

"I guess I did learn a few things," Hannah reflected. She stared at the brushed nickel water bottle. "And if I knew what I wanted to do with my life, I could make a plan. But so far all I know is that weddings are expensive, guns are dangerous, and love doesn't fix everything."

213

Andrew wrapped an arm around her shoulders and kissed the top of her head. "You're wiser than most twenty-five year olds if you've already learned all that." He stood up and made his way to the door. "We're going to miss having you around. The house just won't be the same without you trying to run a hole in the floor."

Hannah laughed. "Is that supposed to be a compliment?"

"Just an observation." Andrew reached for the door and gently sealed it behind him.

Hannah took a deep breath and let it out slowly. She would miss living here too, but not enough to change her mind about marrying Ray. Standing up, she plucked at the front of her yellow tank top and crossed the hall to her parents' bedroom, where Jeanette was putting away laundry.

"Hey, mom."

Jeanette looked up, startled, a stack of dress pants resting on her open palms.

"I heard the treadmill," she said, turning toward the dresser. "How was your workout?"

"Good. I'm down five pounds." Hannah glanced at the chaise lounge in the corner of the room, currently home to a half-packed suitcase. "Isn't it a bit early to start packing?"

"It is, but I'd rather get it over with," Jeanette replied.

"Fair enough."

"How's the immigration research coming?"

"Slowly. I'm actually a bit worried about how long the process will take, although if Ray sponsors me it'll shorten the timeline considerably. But, of course, we have to be legally married in order for him to *be* my sponsor…" Hannah perched on the corner of the lounge, her eyes clouding over in a storm of unuttered thoughts. "Sometimes I wish this was easier. You shouldn't have to jump through so many hoops to prove you love someone."

"Immigration law is complicated. And not everyone is motivated by love and happiness."

"I know."

Jeanette sorted through the last of the clothes and shut the drawer, returning the laundry hamper to its usual spot in the walk-in closet.

"Mom?"

"What?"

"Is everything okay with you?"

Jeanette crossed her arms. Going off of body language alone, Hannah thought she already knew the answer. "Why wouldn't I be?" Jeanette replied.

"You've been working a lot lately, and I just wanted to check in. Plus, with the wedding coming up, and you and dad being required to travel, I know you probably have a lot on your mind."

Her mom relaxed her shoulders.

"Oh. I see." Jeanette brushed some hair out of her eyes with the back of her hand. Hannah remained silent, and eventually, Jeanette volunteered some more information. "That's very perceptive of you. I'm fine, though."

"Are you sure? Because after I marry Ray, things are going to be a lot different."

The lines in Jeanette's forehead smoothed away. She lowered her gaze. "I know."

Hannah rose and moved to sit on the bed, just as her dad had done a few minutes ago.

"I know you haven't always liked him," Hannah began, "that you think he's bad for me. But when I look at Ray, I don't see a pile of immigration papers or some cowboy... I see the best thing to come out of the worst time of my life."

Jeanette's body sagged, and a smile rose on her lips. "I never said he was bad, or bad for you. I know what you're capable of, and I don't want you to settle for less than you deserve."

"But I won't. Ray and I lift each other up. He's starting his own business now, and I'm… well, I don't know what I'm doing, but I know I can figure it out." Hannah blinked several times before turning away. "Anyway, I should go take a shower."

At the door, Jeanette called her back.

"You should call Joanna. I know you've missed her, and it might be nice to have a friend." Jeanette faltered, confused by Hannah's silence. "That was all I wanted to say."

Hannah nodded and forced a smile. "Maybe I will."

Twenty-eight

A warm wind rushed past Ray's ears as he cantered along the ridge overlooking the north field. Below him, the spring calves, now three months old, had gained enough weight to resemble the adult cows in shape, if not size. Ray pulled his horse up and surveyed the scene for signs of trouble, but spotted nothing out of the ordinary. That was a good thing, and if Hannah were here, she'd tell him to focus on the positive. Easier said than done, especially since this was where the shooting had happened. Marcus had told him everything—about Wilbur and Laney's past, and how Wilbur had used Ray to get back at her for something that had happened years before Ray was even born. Then Marcus had called Wilbur a coward and told Ray it was time to bring in the horses, just like he always did when he knew he was right about something and the conversation was over.

Turning away from his memories, Ray rode at a brisk trot up the hill, where Marcus and Abby were waiting.

"How do they look?" Marcus asked.

Ray squinted at the sea of black bodies in the distance. "They look good. Healthy, at least." He motioned to the raven mare. "How's Abby?"

"She's okay. I was worried that cut might've gotten infected, but I think we got lucky." Marcus hinged forward to pat her neck before turning to Ray with a prying expression. "How's your shoulder?"

"Fine."

"You sure? I thought I saw you rubbing your arm a few minutes ago."

"That has to be the most unscientific observation anyone's ever made," Ray argued, "maybe I was cold, okay?"

"Maybe. Or maybe you should have listened to me when I told you to talk to your doctor about any weird pains." Marcus tried to meet Ray's gaze, but he was watching the herd spread out in search of grass. "I'm just looking out for you."

"I know." Ray leaned back slightly and dug his phone out of his pocket, frowning when he read the name on the screen. "It's Mickey." His heart was racing as he lifted the phone to his ear. "Hello?"

"Hi, Ray. It's Mickey Hammond."

"How are you?"

"I'm good. The more important question is, how are *you*?"

"I'm fine," Ray replied, darting a glance at Marcus.

"Great. Listen, I'm going to be in town for a few days next week, and I was wondering if it would be possible for me to stop by your place. Just to talk."

"Sure. Do you have our address?" Out of the corner of his eye, Ray saw Marcus stiffen. Marcus had never liked Mickey, even after Ray started working with him, and he was even less fond of him now, to the point of openly scowling at their conversation. Ray made a point to ignore him, just like he ignored the grating ache in his left arm.

"I do. I might not be able to get there until the afternoon, though."

"Okay. We'll be here." As Ray hung up the call, he asked his brother, "What's your problem?"

"I don't want him coming here. I don't care if you talk to him, but no friend of Wilbur's is welcome on our property."

"So, what do you want me to do? Call Mickey back and say, 'Hey, change of plans—my brother has trust issues'?"

"No. I want you to tell him you'll meet him at a neutral place. I just don't think it's a good idea right now to talk about what happened, especially with someone who knows so many people."

As much as Ray hated taking Marcus's advice, this made sense to him. Truthfully, Ray wasn't in a mood to talk about the shooting either. Hannah had suggested journaling as a way to relieve stress, but committing his thoughts to paper seemed like a good way to ensure the memories of that night always remained fresh in his mind, rather than fading away over time. Then there was the issue of his arm pain, which, though not severe enough to limit his productivity, served as a constant reminder that his life was still under threat. But maybe meeting Mickey would be good for him: at the very least, it would show him who his friends were, and who he should never do business with again.

"You're right," Ray said. "I'll call him back when we finish here."

*

Ray wasn't sure what to expect when he walked into the diner where Mickey had agreed to meet him. Old-fashioned vinyl booths lined the restaurant's perimeter, and the walls were covered in newspaper clippings trapped in skinny, black frames. At a table in the corner, Mickey was hunched over his phone, his normally sharp features softened by the light streaming through the window on his left. Ray took a deep breath and made his way across the diner.

"Mickey?"

The Horse God looked up and grinned.

"You made it. Have a seat." As Ray slid into the empty space across from him, Mickey set his phone aside, his mouth straightening as he looked his former co-host over. "So. How are you?"

"I'm okay."

Mickey nodded. Ray didn't look any different on the outside, but the changes to his personality, conveyed through the micro expressions on his face, were clear as day.

"I heard what happened," Mickey hedged, lowering his voice, "I guess that's mainly why I'm here."

"I assumed as much." Ray relaxed into the booth, pressing his back against the padded seat. His gaze flickered to the window and spotted Mickey's truck sandwiched between two others, not far from where Ray had parked his own.

"Yeah. You think you know someone, until something like this happens. I'm referring to Wilbur, by the way, not you."

Soon, a waitress approached their booth and removed a notepad and pen from her apron. "Can I start you off with something to drink?" she offered, looking at Ray first.

"Coffee, please," he replied.

"The same. Oh, and a slice of blueberry pie, if you have any." Mickey waited until she'd vanished through the kitchen's doors before turning his focus back to Ray. "This place is famous for their pie. You should try some."

"I'm not hungry."

"Wedding jitters?"

"I'm surprised you remembered."

"Well, I am rather good at that," the Horse God boasted, slinging his right arm along the back of the seat, "among other things."

"It's not just the wedding. It's… everything. I'm not really supposed to be discussing the shooting while the investigation is ongoing, but this whole thing with Wilbur made me realize that just because you know someone, doesn't mean you know what they're going to do. I guess I thought I could trust him because he knows Laney."

"How's she handling all this?"

"Not well. It's even worse because her health is already poor."

"I'm sorry. Is there anything I can do?"

"I don't think so." Ray's gloomy expression sought purchase on something in the distance. As he sank deeper into his thoughts, he raised his right hand and absently kneaded his left shoulder until the stiffness abated.

The same waitress from before emerged from the kitchen bearing two white mugs and a pot of coffee. She placed a mug in front of each customer and filled them both with steaming black liquid before saying to Mickey, "I'll be right back with your pie."

"Thank you." Mickey watched as Ray emptied a sugar packet into his coffee, then asked, "Is your shoulder bothering you?"

220

"What? Oh, yeah. It's fine. Just tingling a bit."

"Tingling, eh? Sounds like nerve damage."

Ray shook his head emphatically. "No, my doctor said there's no long-term damage."

"Doctors sometimes get it wrong. If you've got any pain, you should take care of it now—before the wedding, I mean."

As Mickey said this, a wedge of pie appeared in front of him, ribbons of steam unfurling from its golden crust. He picked up the fork, pierced the tip of the flaky dessert, and lifted the all-important first bite to his mouth. "Mm. Good as always."

"Have you talked to Wilbur recently?" Ray asked.

Mickey shook his head down at his plate and carved off another mouthful. "No, and I don't intend to. After what he did for that guy— Dave or Darrel or—"

"Don."

"Yeah, that's it. Point is, I won't be recommending Windreach to anyone going forward, assuming the place stays open much longer."

Ray deflated. "You don't have to do that."

"What?"

"You don't have to burn a bridge for my sake. I mean, this whole situation is kind of complicated—and this is really between me and Don, not you and Wilbur."

"Doesn't matter. I said I liked you, and I meant it. Wilbur should've known better than to get involved in shady business. Trust me, a reputation is a very fragile thing..." Mickey's voice trailed off, and he plunged back into his sweet diversion.

Ray didn't dispute this—how could he? His own horse training career had barely begun, and his reputation was already partially ruined by a simple misunderstanding. Hannah had said that Don had called him a horse thief, all because he'd stepped in to help Red. But perhaps the consequences would've been greater if he hadn't.

Scraping the lingering crumbs off his plate with his fork, Mickey washed his last bite down with a sip of coffee. His phone had been going off almost continuously since Ray had sat down, with text messages and social media notifications filling the screen. Curiosity compelled Ray to glance over at the device, but Mickey merely slipped it into his pocket with the habitual urgency of someone who was always on the move.

"Anyway, I've got to go pick up a few horses. Foals, actually. Ever heard of Premarin?"

"No."

"Then you're one of the lucky ones. There's a whole industry dedicated to breeding mares strictly for their urine, so it can be redirected to pharmaceutical uses."

"What happens to the foals?"

"Depends. Most go to auction—that's where I'm getting mine. The rest either die within their first year due to being weaned too soon, or they're sent to slaughter." Mickey rubbed the side of his nose with his finger. "Terrible stuff, really. The worst part is knowing you can't save them all, but I'll be damned if I don't at least try."

Ray leaned forward, horrified and intrigued. "And anyone can buy them? Just like that?"

"Sure. You thinking of jumping on the wagon?"

"I might."

"You should," Mickey said as he prepared to leave, "a lot of the foals are pure-bred Quarter horses, so they'd make great ranch stock. You could even start a series on your channel—call it 'Gentling Foals 101,' or something like that. People would go nuts."

"Myself included—foals are a handful. But Hannah would love them."

Mickey's face split into a grin.

"There he is," he said, almost to himself, "even when everything is a mess, you still think of the horses. A true cowboy."

"I guess you're right," Ray agreed, his cheeks reddening at the compliment.

"You're going to love being married. It's like having a project every day for the rest of your life." Mickey exited the booth and stood over Ray with his hand extended. "I've gotta go. But if you ever need work, you call me, okay?"

Ray shook his hand. "Okay."

Mickey crossed to the door and stepped outside. Ray watched him climb into his truck, the red paint job glaringly bright against the iron grey clouds that portended a coming storm. The Montana license plate, and the truck it was attached to, quickly faded to a speck in the distance.

Ray picked up his coffee cup, smiling as he put the ceramic vessel to his lips. Maybe things just had a way of working out after all.

Twenty-nine

They arrived in a row, with Hannah in the middle between both her parents. Rather than sitting in one of the chairs, Ray had chosen to stand in the same place Hannah always looked for him. It was a balmy summer day outside, and the sun's heat was rising off the sidewalk in waves, smudging the trees and mountains in the background.

As they cleared the arrival gates, Hannah swiveled her head toward the windows and grinned.

"Long time, no see," Ray joked as he met her halfway. She ditched the carry-on and wrapped her arms around his body, then rose up to kiss him. Embarrassment flowered in Ray's cheeks as Jeanette made a face at their very public display of affection. But he didn't pull away.

Andrew chuckled, "And so it begins."

Hannah unwound her arms from around Ray and gestured to her parents. "You remember my dad, Andrew, and my mom, Jeanette."

"Of course." Ray stepped forward with his hand outstretched toward Andrew first. Rather than shaking it, he took Ray into a hug, slapping his soon-to-be son-in-law on the back a couple of times for good measure. Hannah had never understood why male affection had to be so painful, but in this moment, she was too elated to question it.

At last, Andrew pulled away, and the momentary relief Ray had felt in his embrace faded as he turned to Jeanette. She'd been aloof during the flight, answering emails on her phone while Hannah stressed about last-minute wedding details. To be fair, Jeanette hadn't tried to hijack the plane in a desperate attempt to thwart her daughter's marriage. But she also hadn't offered any kind of encouragement when Hannah began to worry about whether the heat would cause Laney to suffer another stroke, so Hannah continued to withhold optimism that everything would turn out okay.

"It's good to see you again, Mrs. Lowry," Ray said.

Jeanette smiled and offered her hand. "It's good to see you, too."

"We should get going," Hannah said, wrapping a hand around Ray's arm. She lowered her voice. "Can I talk to you?" They wandered a few paces away, leaving Andrew and Jeanette to guard the luggage.

"What's wrong?" Ray asked as they stood near the windows.

"Nothing. And everything." Hannah laughed unconvincingly. "My mom's worried about us, as usual. And I know that's nothing new, or anything, but I really thought this week would be different. I *hoped* she'd come around and be happy for us." She shook her head, her gaze stuck on something outside. "I guess some things never change."

Ray grasped her shoulders with his hands and squeezed lightly. "I'll talk to her. I'll tell her this is what we want. Maybe she just needs to hear it from me that everything's going to be okay."

"Maybe."

"I'm happy you're here. I've missed you." Ray took her into his arms and kissed the top of her head, disapproving looks be damned. "Let's go home."

All the way to the ranch, Hannah kept her window rolled down, letting the gusts of air cool her skin and kill the awkward silence. Marcus had permitted Ray to borrow his truck, promising it would be more comfortable than his dusty Chevy, not to mention less likely to break down. Andrew and Jeanette sat in the back, chatting with Ray about the state's history, and his family's history, through every breathtakingly beautiful mile.

"My great-grandfather bought the land in 1930. That's when he started building the house," Ray explained, glancing at his rear view mirror. "His neighbours helped him build the barn, but it burned down a few years later, so they had to rebuild."

"What caused the fire?" Andrew asked.

"We don't know. My grandpa was only five or six when it happened. He used to tell us this story sometimes, and according to him it happened during a drought, so we think it might've been some hay that caught fire." Ray added, "The second barn was a lot sturdier. In fact, we still use it."

He steered into the driveway. *This is it,* Hannah thought, subconsciously gripping the door as they bumped along the dusty, stone-littered road. She glanced at the side mirror to see Jeanette in the backseat, holding that stiff, unnatural pose that always managed to spread to her face. Hannah took her mom's lack of comment as an opportunity to start a conversation.

"Hey, mom, maybe later you and I can go for a hike. There are lots of great trails around here," Hannah offered, her tone hopeful.

As they rounded the side of the house, Jeanette monotoned, "I didn't bring my hiking shoes."

Hannah shot a pleading glance at Ray, who consulted the rear view mirror before saying, "That's okay, we have some boots you can borrow. I'll bring them to the bunkhouse once you're settled in." His eyes shifted to his fiancée as he shrugged. Hannah merely shook her head, then turned her attention over to the paddocks.

Rather than stopping at the house, Ray kept driving until they'd reached the barn. The path to the bunkhouse was about fifty feet past it, half-hidden by the overgrowth of trees and ferns. Marcus was in the round pen, a bib of sweat darkening the front of his grey shirt, another line of it down his back. He was working with one of the foals, a spindly bay filly with a dark snout and hooves like black stilettos, who was fighting against the rope with every ounce of her spitfire energy. Ray parked the truck.

"Why are we stopping here?" Hannah asked. The corner of her thumbnail was ragged. She started picking at it.

"I want to say hi to Marc." Ray could see Jeanette out of the corner of his eye, watching him like a hawk. "Be right back," he said as he opened the door. A dull echo lingered in the air as it closed behind him. He walked over to the enclosure and leaned on the gate, keeping his back to the truck and its passengers.

"Who is that?" Jeanette asked.

"It's Marcus. Ray's brother."

"He looks disheveled."

"He's working, mom."

Jeanette refrained from further scrutiny.

"So, this is where you're going to be living," Andrew said. Hannah couldn't tell if he'd meant for it to be a question or an observation, but she nodded anyway. A shred of fingernail came off in her hand.

"It's a nice place, honey. But you might want to consider remote work, like tutoring. That driveway looks like it gets icy in the winter."

"That's a great idea," Hannah said automatically, starting in on her pinkie. The nail was soft, vulnerable. As soon as it broke, Hannah felt an odd sense of relief. Ray had finished talking to Marc and was walking back to the truck, his head slightly lowered as he watched the dust rolling around his feet.

Hannah tore off the half-moon of her little finger nail just as he climbed behind the wheel.

"When did you guys get foals?" Hannah wondered.

"A couple of weeks ago. It was Mickey's idea. I'll tell you all about it tonight."

The sweet smell of wildflowers flooded through the open windows as they approached the bunkhouse. It wasn't exactly a five-star hotel, but it was quiet, clean, and private—perfect for getting some work done, or simply forgetting about responsibilities altogether. Ray parked the truck, and the four of them got out.

"I'll take your parents' stuff inside," Ray told Hannah as he came around the vehicle.

"Thanks."

"I'll give you a hand," Andrew offered, and the two of them disappeared into the cabin bearing a suitcase in each hand.

Hannah took a deep breath. The hardest part of this trip—getting her parents to come to Colorado—was over, but the thought brought her no relief. From now until the wedding, she'd have to convince her mom that this wasn't a mistake—that marrying Ray, and settling for a life that most people would never get to experience, was the right thing to do.

Jeanette was standing down by the firepit, where a ring of flat, grey rocks encircled a shallow hole dusted with fine white ash. Hannah approached her slowly, leaving Ray and her dad to continue their male bonding in the bunkhouse.

"Mom." Jeanette turned around as Hannah lightly touched her arm, asking, "Are you okay?"

"Me? I'm fine. I'm just not sure what to make of all this yet."

"I found it disorienting when I first came here, too. It's a lot different than what we're used to, but I promise, this place will grow on you." *And so will Ray, hopefully.*

Just then, Andrew emerged from the cabin behind them, a grin stretched over his face.

"Hey, honey, they have one of those Internet sticks. You know, like we were thinking of getting for the cottage."

"Terrific," Jeanette enthused dryly.

As Ray sauntered over to them, Hannah looked at both her parents and said, "We normally have dinner at six—Marc's thinking of having a barbecue tonight. We hope you'll join us."

"We wouldn't miss it," Andrew replied, collecting his wife under his arm. These open displays of affection were rare for them, but Hannah didn't miss the smile that flashed across her mom's mouth. Maybe this week would be different, after all.

Soon, Andrew and Jeanette disappeared into the bunkhouse to settle in and freshen up, and Hannah and Ray departed shortly after.

"That's one crisis down," Ray said as they climbed into the truck.

"Why do you say it like that?"

"What?"

"You called my parents a crisis," Hannah stated, "why?"

He smirked and directed his gaze at the bunkhouse. "I guess I expected things to be worse."

"Yeah. Me too," she admitted, sinking back into the seat.

"You said they weren't even going to come. This is a big step up." Ray started the engine, then turned the truck around and headed back toward the barn. "You know what your dad said to me when we were taking in the bags?"

"What?"

"He said it'll be nice to have a son."

Hannah grinned at her reflection in the window, her heart lifting. "Yeah. It will."

Thirty

Hannah had not come to Colorado with any delusions of rest and relaxation. Thankfully, she'd come prepared—with lists, itineraries, and a bottle of extra-strength Tylenol. As she and Ray walked back to the truck, Hannah pulled up the schedule on her phone. *Wednesday — arriving in Aspen. Thursday — errands with Ray. Friday — rehearsal dinner. Saturday — Wedding @ 2:00.* She scanned the list of tasks they'd been working through at the same time that Ray unlocked the Chevy. All around them, the usual crop of summertime tourists flooded the sidewalk with bulky shopping bags and trailing clouds of marijuana. Hannah wrinkled her nose, making Ray laugh.

"You'll get used to it," he promised, opening the driver's door. "I mean, you kind of have to, if you want to live in Colorado." As they ducked into the truck, he reached around for his seatbelt, asking, "What's next on your trusty list?"

Hannah checked her phone. "Pick up marriage license—check. Finalize payment with florist—check. Pick up arthritis pills for Laney—"

"Check," Ray said, rummaging through the grocery bag in search of the pain relievers. "And Marc's allergy medication was on sale, so I bought two of them."

"Great. So, what's left?"

"You're the one with the list," Ray said, leaning forward to turn over the engine.

As her focus returned to the phone, Hannah's smile evened out. "Oh, my God."

"What? What's wrong?"

"Joanna replied to my message—my email."

"What did she say?"

Hannah's eyes moved quickly, darting back and forth across the screen. Ray had pulled back into traffic, unsure of where they were headed next. Instead, he simply drove, taking in the sights and a chance to catch his breath.

"Joanna's in Peru," Hannah said at last, "she said she's been building houses, and that's why she hadn't contacted me earlier." She read to the bottom of Joanna's reply, then leaned back in the passenger seat, watching the town pass in a meaningless blur.

"Is she still coming to the wedding?" Ray asked.

"I don't know. I mean, I don't want to ask her to fly here from South America. Weddings are stressful enough without adding jet lag to the mix." Ray nodded at this sensible approach. Hannah continued, "But she's my Maid of Honour. And Joanna's always come through for me."

"Why don't you call her, see what her plan is? By the way, where are we going?"

As if suddenly remembering they were on a schedule, Hannah consulted her phone again. Their last-minute wedding plans included penning thank-you cards to their guests and stuffing the tip envelopes for their vendors, but all Hannah could think about in that moment was Joanna being in Peru and what it would take to get her to Colorado in time for the ceremony. "We need to stop at the post office and pick up stamps."

Ray nodded and set them on that course. Out of the corner of her eye, Hannah saw his jaw muscle tense. He hadn't said it out loud, but she knew having her parents here had only added to Ray's existing stress about the wedding, Wilbur, and whatever madness Mickey had roped him into with those foals.

"Peru," Hannah said after some reflection. "Can you imagine?"

"I'm not good at imagining," Ray admitted, "but I'm sure it's probably very different from here. Didn't you want to go to Peru a few years ago?"

"Australia. You made fun of me for it."

Ray smiled wryly, his gaze fixed on the road. "To be fair, I never said you shouldn't go."

"That's true. And I guess I shouldn't be so surprised that Jo's building houses—I mean, she went to school for interior design. What I don't understand is why she didn't tell me sooner…"

At this, Ray pried his focus from the busy streets and let it settle on his fiancée, wilting with disappointment on the opposite side of the truck. There'd been plenty of times in university when Hannah had lamented her lack of a best friend, to the point that Ray had even teased her about liking Joanna more than him. "It's normal—people grow apart as they get older. At least, that's what Marcus always told me. He said adulthood is where your real friends are."

"I know, but I thought we'd keep in touch more. I'll bet she talks to Logan all the time."

"So what if she does? That doesn't mean she's not your friend, too."

Hannah softened at his wisdom, and the way the afternoon sun cradled the edges of his face. "This is why I'm marrying you: you always know what to say."

"And let's not forget that I'm also handsome, funny, and sensitive."

"You are."

Ray turned to her, grinning, one hand on the steering wheel and the other hanging out the window. Hannah faced the windshield again, and her heart lifted with hope at all the good things that were still to come.

*

It was later that day, as Hannah and Ray were compiling thank-you cards and wedding favours at the kitchen table, that the logistics of Joanna's voyage revealed their many hidden complexities, along with Marcus's doubt.

"So, let me see if I have this right," he said, clutching a beer bottle in one hand while the other worried his pocket. "Joanna's going to fly from Peru to the US and arrive the day before the wedding, and when she gets here, she's going to sleep where, exactly?"

Hannah ignored the motion in his pocket, having enough of her own anxiety to deal with. "She can stay in the guest room."

Marcus leaned toward her. "*I* sleep in the guest room."

"Look, it would just be for a few nights. Please, Marc, just try to be flexible."

"She's right. Now's not the time to argue," Ray chimed in, adding another gift bag to the growing pile. Delicate gold crepe paper rose from each of the square packages like the flickering tongues of a winter fire. "How many more of these do we have to do?"

"At least thirty." Hannah slid another thank-you card across the table to him.

As Ray added it to the bag, he told his brother, "When Hannah came to visit a few years ago, you slept on the couch the whole summer. I know it's not ideal, but we don't have any other option."

"I didn't even think I'd *have* a Maid of Honour," Hannah went on, "or I'd have come up with a better plan."

Marcus sighed. Bringing the bottle to his lips, he watched as his brother and future sister-in-law resumed their work in silence. Hannah had agonized over every tiny detail, from the size of the gift bags to the font on the cards, and seemed almost transfixed by the act of stuffing, sealing, and stamping a hundred and fifty envelopes. Marcus wasn't sure whether to be impressed or intimidated by her unwavering determination.

At last, Hannah said, "If you really don't think you can handle a change in the sleeping arrangements, then Jo can sleep on the couch. But I have to warn you, she tends to stay up really late watching TV."

"Then the bride shall have what the bride demands," Marcus relented with a steep bow.

Ray asked, "Are you going to be an ass for the rest of the night, or can we just agree that Joanna gets the guest room?"

"Were you not listening? I said the bride shall have what the bride demands." Despite his snide tone, a smirk emerged on Marcus's face, calming some of Hannah's fears about a potential conflict. Soon, Marcus left to check on the horses, leaving the couple to their last-minute preparations.

Hannah looked up. Across the table, Ray had paused in the middle of crumpling a sheet of tissue paper to massage his shoulder, a pained expression written on his face. His left hand made a tight fist, like he was holding on to one of the foals' lead ropes, then gradually relaxed as the circling motion of his right palm soothed away some of his discomfort.

"Are you okay?" she asked around the lump in her throat.

Ray removed his hand from his shoulder and picked up the paper again, kneading its razor-thin edges into a jagged sphere. "Yeah. I'm fine."

"I thought you said you talked to your doctor."

"I did. He said nothing's wrong."

"He must not be a very good doctor then. Even I can tell that's not true."

"Look, I can't just keep going back to him. They charge for that sort of thing here. And the pain's not that bad."

Hannah shook her head, looking at her reflection in the kitchen window. Denial—the first stage of grief. She knew it well, and she knew getting past it was the hardest step.

"I'll be fine," Ray assured her, jamming the paper flames down into the bag and reaching for another envelope. "I've been through worse."

"You got shot. I know cowboys aren't supposed to talk about these kinds of things, but you and I both know this isn't going away anytime soon." She met his impatient frown with a teary smile. "I don't want you to hide things from me. There are going to be scars, Ray—physical, emotional, *and* psychological. You could've died that night! And instead of being angry about it, you're stuffing wedding favours."

"I thought that was what you wanted."

"I want you to be okay. I want *us* to be okay." Hannah reached across the table to grasp his hands. Her thumb traced a callous at the base of his fingers. It wasn't quite a scar, but she knew the pain that had carved it into existence, layer by layer. "Promise me you'll go back to your doctor and tell him you want a referral to a physiotherapist. Or you aren't going to be able to train horses professionally."

His gaze dropped to her hands. Smiling, he covered them with his own.

"I promise," Ray whispered. He glimpsed the gift bags and the thin stack of envelopes near Hannah's elbow. "You said we have to do thirty more of these?"

"Give or take."

"Then I guess we shouldn't waste another minute." Ray leaned forward, kissing the point of her nose, then settled back into his chair to finish the job.

Thirty-one

Of all the foals Ray had purchased at the auction, he was especially fond of the pinto colt, although it had clearly been taken from its mother way too soon. When it was standing next to him, its back barely reached Ray's hip. An improperly weaned foal was one that would never reach its full size or potential, so Ray had no choice but to bottle feed it and hope for the best.

"You're hungry this morning, eh?" Ray said, holding a bottle of mare's milk replacer so that the foal could suckle. Its short, skinny tail swished back and forth as it drank. "Keep this up and you'll be eating grain before you know it."

As he said this, Marcus appeared in the barn doorway. Of all the days he would've permitted Ray to slack off, this one was at the top of the list—yet, when he'd woken this morning, the lights were on at the barn and Ray's boots were missing from the entryway. A smile worked its way across Marcus's face as he approached the stall where Ray was nursing the colt, and leaned on the top of the door to observe his progress.

"How's he doing?" Marcus asked.

Ray replied, "Pretty well. He's got a lot of energy, so the formula's doing its job."

"What are you doing down here anyway? It's your wedding day. You should be getting ready."

Straightening, Ray opened the stall door and stepped out. "I know, but I couldn't sleep, so I came down early to start mucking out. The work doesn't stop just because it's a special occasion." He placed the empty bottle on the bench and faced his brother. "Have you talked to Hannah this morning?"

"Yeah. She and Joanna are packing for Jim and Laney's as we speak."

Ray nodded. Without anything to occupy his hands or distract his mind, the jittery feeling that had roused him before dawn came surging back. His stomach wormed with nerves and his palms were instantly slick with sweat. The wedding was in seven hours—seven short hours, and he'd be a married man. Nothing was ever going to be the same again.

"If you wanted to head up to the house, I can take over down here," Marcus offered, gesturing to the stalls, "although it looks like you already put quite a dent in the chores."

"Okay. Make sure when you put the weanling out, you take off his halter—the pinto keeps grabbing it when they play. And I think we're running low on salt licks—"

"*Go*," Marcus ordered playfully, "I know what I'm doing. You just worry about yourself and Hannah today, okay?"

"Right." Ray hesitated a moment longer, as if Marcus might suddenly ask him to fix a gate or move some hay. Instead, he merely trained his cool blue eyes on Ray and waited for him to leave.

As he trekked up to the house, Ray concentrated on drawing air into his lungs. It wasn't that he didn't want to get married—on the contrary, he'd been dreaming of this day for years—but Laney had invited practically everyone she knew, and as Mickey's clinic had proven, Ray wasn't used to speaking in front of a crowd. Today, more than ever, he wanted everything to be perfect, so that Hannah (and her parents) could see what he was capable of. He climbed the porch steps and entered the house, where he was greeted by Joanna's anxious chattering. Ray kicked off his boots and crossed to the stairs, following the sound to its source.

"It's perfectly normal to be freaking out. I mean, who wouldn't? All that pressure—well, it's mostly society's fault for making such a big deal out of weddings in the first place, but still—"

"Jo, I'm fine. Really. I've got everything planned out."

"Of course you do. I was talking about myself here."

Hannah rearranged the contents of her makeup bag. Scattered around the bed were piles of last-minute necessities as well as a copy of the day's schedule, which she was determined to follow to the letter. She tucked her travel-sized sewing kit in the bag and looked up to see Ray standing in the doorway. "Hey. There you are."

"Marcus ordered me to come and check on you," Ray said. "The foal's doing well, by the way. I just gave him another bottle."

"Oh, who cares about the foal?" Joanna snapped, turning her head so quickly that the towel wrapped around her damp hair nearly unwound. "We're in the middle of a feminist nightmare over here."

Quirking his brow, Ray glanced at Hannah and said, "Hey, Jo, would it be alright if I talked to Hannah for a minute?"

"Fine. If you need me, I'll be downstairs, having a mental breakdown in peace." Joanna shuffled down the hall in her bathrobe and fuzzy slippers, muttering to herself until she disappeared.

Ray faced his fiancée. Compared to him, she didn't look nervous at all. Then again, she'd always been the brave one in their relationship.

Hannah smiled. "I was worried when I woke up and you weren't here. I thought you might've been sick or something."

"Just wanted to get a head start on the chores." Ray took a couple of steps into the room. "How are you feeling?"

"Better than Jo, I think. But I'm sure I'll feel differently once we get to Eve's place."

"Can you believe we're actually getting married today?"

She shook her head. "Not really. I keep thinking about how everything is going to change, and I think I'm ready for that, but I'm still scared."

Ray took her into his embrace, where the thumping of his heart filled her ears. As she wrapped her arms more tightly around him, Hannah squeezed her eyes shut as hard as she could and swallowed the sob threatening to crack her open. She'd chosen Ray and the ranch, but that didn't mean she loved her old life any less.

"Nothing's going to change between us," Ray promised, "in fact, I think they're only going to get better from here."

"I hope so. But Jo's right—it's a lot of pressure. For both of us."

Suddenly, Joanna called, "Someone just pulled in. A blue SUV."

"Shoot," Hannah muttered, gazing down at her half-packed bag. "I haven't even showered yet, Jo's having a mental breakdown, and Addy's half an hour early. So much for following the plan."

"Everything's going to be fine. What do you need me to do?"

"Check on my parents—especially my mom. She'll never admit it, but this day's as stressful for her as it is for me."

"I'm on it." Ray leaned down to kiss her cheek. Jeanette still hadn't warmed up to him, but he wasn't about to let her aloofness stand in the way of Hannah's sanity.

When he arrived downstairs, he saw Victor and Adrianna walking through the door, and Joanna, her towel slightly askew, sitting on the couch and taking deep breaths. *One crisis at a time*, Ray told himself, taking a page from Hannah's book.

"Sorry we're so early," Addy said, closing the door behind her. "Are you okay, Joanna?"

"Me? I'm fine. Just taking my role as Maid of Honour very seriously."

"Where's Hannah?" Victor asked.

"Upstairs, packing," Ray answered. "Marc's at the barn. I need to talk to Jeanette."

"What do you want us to do?"

"Whatever Hannah needs." Ray consulted the clock on the microwave and nodded to himself as he reached the door. The closer they got to two o'clock, the faster time seemed to go. Leaving Victor and Adrianna to handle matters at the house, he stepped through the screen and trotted down the steps, determined to keep his body moving so the fear couldn't catch him.

*

Ray didn't recognize his own face staring back at him from the mirror, or the angles of his body under the crisp lines of the tuxedo jacket. Beneath the white dress shirt, his heart hammered steadily against his ribs. Breathing was a struggle, like the outfit was a tiny room to which he'd been confined. He adjusted the bowtie again, trying to find some trace of himself in the glass. He was clean-shaven and tanned, mostly on his hands and cheeks, and his eyes were bright and clear. Ray let his fingers drop from his throat. When Hannah came down the aisle, this was what she'd see: his tall frame and broad shoulders, all enclosed in a black-and-white ensemble that had cost him a fortune.

Marcus knocked on the door. "Are you decent?"

"More than decent, I hope," Ray replied.

As Marcus entered the room, Ray turned away from the mirror. He watched his brother's gaze cover him from head to toe before coming to rest on his face.

"How do you feel?" Marcus asked.

Ray forced himself to take a breath. "I feel like I'm about to get married. Where's Victor?"

"He's waiting for us downstairs." Then Marcus smiled, not his usual smirk, but something more sincere. "You ready to do this?"

"Yes. I mean, I'm terrified, but not of marrying Hannah, you know?" Ray faced his reflection once more. Today marked the beginning of their lives together, but it was also an end, and Ray sensed that Marcus knew this, too: they would still be partners in business, but Hannah would be Ray's main advisor in personal matters now. By the time Ray turned back around, Marcus had already left the room, as if he'd come to the same conclusion.

When Ray went downstairs a few minutes later, Victor was sitting on the couch and Marcus was standing next to the fireplace. Joanna's belongings had been cleared from the coffee table, and in their place was a large, unmarked envelope. Ray eyed it warily.

"That's for after the wedding," Marcus said.

"What is it?"

"You'll see."

Victor stood up and straightened his jacket. He normally hated crowds and loud, raucous partying, but for Ray, he was willing to make an exception.

240

"You look good," Victor told him.

"Thanks."

"So, are we ready to go?" Marcus looked from Ray to Victor and back again, and Ray thought he heard the faintest hint of impatience in Marcus's voice.

He smiled at this tiny, unchanging detail. "I am."

*

Every wedding Eve Sparrow had hosted had ended happily, and she was certain this one would, too. The guests had been arriving steadily, cars filling the designated parking area under the trees and along the grassy strip behind the barn. The chandelier had been lit, the chairs arranged in their usual white phalanx on the hilltop, and the flower petals scattered. She consulted her checklist again and started toward the lady with the cane, who sat on the bench next to the hand-dug pond. The godmother of the groom.

"How are you, Mrs. Fitzgerald?" Eve asked as she sat down.

"Well, don't tell my eldest godson, but my arthritis is troubling me today. That being said, I've never let the pain stop me from doing what I wanted."

"Is there anything I can get you?"

"I'm all right," Laney answered, absently tracking a tadpole's course around the pond's edge. "Just enjoying the sunshine, really. I don't get out much these days, as I'm sure you can imagine."

As she said this, Marcus's truck drove through the leafy tunnel and emerged a short distance from where Laney had chosen to observe her surroundings. Jim had been milling around in the area, never wandering more than twenty feet from his wife, but when he saw the truck, he was by her side in an instant, keeping a gentle hold on Laney's elbow as she stood.

Ray got out first. In direct sunlight, the tuxedo practically glowed, slashed with gold around the shoulders. When he saw Laney, he spread his arms and grinned, feeling bashful.

"Look at you!" she gushed. Her eyes were moist with tears that she quickly blinked back. "Jim, look at him. Doesn't he look dashing?"

"He sure looks like something," Jim replied.

"And you two" – Laney stepped forward to hug Marcus and fiddle with the lapels of Victor's jacket – "oh, I can't believe this. You're all so handsome."

"Is Hannah here yet?" Ray asked.

"I've been keeping an eye out for her," Eve said, coming forward. "When she arrives, we'll start the procession. I'll be on hand to make sure everything goes smoothly, so don't worry about messing anything up."

The chairs were filling quickly. One hundred and fifty people had seemed like a mob on paper; in reality, it was even more impressive. But Eve had managed to corral them all into one area without compromising breathing room. Ray stared at the back of everyone's head, their casual chatter rising like a flock of birds on the warm currents of air, and reminded himself that no matter what happened today, good or bad, there was only one thing he needed to focus on. He subconsciously dried his palms on his pants and waited for Eve's signal to proceed, which came about ten minutes later.

"The bride's limo just pulled in," Eve informed him. Ray was standing in the barn's shadow along with Marcus and Victor, as Jim and Laney had already been escorted to their seats. "Is everyone ready to walk?"

"I am," Marcus said. Victor nodded.

"Me, too," Ray replied. He focused on the path ahead, sprinkled with the white roses Hannah had picked out. In the distance was the altar, and Isaac, the first wedding detail Hannah and Ray had agreed upon.

Jeanette went first. Ray watched her walk down the aisle toward the first row of chairs, her slender figure sheathed in a tasteful beige dress that ended below her knees.

Ray felt the throbbing of his pulse as Eve directed him up the path toward the altar, dripping in sprigs of baby's breath and more white roses. He felt the guests' eyes on his back and the cool caress of the wind under his shirt collar as he walked. Isaac offered him a reassuring smile as he took his place and faced his friends and family—a sea of smiles and flushed faces. Marcus's hand was on his shoulder, and his voice was in Ray's ear, just as it had been his entire life.

"Breathe."

Ray did.

*

He saw her. Dressed in white, with Andrew at her side. Everyone stood up at once.

Hannah clutched the bouquet in one hand, while the other was wrapped around Andrew's arm. Sunlight broke through the trees as they walked along the forest path, the ground soft under their feet. Ray had entered the meadow a slightly different way, but this scenic route was strictly for the bride's benefit: a chance to catch her breath without feeling smothered by the guests' expectations. Eve had truly thought of everything.

Andrew leaned toward his daughter. "This is it."

"I know."

"Promise me one thing." Hannah looked at him. "That you'll always remember who you are."

She smiled. "I will. I promise."

When Ray caught her gaze, his face lifted, overcome by the sight. The twenty feet separating them shortened to ten, then five. And then he was directly in front of her, and she no longer felt the curve of her dad's elbow in her hand.

When they were standing side by side in front of Isaac, Ray leaned down to whisper, "You look beautiful."

"Shall we begin?" Isaac asked.

Hannah and Ray exchanged looks. They both nodded.

Isaac began, "Welcome, dearly beloved. We are gathered here today to join Hannah Lowry and Raymond Fisher in holy matrimony. Through the years your love and loyalty have proven that neither time nor distance can stand in the way of what you feel for one another. With that said, we will now proceed with the vows. Ray, would you like to go first?"

"Yes." He reached into the pocket of his pants and pulled out a sheet of paper, folded into quadrants, and opened it.

"Hannah, I started writing these vows a few weeks before... well, everything. Even though a lot has changed since then, the way I feel about you never will. Seven years ago, you came into my life and taught me that we're more than our pasts and greater than our mistakes. You gave me a reason to believe in myself, and it is this faith that I carry with me every day, through the darkest moments and the hardest breaths. You're the one thing I've never questioned. You're more than my rock— you're the mountains in the morning and the stars at night. You're everything I call home. I promise I'm going to do whatever it takes to give you the life you deserve. Even if I have to break a hundred horses or drive a thousand miles, I'm always going to come home to you." Ray refolded the page, a faint rosiness rising in his cheeks as he smiled.

Isaac smiled as well, and, after an appropriate pause, turned to the bride. "Hannah. Whenever you're ready."

She looked at Ray. Unlike him, she hadn't written her vows down— not on paper, anyway, but they came to her as effortlessly as breathing, carried in every cell of her body instead.

"Ray, sometimes, the best things in life are the things we don't plan at all. You were one of those things. You taught me that love is worth fighting for. You took the pieces of me that were broken and glued them back together again in ways I never imagined could be so beautiful. It's been a long seven years and I know they haven't always been easy. But if I had to start over, I wouldn't change anything. I vow to be here for you always, to see the best in you even on the worst days, and to trust that whatever we face now and in the future, we will get through it together."

After another brief pause, Isaac announced, "And now for the rings and declaration of intent."

They'd opted not to have a ring bearer, instead entrusting the task of the rings' delivery to Marcus and Jeanette. Ray turned to his brother, who slipped his hand into one of the tuxedo's inner pockets and handed the gold band to Ray.

As he held the small, metal circle between his first two fingers and thumb, Isaac prompted, "Ray, please repeat after me: Hannah, with this ring, I promise to love and honour you, in good times and in bad, in sickness and in health, in poverty and in wealth, until death do we part."

"Hannah, with this ring, I promise to love and honour you, in good times and in bad, in sickness and in health, in poverty and in wealth, until death do we part." He placed the ring on her finger, running his thumb over the top of it as it rested against her knuckle.

Jeanette stood, looking sheepish, and from her matching beige clutch, pulled out the slightly larger band destined for Ray's finger. Hannah accepted it with a soft "thank you." Jeanette hurriedly sat back down.

"Now, the same from you, Hannah. Ray, with this ring, I promise to love and honour you, in good times and in bad, in sickness and in health, in poverty and in wealth, until death do we part."

"Ray, with this ring, I promise to love and honour you, in good times and in bad, in sickness and in health, in poverty and in wealth, until death do we part." Hannah slid the ring onto Ray's finger, where it sat snugly against the bronze hue of his suntanned skin.

And then the ceremony was over, and Isaac was saying the only part that seemed to matter, the words that would be forever engraved in her memories as she and Ray moved forward in this new life together.

"By the power vested in me by the state of Colorado, I now pronounce you husband and wife." Isaac's gaze flicked between them, this young couple around his age, and grinned at the look of restrained delight that came over Ray's face. In a tone that was more friendly than formal, Isaac said, "Well, you know what comes next."

Ray leaned down and kissed her as their guests broke into applause.

As the clapping reached its crescendo, Ray pulled back and whispered, "We did it."

"Yeah, we did." Hannah grinned. Ray reached down and took her hand.

The walk down the aisle felt shorter. Overhead, the sky was a vanishing shade of blue, soft around the edges and calm. It seemed like a good omen, but Hannah wasn't looking to the sky or the stars for guidance this time. This time, she was looking inward, toward her heart. Ray's fingers tightened on her hand, and she squeezed back, until their pulses beat as one.

Thirty-two

"In hindsight, leaving Jo alone with Marc was a terrible idea," Hannah reflected. She watched from across the dance floor as the Maid of Honour blissfully antagonized the best man. Though she couldn't hear what Joanna was saying, Hannah imagined that the scolding had something to do with a comment he'd made about one of the guests—or maybe even Joanna herself.

"Yeah, but it's fun to watch, isn't it?"

Hannah shot Ray a clandestine grin. "Is judging people going to be our new married couple hobby?"

"I don't see why not. We're so good at it."

"Cheers to that." Hannah raised her glass and clinked it against Ray's, feeling a wonderful thrill at this silly diversion they'd created for themselves. "Can you believe all these people came out to celebrate with us?"

"Well," Ray said, setting his glass on the white tablecloth, "I think most of them are here for Laney, but no, I can't believe it. The whole day's been kind of a blur, to be honest."

In this moment, Joanna stormed over to them. Her hair hung limp from the heat, and her cheeks were scarlet from edge to edge. Worry straightened Hannah's spine.

Joanna's eyes snapped to Ray. "Your brother," she stated, "is a pig. I just thought you should know that."

"I know he is. Do you want to sit down?"

"I can't. I'm three glasses in and my bladder is expanding faster than the universe. Where are the bathrooms?"

Pointing to the doors, Hannah said, "Through there and to the right."

"Good. When I come back, I'm going to party like it's 2008." Joanna crossed the barn to the doors, where she soon disappeared into the gathering violet of early evening.

Ray shook his head. "You know what *I* can't believe? That Joanna Gillard is your best friend. I mean, she's nice enough, but everything about her is the opposite of you."

Hannah pulled her gaze from the crowd as a sobering realization dawned on her. Ray had shed his jacket a few hours ago, inviting the chandelier's starry glow to dance on his white shirt. "Joanna's not my best friend anymore. You are."

He smiled, then leaned sideways to rest his arm on the back of her chair. "What does 'party like it's 2008' mean, anyway?"

"Who knows?"

Ray's grin widened. He pointed to table eight, around which a number of older relatives were seated. "See the guy on the left, with the silver cufflinks?" Hannah nodded. "I always thought his moustache made him look like Yosemite Sam."

"Okay, *now* we're taking it too far," Hannah said around an impish grin. It was no use: the visual had stuck, and Ray was obviously pleased with his observation. A laugh spilled out of her before she could stop it. "He really does, doesn't he?"

Soon, a faint tinkling noise rose above the clamor. Hannah quickly searched for its source as Joanna staggered in and unabashedly seated herself at a table with Andrew and Jeanette, who suffered her presence with mild expressions of disapproval.

"Could I have everyone's attention for a minute?" Marcus waited for the ruckus to die down. He held a microphone in one hand and a champagne flute in the other, striking the perfect balance between effervescence and sobriety.

"Thank you." His voice echoed in the silence. As a smile lifted his face, he began, "I'm actually amazed that Ray asked me to be his best man, knowing I'd have to get up in the middle of the reception and embarrass him like this." Laughs bubbled up from the crowd.

"Nevertheless, I'd like to say a few words. As many of you know, when my brothers and I were a lot younger, our mom passed away. And it was really hard. If Jim and Laney hadn't stepped in when they did, I honestly don't know what would've happened to us.

"I remember being worried about both of my brothers, but especially Ray. No offense—" Marcus broke off mid-sentence to dart a glance at Victor, who shook his head without reproach. "According to Laney, when I was four, I pestered my parents for a baby brother, and, well, there he is." Marcus gestured in the direction of the head table, toward Ray and Hannah. "Ray, you've always been a good kid. And as your big brother, I've had the privilege of watching you become the person you are today. Of course, I can't take all the credit, but I know that if mom were here, she'd be really proud of you. And Hannah: I know what you've given up for him. What you and Ray have found in each other is nothing short of incredible. Tonight is about celebrating a beginning, but it's also the end of a lot of uncertainty. I think maybe I'll finally be able to sleep a little easier, knowing that you have each other's backs." Marcus lifted his champagne in toast. "To the bride and groom."

Everyone drank to this. When the speech was over, the conversation, laughter, and nostalgic recollections came surging back, blanketing the room in a warm, comfortable murmur. Music filled the leftover pockets of silence. *This is perfect*, Hannah thought—or as perfect as it could be given that there were still so many unknowns. For tonight, she was happy to be married to Ray and to celebrate the conclusion of their years-long courtship. Eventually, Joanna coerced her onto the dance floor, and Hannah allowed herself to be led into a circle of other young women who were just as eager to pretend this party would never end.

"I couldn't help but notice you didn't get us a wedding present," Ray said as he slid into the empty chair next to Marcus. While Hannah was dancing, he'd been going around the room, talking to some of their guests and answering the usual questions about when he and Hannah were planning to have kids.

Marcus scoffed. "Why would I get you a wedding present? If anything, *I* should be getting a present for putting up with you for as long as I have." Ray shook his head as he looked out across the sea of flushed faces. "Are you happy?" Marcus asked.

"I am."

"You should be. You have a beautiful wife and a family that loves you." Marcus set down his glass, turning the stem in his fingers. "I've been doing a lot of thinking lately. Seeing what you and Hannah have—and what Victor and Addy have—made me realize what's missing from my life. I think maybe I'm ready to put myself out there, you know, start dating again."

"Really?"

"Really."

Ray smiled. Hannah had detached herself from Joanna and was orbiting the dance floor solo, humbly accepting whatever compliments came her way. Seeing her, Ray understood exactly what "missing piece" Marcus was referring to. It wasn't something tangible like money, but it was every bit as valuable, if not more so.

"I should get back out there," Ray said at last, rising from his seat.

"You should. And Ray?" Marcus waited until Ray had turned back around before saying, "Congratulations."

Hannah's skin prickled with sweat. Even with the doors wide open, the heat of over a hundred bodies was stifling. She swished from one pocket of empty space to the next, smiling as people reached out to touch her arms or her shoulders, but the relief was negligible. She lifted her hair off the back of her neck and took a deep breath just as Ray was making his way toward her.

"Want to take a breather?" he offered, seeing the rush of blood pooling under her cheeks.

"Yes, please." She took Ray's hand, and they navigated the tireless gyrations of the crowd until they reached the exit.

Outside, the air had a sweetness to it—not in taste, but in disposition, like the tender motions of a mother's hands. The grass tickled Hannah's feet as they walked toward the bench. She sank onto the wooden boards in a heap of tulle and breathed in the dank scent of reeds that swayed at the pond's edge. Ray pinched the front of his pants and sat down on her left.

"Kathy and Neil want to know when we're having kids," Ray said after a minute. "Can you believe it?"

"We've been judging everyone all night. I guess it's okay if they judge us, too."

Ray's eyes settled on her. "I love you. I know I say it all the time, but tonight feels different, you know?"

"I know." Hannah stared out across the silvery ripples.

"I meant every word of my vows," Ray went on. "I think it's important to be honest about things like that."

"Me too."

They sat for a few minutes longer, enjoying the silence and each other's company, until Eve approached from somewhere nearby. She'd unobtrusively been keeping an eye on the festivities, popping up now and then to check on the caterers or adjust the volume of the music. As she made her way toward the couple, Hannah stood up and smoothed down the front of her dress.

"It's beautiful out here at night, isn't it?" Eve said.

"It is. Ray and I can't thank you enough for this. It's everything we could've dreamed, and more."

"I'm glad you love it so much. If you need anything else, I'll be around."

"Thanks." Ray rested his hand on the small of Hannah's back.

"We should get back to our party," she said.

Ray offered his arm to her, his smile lighting up the darkness. "Lead the way, Mrs. Fisher."

*

Hannah and Ray returned home to an empty, quiet house. The rooms were dark, soaked through with the shadows of the furniture and the absence of sleeping bodies. Ray switched on the lamp next to the sofa and tossed his jacket onto the armrest.

"Are you tired?" he asked.

Hannah, in the middle of removing her shoes, said, "I guess that depends on why you're asking." She peeled off the white heels, pierced here and there with bits of grass, and relished the cool, slightly uneven planks that made up the hardwood floor. She was sitting on the bench, her back pressed up against the sweaters lining the wall behind her. Their familiar musk crept into her nose, along with the spicy undercurrent of Ray's cologne, which she'd been too distracted to notice before.

He shrugged, dismissing his implications. "Just wondered."

Hannah stood up. "I think the marriage is still valid even if you don't consummate it right away," she said, adding, "Of course, I expected to be a virgin on my wedding night, so I'm not sure what the protocol is for skipping that step."

Ray feigned horror. "You're not a virgin?"

"Oh, shut up." She finally noticed the envelope on the coffee table and picked it up. "What's this?"

"No idea. Marc said it was for after the wedding."

"Well, it's after the wedding." Hannah slipped him a sly smile. "Come on, aren't you just a little bit curious?"

"It's not even addressed to us."

"Yeah, but why would he leave a random envelope sitting around if he knew we were going to be the only ones in the house tonight?"

"You're right: he probably left it out because he knew you were a big snoop."

"I am not a snoop!"

Ray broke into a grin. Stepping around the couch, he lowered himself onto the cushion next to her and threaded his finger under the envelope's

252

flap. Inside was a sheaf of pages, bound with a metal clip. He removed the contents and laid them on the table, where he flipped through the pages in silence.

"What is it?" Hannah asked.

Ray got to the last page and skimmed it quickly. "It's the deeds to the house."

She picked up the envelope again. Its peculiar weight prompted her to reach for whatever was still inside. "Look, there's a note." Hannah unfolded it and read out loud:

"Dear Hannah and Ray. If you're reading this, then that means you've found the deeds. As of today, I'm officially transferring the land title over to you. Ray, please make our childhood home the one in which you raise your family. As for me, I have a few plans of my own. You always said I should get my own life and stop worrying about yours, so… I'm moving to Wyoming."

"Wyoming?"

"That's what it says." Hannah kept reading: "I'm sorry that mom couldn't be here for any of this, but I know she's looking down on you and that everything is going to be okay. I hope this makes up for everything. Love, Marc. P.S. I've included the key to the safe deposit box. You can put the deeds in there whenever you're ready."

She placed the note on the table. The silence suddenly felt delicate, like a bloom balanced on the end of a stem. Hannah reached for Ray's hand.

"It looks like Marc did get us a wedding present after all," she whispered.

Ray took her into his arms, pressing his lips to the warm dome of her head.

"Yeah," he said, holding her tightly, "yeah, he did."

Thirty-three

The following morning began like any other, albeit later than Ray was used to. He awoke around 10:00 to the sight of Hannah's wedding dress splayed over the chair in the corner—a puff of white against the dark cinnamon of his bedroom walls. His own clothes had been relegated to the empty spaces on the floor and the top of the dresser. Ray's head sank back into the pillow, then turned to look over at Hannah, her body loosely covered by the quilt.

Last night, after learning of Marcus's plans, Ray had been overcome with a sadness so intense, it had been hard to breathe. He'd wondered if they'd made a mistake in opening the envelope so soon, though clearly his brother had intended for them to find it. Hoping to salvage the remainder of their wedding night, Hannah had led him upstairs. As Ray was helping to undo the buttons on the back of her dress, a thought had crossed his mind.

"We could go and visit him. I've never been to Wyoming."

Hannah had had her head tipped forward, holding her hair out of the way with one hand. A tiny smile had reached around the side of her face. "I thought you said you couldn't take a vacation from a working ranch."

"Not a vacation per se, but like… a road trip." He'd undone the last button and skimmed his fingers across her back, then leaned down to kiss the curve of her shoulder.

She'd turned around, the dress moving with her in a slow twirl of dusky white mesh and shimmering ivory beads. She'd removed her hand from the bodice and it fell away from her chest unresistingly, exposing a vaster territory of skin.

All thoughts of road trips forgotten, Ray's hands had migrated and explored, covering the small hills and valleys of her figure with the rough tracks of his fingers. Hannah had unbuttoned his shirt and laid it at the foot of the bed. Then she'd lifted the undershirt over his head, and there was the scar, still pink, a few inches below his collarbone. She'd traced its shape with her fingers, the skin so different from the rest of his body that she had the sensation of touching a stranger, and pulled away out of embarrassment.

"I'm sorry," she'd whispered.

"Don't be." Ray had brought his hand up to the mark with some hesitation. "I can feel it, but it doesn't hurt." He'd grasped her hips between his hands, his thumbs gliding up to claim the faint runes of years-old stretchmarks. "Do these hurt?"

"No."

He'd smiled. "Then I guess we're okay."

Ray was in the middle of making breakfast when Marcus stepped through the front door and set his duffle bag down on the bench. Moments later, when he appeared in the kitchen, Ray looked up from the scrambled eggs he was cooking and waited to see if Marcus mentioned the note.

"Sorry I'm late," Marcus said, going straight to the coffee pot.

"That's okay. We slept in." As Marcus filled one of the mugs, Ray set down the spatula, tucked his hands in his front pockets, and said, "I got your note."

"Oh, good. I wondered about that."

"When do you leave? For Wyoming, I mean."

"September. I've got a friend who can hook me up with a job once I'm settled."

"Right before the fall calving season," Ray remarked. In saying this, he felt a small spark of hope: maybe if Marcus saw how bad the timing was, he'd feel compelled to stay.

As if divining Ray's thought process, Marcus explained, "You'll be fine. I've already pulled a team together, so you'll have lots of help. And don't forget: Hannah's got some branding experience too, thanks to me."

But his explanation was less than satisfactory to Ray. This was all wrong—he and Marcus were supposed to be in business together, and that simply wouldn't be possible if Marc wasn't here. "Yeah, I guess."

As Ray went back to cooking, Hannah came downstairs. She'd just had a shower, and her hair hung in wet clumps down her back. Seeing Marcus, she smiled and cut a beeline to the stove, where she landed a swift peck on Ray's cheek.

"Morning," she said to her husband, reaching over his head for a mug. "Hey, Marc."

He chuckled, "Looks like someone slept well last night."

"I slept like a baby. All that dancing took it out of me."

"Dancing. Right."

"Marc's leaving us in September," Ray announced. He scraped eggs onto three plates and handed one to Hannah, who carried it to the table.

"I'll bet Wyoming's beautiful in the fall," she remarked.

Marcus shrugged. "I wouldn't know. I'm a born and bred Coloradoan."

"Are you nervous?" She'd heard that question so many times in the past couple of weeks that it felt good to finally be on the other end of it.

As usual, Marcus was quick to smirk. But beneath the carefully-crafted veneer of half-smiling indifference, Hannah thought she noticed a glimmer of uncertainty, pulling the muscles in his jaw tight like a string. "Why would I be? It's only a few hours away."

"Right," she replied in the same disbelieving tone he'd used on her moments earlier. "Well, I wish you the best."

"Thanks." Marcus drained his mug and placed it in the sink before heading for the door. "I should go. I've got a lot of work to do today."

"You're not having breakfast with us?" Ray asked.

"I ate at Victor and Addy's." Marcus poked his head back into the kitchen. "By the way, you should go and see them later. They have some stuff they want to give you."

"I can't. I have to work, too."

"I'm sure it can wait," Hannah said, "it'll be like a mini road trip."

"A road trip?" Marcus repeated, furrowing his brows.

"It's nothing, just something Hannah and I were talking about last night."

Marcus disappeared from view, only to pop up a few seconds later halfway down the driveway. Ray stood by the window, caught up in a web of feelings that were uncomfortably new to him.

Hannah placed a soothing hand on his arm. "Come on. Let's eat."

*

It had been a few months since Ray set foot in Victor and Adrianna's house, with the wedding plans taking up most of Ray's free time and Victor being a naturally private person. While Hannah and Adrianna sat in the backyard enjoying the sunshine, Ray and Victor headed out to the garage.

"I know Addy and I already gave you a wedding present, but we thought you might like to go through some of this stuff. Most of it's from Heather and Jeff, but it's all in pretty good condition."

Victor lifted the garage door, and out came a rush of cool, dusty air. The stuff in question sat in boxes along the back wall, some open and mixed, and others still sealed in their original packaging. Ray examined a small air conditioning unit half-heartedly as Victor rooted through a seemingly unrelated tote filled with tools and duct tape.

"If they wanted to get rid of it, why not just take it to the landfill?" Ray asked, deciding to pass on the fan.

"People tend to get attached to stuff. It's easier to give it to someone else than to get rid of it altogether."

Ray ferreted around in another box, but couldn't get his mind to focus on the task at hand. He didn't want any of Heather and Jeff's old junk: what he wanted was to pretend he hadn't seen Marcus's note, and for his life to stay the way it was for just a little longer.

"Did you know Marc's moving to Wyoming?" Ray asked.

"Yeah, he told me a few weeks ago."

"Why didn't you tell me?"

"He wanted to tell you himself when the time was right. Probably didn't want to ruin the wedding." Victor perched his hands on his hips as Ray wandered aimlessly around the garage, looking at nothing in particular. Sunlight glinted off the gold band on his ring finger; the unfamiliar sight hit Victor like a slap to the face.

Without meaning to, he found himself saying, "Marc deserves a chance to be happy too, Ray. And if going to Wyoming will help him achieve that, then I want him to go."

Ray spun around, wide-eyed. "You *want* him to go?"

"No, but I want him to be happy."

"But why does he have to leave Colorado? I can see moving to another city, but crossing a state line seems like an overreaction."

"Is it? A lot of things have gone wrong for Marc here, but he stuck around for you. Honestly, I don't blame him for wanting to start over in a place where no one knows his name." Victor cocked his head. "Is any of this sinking in?"

"Yes. Are we done here?" Ray waved a hand at the boxes.

"It's going to be okay. Addy and I are always around if you need us, and so are Jim and Laney. You and Hannah are married now—things are going to have to change."

Ray stared down at the floor, then out at the driveway, where the shadows of the trees flickered on the hood of his truck like a reverse disco ball. "I know. But I'm not ready."

Victor smiled, his mouth quirking a little higher on one side than the other. He indicated the second-hand cookware and cast-off bedding and asked, "You sure you don't want any of this?"

"I'm sure."

With that matter settled, Victor led them back across the garage. He reached for the rope affixed to the door and yanked it down, then followed Ray toward the backyard.

Thirty-four

Hannah had done everything she could think of to try and take Ray's mind off of Marc's leaving. Despite her efforts, Ray had persisted in his desultory state. At mealtimes, he'd stare gloomily at his plate or out the kitchen window, even if Marcus was right there in the room. Lately, Hannah had found herself toying with her wedding ring, wondering if she truly understood what she'd signed up for. Yes, this was a working ranch. No, they didn't take vacations or go on honeymoons. But the Ray she'd seen on her wedding day, who'd danced with her under a three-tier chandelier and poked fun at his relatives in a champagne haze, had seemingly disappeared overnight.

Winter was coming. Hannah could feel it in the air that funneled down from the mountains, bringing its skeletal fingers of ice and shorter, chillier days. She'd been somewhat surprised when, after completing morning chores, Ray had asked her to help with one of the foals. Nonetheless, Hannah had agreed. There was so much to learn about running a ranch—way more than Marcus had been able to impart during the spring branding—and if she was going to be Ray's business partner, she wanted to be prepared.

Hannah ran a hand down the foal's neck and snuck another glimpse at Ray. Out here, his sullenness didn't seem so noticeable—training horses required a quiet strength that few seemed to master. Still, he kept his back to the house, as if by not looking at it, he could ignore the reality of Marcus's departure.

She broke the silence by saying, "It's okay to miss him. This is the first time you guys have ever been separated for more than a few days."

"What? Oh." Ray's expression cleared upon hearing her voice. He shook his head, gazing at the colt up and down. "Does he look underweight to you?"

"I don't think so."

"Hmm." He stepped forward, throwing an arm across the animal's back and rubbing its opposite shoulder with a gloved hand.

"I did some research. Cheyenne is only five hours away by car. Marc will actually be really close to home, even if it doesn't feel that way."

"Five hours is still five hours. And what's going to happen once he settles in? Gets a job? He won't have time to check in with us."

"Then we'll check in with him. I know this is scary and different, but it's not as bad as your imagination makes it seem."

As she said this, the front door of the house opened and Marcus emerged bearing a duffle bag in each hand. He tossed both into his truck, then trekked down the laneway to the barn, his boots crunching across the wet gravel in a heavy, but familiar rhythm.

"Did you give the little runt a name yet?" Marcus asked, stopping at the isolation paddock.

"No. I've been too busy adjusting to my increased workload," Ray replied.

Ignoring the passive-aggressive jab, Marcus suggested, "You should name him after me."

"I don't think he answers to 'Annoying pain in my ass.'" Ray removed the halter and sent the colt away with a soft flick of the rope. Then he turned toward the gate, training his eyes on the ground as he walked. "You heading out?"

"Yeah. I promised I'd stop by Fitzgerald Farms and say goodbye to Jim and Laney."

Hannah exited the paddock first, leaving Ray to close the gate behind them. Autumn leaves fell in golden spades toward the ground, and everywhere Hannah looked, she was greeted by the dull grey of change. She placed her feet carefully in the muddy ruts of days-old tire tracks and watched Marcus approach the main paddock, where Abby was standing by the fence.

"Hey, old girl. We've been through a lot together, haven't we?" Marcus patted her neck.

Hannah walked up to them. "Don't worry about Abby—we'll take good care of her while you're gone."

"I know. I just can't believe I'm leaving after all this time…" Marcus's hand fell away with visible reluctance.

Ray said, "You have to go. Not because we want you to, but because if you don't, you'll never know what your life could've been."

"He's right," Hannah added, "sometimes, the best plan is not having a plan at all."

"That is the most ironic thing I've ever heard you say," Marcus told her, his mouth quirking at the corners.

She shrugged. "I speak from experience."

As Abby retreated to join the other horses, Marcus led Hannah and Ray back up the hill toward the truck. He had a full tank of gas and two bags containing his worldly possessions. It wasn't much, but it was enough to start the life he'd postponed in order to fill the hole of their parents' absence.

"Any last-minute lectures I should be subjected to?" Ray asked.

"Nah. That's Hannah's job now." Marcus switched his focus to her. "I know *you're* going to be okay. That's why I'm counting on you to check in on everyone while I'm gone."

"I will," Hannah promised. She wrapped her arms around Marcus's shoulders, pulled him close, and whispered, "Don't worry about Ray. I'll take care of him." As she drew back, she flicked her eyes at her husband and said, "I'll give you two some privacy. Safe travels, Marc," she added, touching his arm. Then she climbed the steps and went into the house.

For a long time, Ray couldn't think of what to say. A simple "goodbye" seemed too casual for the occasion, and "thank you" didn't seem sufficient to express his gratitude. After all, where would he be without Marc? Everything Ray had become—a cowboy, a horse trainer, a husband—was because of everything Marcus had given up, and then some.

"Well, this is it," Marcus said, concealing his hands in his pockets. "Cheyenne's only a few hours from here. I can practically smack you in the head from that distance."

Ray forced himself to smile. "You might have to. I'm bound to do something stupid before my first wedding anniversary."

A sharp laugh issued from Marcus's chest. He sobered rather suddenly and looked at the ground between his feet, where the slick, grey stones stared sightlessly back at him.

"You gonna be okay?" Ray asked.

"If you're going to worry, worry about Laney. I know she's only saying she supports my decision to leave because admitting how she really feels would be selfish—and Laney doesn't do selfish." Ray nodded. "As for you and Hannah, you only have to worry about one thing, and that's always being honest with her. Especially if you screw up."

"For a guy who never married, you sure seem to be an expert," Ray observed.

"It's common sense—don't lie to the people you love." Marcus appeared to hesitate, then stepped forward, pulling Ray in for a hug. "And don't go jumping in front of any more guns. I'm serious."

Ray didn't speak. They hadn't talked about what happened that night, and they probably never would, but its presence was unmistakable, like the chill that occupied old houses and empty rooms. The pain in his shoulder was coming back again, but it might've just been from how hard Marcus was squeezing.

Eventually, Marcus released him and proceeded to the driver's side of his truck. As he ducked behind the wheel, Hannah emerged from the house to stand by Ray's side, meshing her fingers with his.

"Tell me it's going to be okay," Ray murmured as Marcus started the engine.

"It's going to be okay."

He swallowed, drawing in a sharp breath. The truck was backing away from the house, and he couldn't feel his hands or his feet.

"I'm not ready for this," Ray said, staring at the taillights.

Hannah let go of his hand and fitted herself under his arm, leaning in to his warmth. What did it mean to be ready for anything? All the planning in the world couldn't lighten the burden of a broken heart, but from those broken pieces came the chance to build something new. Marcus had left them the ranch: together, they would find a way to adjust—to be ready for whatever the future had in store.

"I know," Hannah said as the truck rounded the bend and disappeared. "But I am."

Other books by Jessica Ingold:

Fate Unwritten (Moving Mountains, book 1)

Roads Untraveled (Moving Mountains, book 2)

Words Unspoken (Moving Mountains, book 3)

—

The Spirit Catchers

Captured

—

The Absentees

—

Our Infinite Depths

—

Quiet: Poems about love, loss & healing

Listen: Poems for a noisy planet